UNPROTECTED WITH THE MOB BOSS

A DARK MAFIA ROMANCE (ALEKSEIEV BRATVA)

NICOLE FOX

Copyright © 2019 by Nicole Fox

All rights reserved.

No part of this book may be reproduced in any form or by any electronic or mechanical means, including information storage and retrieval systems, without written permission from the author, except for the use of brief quotations in a book review.

❀ Created with Vellum

MAILING LIST

Sign up to my mailing list!
New subscribers receive a FREE steamy bad boy romance novel.

Click the link below to join.
https://readerlinks.com/l/1057996

ALSO BY NICOLE FOX

Kornilov Bratva Duet
Married to the Don

Til Death Do Us Part

Heirs to the Bratva Empire
Can be read in any order

Kostya

Maksim

Andrei

Tsezar Bratva
Nightfall (Book 1)

Daybreak (Book 2)

Russian Crime Brotherhood
Can be read in any order

Owned by the Mob Boss

Unprotected with the Mob Boss

Knocked Up by the Mob Boss

Sold to the Mob Boss

Stolen by the Mob Boss

Trapped with the Mob Boss

Volkov Bratva
Broken Vows (Book 1)

Broken Hope (Book 2)

Other Standalones

Vin: A Mafia Romance

UNPROTECTED WITH THE MOB BOSS

A DARK MAFIA ROMANCE (ALEKSEIEV BRATVA)

By Nicole Fox

My enemy's daughter. My unprotected bride.

Allison thinks that this is a fair world, that justice exists.

I'm here to show her there is no such thing as innocence.

In my world, it's might makes right.

Kill or be killed.

And I've caused my fair share of bloodshed.

But when I discover her with an innocent man's blood on her hands,

We both know that there's only one way out of this mess:

On her knees before me.

So I give her an offer she cannot refuse.

Become my wife.

Carry my baby.

Or prepare to suffer the consequences.

1
LEV

She's still here.

When I step back out into the hotel room, the steam from the bathroom creeps out. Krystal, lounges on the bed, still naked.

Her blonde hair, soaked in sweat, sticks to her skin and she's wearing a smile that might be considered seductive by some. Not by me, though. She served a purpose. Now we're finished.

"I told you that you need to return to the party," I say. As I get dressed, I keep my gaze on her, waiting on a reply. Her tongue flicks over her bottom lip. Her hands curve around her breasts. She thinks we're playing some kind of game—my willpower versus my libido.

What she doesn't know is that, if she really saw the kinds of games I like to play, she'd run screaming.

"Oh, but I thought we could go for round two," she purrs. "I bet you can't fuck me as hard the second time."

I don't bother replying to her obvious bait. I pick up her dress and throw it at her before finishing buttoning my shirt.

"Get dressed and go."

She gets up onto her knees, the bed shifting under her weight. She rubs her hands down from her breasts to her thighs, her thumbs crossing over her slit.

"Come on, Lev. Please? Let's visit your place. I've heard it has enough rooms that we could be having sex for hours. I just want to see the lion's den. I could be your little kitty cat, you know?"

She smiles again, oozing sex from every pore.

I just stare back.

"Are you a journalist?" I snap after a tense silence.

She blinks, her hands dropping down to her sides. "What? Like … newspapers?"

"Or do you work for another vodka company?"

She wrinkles her forehead in confusion. "I told you when we met. I'm a model."

"Why are you so invested in coming to my house? Is there something that you want?"

She laughs, a high-pitched giggle.

"I want you, Lev," she drawls. "Don't be so surprised. You've got that boxer's body, you know? All muscle. But without those gross ears."

She pauses, gnaws at her lip, then glances up at me again through heavy-lidded eyes. "I just thought I could see your house, that's all. If you don't want that, we can stay here and I'll show you what I can do with my tongue."

"You're not going to my house," I state. "I don't know if other people think this dumb bitch act is endearing, but I don't care what you want. I didn't get to where I am by catering to the needs and desires of obnoxious, boring women whose only talent is spreading their legs."

It takes a moment for my words to register. When they do, her smile slips away like I slapped it off her face. A flush of red fills her cheeks.

"You son of a bitch!" she screams, yanking her dress on over her head. "You narcissistic asshole!"

She stumbles off the bed, which only pisses her off more. I try not to laugh.

Krystal snatches the bottle of wine off the nightstand. Her arm cocks back. I step to the left as she throws the bottle. The bottle slams against the bathroom doorframe. Somehow, miraculously, it doesn't break. It just falls to the carpet with a thud.

"I hope you die!" she screeches. "I hope—I hope you know I'm going to the media about you. I'm going to tell them all what a cold, sexist, self-absorbed asshole you are. I'm going to tell them that you were terrible in bed and that your vodka tastes like shit."

I smile thinly. "The media has said far worse things about me. And if you knew which parts were true, you'd get out of my goddamn room."

I point to the door.

She huffs and puffs, but when I don't even blink, she just hisses and stomps out.

As she passes by me, she tries to take a swing. I grab her wrist before her fist reaches my face.

We stare at each other for a second before she drops her gaze and her hand relaxes. I let her wrist go. She skulks out of the room, pouting.

When she's gone, I pick up the wine bottle. There's not a single chip out of it. I pour a glass and take a sip. It's not strong, but I've been drinking all night.

The hotel room has large windows that allow New York City's lights to shine through. Other people might call it beautiful. All I see is territory that either belongs to me already, or will belong to me soon enough.

I see a city that wants to be under somebody's thumb. It just doesn't know it.

Yet.

I pluck my wallet from the nightstand, sliding it into my back pocket, and head out.

When I leave the hotel room, a drunk couple walking by lift their half-empty bottle of Mariya's Revenge to greet me.

"Good shit, brother! Best yet!" the man bellows drunkenly. His girlfriend laughs and shushes him.

I ignore them and take the stairs down to the ground level.

Booming music from the hotel's main ballroom shakes the floor. When I step into the ballroom, it's a world of bad decisions.

My event coordinator, Anya, insisted on an orange theme to fit the celebration, given that we're releasing our newest product: orange cream Mariya's Revenge vodka. But all of the models dressed in shades of tangerine look repulsive under the lights. I should have kept a closer eye on the details, but Anya should know my expectations better by now. I'll have to express my displeasure to her in the morning.

A man walks up to me before I get far. His baby face and spiky hair seem familiar, but I can't place who he is.

"Quite the vodka, Mr. Alekseiev," he says. "And quite the party. You should have these every week."

"On whose dime?" I say coolly. "Maybe you should be the one throwing parties."

He doesn't have the demeanor of a businessman. Where do I know him from?

"Absolutely," he says.

So, he's rich.

"But it wouldn't be good for my image to be throwing parties all the time. My publicist would kill me."

Rich, famous, and can't be seen partying consistently. That can mean only one man: Brett Russell.

I offer a wry smile. "Mr. Russell, everyone knows you're an unkillable man. I've been meaning to thank you for letting us sponsor you for the cycling championship." A tray of vodka shots stops by us. I take two of the shots and hand them to Brett, then pick up two more. "Here's to success without compromise."

Brett winces as he swallows the shots. I down them both before finding another caterer to pass the glasses off to.

"May I get you anything else?" the caterer asks, looking at me through a fan of eyelashes. Another one eager to bare all for me.

"More vodka."

There's a flicker of a frown on her face before she smiles again. "Of course."

Brett raises an eyebrow at me when she's gone and laughs. "Tell me, Lev: when you get to your particular tax bracket, does the IRS just start sending women directly to your bedroom?"

Before I can answer, Charles Schofield, the CEO of Everything Ice, comes barreling through the crowd to stop in front of me.

"Mr. Alekseiev!" He's sweaty, out of breath, and more than a little drunk. He offers me his hand but drops it when I don't react. "Ahem. Well. I've been waiting to meet you. I've thoroughly enjoyed watching how you've led your business to such a success in a short amount of time. As someone who's been in this business for quite a while, I can certainly say you have a one-of-a-kind mind. With that mind and my vision, we could develop something truly great. I want you to consider how Mariya's Revenge and Everything Ice could collaborate—luxury jewelry and luxury vodka. A sophisticated man puts a sophisticated necklace on his woman and they drink until they slip into bed together."

His rambling speech falls on deaf ears. I try not to wince, but I drink two more shots to get through his business proposal. Then I send him off with a curt handshake and a vague promise to connect in the coming weeks, though I have absolutely no intention of following through. I didn't get to my station in life by making ill-advised deals while drunk at a party.

Brett disappears sometime during Schofield's babbling. When I've sent Schofield off, I go do my obligatory lap of the festivities, glad-handing and smiling through gritted teeth. I take shots with anyone I talk to for more than a couple of minutes and keep hoping that more vodka will ease me into a sense of comfort, but there are sharp edges in all of my thoughts that no amount of alcohol seems able to dull.

A hand claps my shoulder. I turn, all those sharp edges ready to cut someone, and release a slow breath when I see Ilya Sevostyanov. He always appears a bit sickly—pale skin, pale hair, shadows under his eyes.

Some think that a right-hand man should be made of sterner stuff. But Ilya is loyalty personified. Nothing is more important in my business.

"Duilio Colosimo and Siro Vozzella are at headquarters," he says.

"Fuck," I mutter. Not the report I was wanting to hear. I finish my last shot and set it down. "Let's go then."

He nods, and we depart.

Duilio Colosimo clasps his hands on the long conference table at Mariya's Revenge headquarters. Between his massive bulk and the city lights glaring through the floor-to-ceiling windows, it's easy to miss his consigliere at his side. Siro Vozzella is a skinny little nobody with a protruding Adam's apple that's begging to be torn out.

"There's no reason for us to trust you, Lev," Duilio drawls. "You have a lot of men with blood on their hands and I have a lot of grieving widows."

I shrug. "Let them cry. I don't see how that's my problem or yours."

His upper lip twitches. "The Calvino Mafia is ... creating complications. They're not as powerful as your Bratva or as influential as my own enterprise, but they're a problem nonetheless. I might be willing to forget what has happened between us in the past if Gio Calvino was dead. You know how certain deaths can offer a somewhat, shall we say, *comforting* amnesia."

"If you want him dead, kill him," I say. "I don't understand what the complication is."

He smiles. His teeth are small and yellowed. "Allow me to explain. The Calvinos won't mess with the Alekseiev Bratva. But they will aggravate my family, if provoked. It's perfect for you to do it—to show our trust with each other."

"I don't see how this scenario proves that you're trustworthy," I point out.

"We're the ones with the dock-loading business—"

"—which you stole from the Irish."

"Regardless, you need us," he insists.

"I don't need you. I don't need anyone, Duilio."

He smiles again and I try not to retch. I can feel his frustration with me growing, but I don't give a fuck. The Italian bastard is clearly trying to back me into a corner. I'm not about to let that happen easily.

"My business will make it easier for you to traffic guns," he says, spreading his hands wide. "Without it, you can't expand your business at all. If you want this partnership to work, I need you to prove that you aren't just going to kill us all the moment we show up with your guns."

His excuses are thin, to say the least. But the death of one minor don might be a small price to pay to keep Duilio fat and happy.

I sigh and raise my hands in mock surrender. "Okay, Duilio. As a token of my goodwill, I can send a professional to do what you need."

His reply is quick. Too quick. "I don't want your 'professional.' I want *you* to kill him."

And therein lies the rub.

On the inside, I'm fuming. This greasy fuck thinks I'll be lured into a trap this obvious? It'd be insulting if it weren't so transparent. Blood on my hands and him with the ability to connect the dots for whoever is interested … It would take a true idiot to fall for this little gambit.

And I am far from stupid.

But I don't betray any of that. All I do is shake my head. "No, I'm not going to do that," I say.

Duilio doesn't seem to notice the rage brewing in my chest. He tilts his head to the side, chins wobbling, and fixes me with his watery gaze. "I was under the impression that you were quite skilled at eliminating threats. I'd heard that you were willing to get your hands dirty for the sake of the Bratva."

"You should stop listening to rumors. They can cloud an old man's judgment."

He sneers. "I don't mean to sound critical. It's just that you're more like your father than everyone thinks."

There it is. The line has been crossed.

No one insults me like that and lives to tell about it.

In one smooth motion, I spring forward, grab a pen from the cup on the table, and jab it deep into the pulse in Duilio's fat neck.

At the corner of my vision, I see Siro lurch forward, hand in his jacket.

I yank the pen out of his boss' throat. Blood spurts out onto my pants as I turn and lunge at the scrawny advisor. He blocks my first thrust, but I swing my fist into his ribs and his body sags to the side. The knife he was reaching for clatters to the ground.

I stab the pen into his neck too, then drop it, putting my hands on his neck and gripping as tightly as I can. His hands grab my wrists, trying to pull me off, but blood is gushing out of his neck and his face is turning ashen.

It doesn't take long before his hands fall to his sides. His body goes limp.

I keep squeezing until I'm certain he's gone.

When I relax my hands, his body drops to the floor. I flex each of my fingers and shake off the stiffness. Adrenaline is coursing through my system. I want to fight, to drink, to fuck, to go to war right this second.

But I force myself to take one deep breath and regain control.

"I'll call the clean-up crew," Ilya says quietly. I turn around to look at him. His facial features are smooth, but there's a tension to his stance that's hard to ignore.

"You don't approve?" I ask. His expression doesn't change. "Speak openly, Ilya. This is not a time for discretion."

"I don't believe it was the smartest decision," he says, the words coming out slowly—a careful man with careful words. "When you killed off Duilio's soldiers in the beginning, it was dangerous. We all knew that, but as you foresaw, it was necessary. But this is the don. This could lead to a war with his family. He has a son and if his son rises to replace his father, he will want to prove his ability to lead by avenging the men you just slaughtered."

"They were already planning to kill me." I wipe blood off my hands. "That's why they were so adamant that I personally murder Gio Calvino. They wanted to kill me or entrap me. Either way, they had no interest in being allies. We'll just have to wait to see how Duilio's son reacts to the murder—if he cares about power and staying alive, he won't test the Bratva. But if he is a fool, then he will end up like them." I point to the bodies on the ground. "Bleeding like stuck pigs."

Ilya nods once. "Understood."

"Good. Call the crew. I have to change."

I take off my tie and head toward my office gym.

∽

"Mr. Alekseiev, welcome back. And Mr. Sevostyanov, always a pleasure."

The doorman bows his head as Ilya and I step back into the hotel. The floor still vibrates from the music coming from the ballroom, but by this time of the night, there are more than a few empty parking spots out front. When I step back into the ballroom, there are only a few stragglers left, each in the later stages of intoxication.

Ilya's wife, Sophie, bounces over toward us. She is an ethereal beauty. Her blonde hair is so pale, it borders on silver. Every one of her features is delicate. I spotted her at one of our nightclubs—a shy little thing, dragged along by her friends—and was intrigued.

But when Ilya saw her, it was like he'd been struck by lightning.

He still looks at her the same way he did five years ago. A softer man might think it's cute, but all I can think is that my lieutenant is going to be shot one day because he's too busy staring at his wife.

"Honey, look what you missed out on." She raises a plate of puff pastries stuffed with beef. Pirozhki. "I can't believe Lev would take you away from your favorite snack."

"My *second* favorite snack," he corrects before kissing her temple. It turns into a playful nibble. She laughs. They start kissing, Sophie's hand barely holding onto the heavy plate.

"Mmm. We should get home," Ilya says. She nods into his chest. He takes the plate from her and looks at me. "We'll talk tomorrow."

"Good night, Ilya," I reply. "Good night, Sophie."

After they leave, I walk over to one of the displays of Mariya's Revenge. I pour myself a couple of shots before downing them.

The last of the stragglers trickle out, one by one. Seated at a table, I watch the cleaning staff come in. They give me quick smiles before starting to clean up. I continue to drink and observe.

One of the crew, an older man, stops by the table to start picking up the numerous discarded shot glasses. He doesn't look at me. I can see his hands nearly shaking as he is forced to get closer to where I'm sitting.

"Is it hard to work this late?" I ask quietly. He nearly jumps, but doesn't dare to make eye contact.

"Um, no, sir. Not exactly." He scratches at his neck. "A little bit, maybe. I have a daughter and son at home. They're at school during the day and I get home after they're asleep."

I sip on a few fingers of vodka poured over ice as I examine the man.

He's thin, wrinkled, with the slightest paunch hanging over his belt. His eyes are drawn tight with exhaustion.

"What is your name?"

"Roberto, sir."

"Are you married, Roberto?"

He nods emphatically. "Yes, sir. We celebrated our twenty-sixth anniversary a month ago."

I take another sip. "Do you love your wife?"

A blush rises into his cheeks. "Yes, of course. She's a good person, she's good to me, she's good to our kids."

I look straight into his face. He is trembling. I wonder what he thinks I will do to him. I toy with the clasp of my watch before I ask him, "Aren't you sick and tired of her pussy, Roberto?"

The color drains from his face immediately. He clears his throat like he's fumbling for words, but when he draws himself up and speaks again, there's a haughty pride in his voice. An undercurrent of strength beneath the fear. "I don't need to go around sleeping with other women to boost my ego."

"Is that what you think I do?" I ask. It was meant to be a joke, but there's too much alcohol in my system to stop the sharp, icy edges from stabbing through.

The bravery that Roberto showed a moment before disappears in an instant. His hands start to quiver enough that the shot glasses clatter against each other.

Pity. I almost respected him for a moment there.

"I'm so, so sorry, sir. I didn't mean it like that. I just meant that ... when I was younger, I might have done that and if I—"

"Do you think I am beneath you, Roberto?"

"Of course not. Oh God. No. Sir, I'm sorry. Sometimes, it's just so late when I work, my mouth tends to get ahead of itself and I say things that I don't—"

"You should go," I cut him off. "Take your coworkers with you. You can come back in an hour."

"Yes, sir, absolutely. Again, I'm so sorry. I didn't mean anything by it."

He hurries away, stopping briefly to talk to his two coworkers before they all leave.

Not a single one of them looks back.

And when they're gone, I am alone.

2

ALLISON

As Jeffrey Douglas walks to the witness stand, he's crying. It must be difficult for him to cry with the fake eyeglasses he scrounged up to look more relatable to the jury.

His lawyer, Ron Ramsey, strides up to the witness stand. Side by side, they nearly look like father and son. The same shade of brown hair, the same broad chest, and the same clean-shaven faces. The biggest difference is that Ramsey sports a deep tan, thanks to his clients' dirty money paying for tropical vacations.

Jeffrey, on the other hand, isn't going to see the sun for twenty years once this verdict comes down. And that's as it should be, I muse. Even though I know better than to make a legal case personal, there's nothing I hate more than a drunk driver. I can't avoid squaring my own past with the terrible crime Jeffrey committed. There was no justice done in my case. At least there will be in his.

"Mr. Douglas," Ramsey says, his voice carrying a faint, ambiguous accent. It's as fake as the rest of him. "We've heard people speculate what happened on the night of June 7. What actually happened that night?"

Jeffrey rubs his neck and swallows back a sob. "Well. It's all ... it's all hard to talk about now, but at the time, I didn't realize it would lead to all this. I didn't realize anything had happened at all. I wouldn't have left a teenager on the side of the road, someone so young and full of life—"

He breaks off, his hands covering his face as his whimpers fill the courtroom. I glance over at the jury. The sympathy on their faces triggers a bullet of anxiety in my chest. There's no way this sob story could sway them. Right?

Nearly three minutes pass before he wipes his face and sits up again.

"I—I'm sorry. It's just ... it's awful. I feel so badly for her parents, for her friends ... for the whole community. Um, I'm not a perfect person. I'm far from it. But I was just ... at the wrong place, at the wrong time. I was ... yes, it's true I was at a nightclub. Maybe I wasn't sober, but I wasn't drunk. At all. I knew I had to get up early for my job. It—it's my fault. Because I wasn't completely paying attention."

I focus on his tear-stained face. I know a confession isn't coming, but there's still that stray hope that wants to come home.

Do the right thing, you bastard, I say to myself silently. *Tell them you killed her.*

"I wasn't paying attention," he repeats, shaking his head. He wipes his face with his hands again. "I saw the car in front of me brake. Those red lights. I thought I saw something rebound off the front of the car. I thought ... at most, I thought maybe it was a dog. I stopped near where I thought the car was when I saw the brake lights. I must have driven past or not far enough ... I looked around the area. I never found anything. I swear, I pray and wish every day that I had looked harder. But at the time, I assumed the darkness was playing tricks on my eyes. So, I left. I drove away and I went to sleep, not thinking anything more about it."

His gaze shifts over to our side of the courtroom. For a second, our eyes meet, but he quickly shifts to looking at the district attorney, Elizabeth Hardick, who is sitting in front of me, furiously writing notes on her legal pad.

"Mr. Douglas, would you have called 911 if you had hit this young woman?" Ramsey interjects.

"There's no doubt in my mind," Jeffrey says with a sudden stroke of conviction. "I wouldn't have hesitated. The … the police brought up that I've crashed my car before and that I was drunk. That's true. But it was three years ago. I'd just broken up with my fiancée, I'd gone to AA, and … it was a Good Samaritan that saved my life that day. His name was Greg Lowe and I've been waiting a long time to pay it forward. I know how much it means to me that Greg called an ambulance for me. I would have done it for anyone else without hesitating. I owe Greg that and I owe God that."

I notice a woman in the jury box nod, like a church parishioner getting into the preacher's sermon. She's wearing a crucifix. If this case ends up with a hung jury, I'll know she had something to do with it.

I can feel the bile rising in my throat. There's a bad, bad feeling in the air.

"Thank you, Mr. Douglas. Your honesty is admirable."

Ramsey sits down.

Elizabeth springs up to her feet and approaches the witness stand like it's her prey.

"Mr. Douglas, you just mentioned your DUI. You talk about it like it's your only DUI, but it's not, is it? Did you break up with a fiancée every time before you were caught drunk driving?"

"I wasn't drunk—"

"The state begs to differ. How many DUIs have you had?"

He blinks, all the grief disappearing from his eyes. For a second, I see the real him, the true him: a man who would run over twenty teenagers just so he wouldn't have to call a taxi.

But then he bows his head, covers his mouth with his hand, and the repentant man is back. "Four."

"Also, as we heard from Officer Maguire, your car was conveniently stolen right after this incident. Still haven't found it yet, have you? In fact, you hadn't even reported it stolen until after the police got involved with this case."

"It was a clunker. It wasn't worth getting the police involved."

"This nightclub you were at—Black Glacier—you visit it frequently, don't you? And the bartender recalls you being drunk there shortly before the hit and run. What do you think about that?"

Elizabeth taught me this method of cross-examining a defendant—volley them with all of the holes in their story. Even if they find an excuse for every one of your points, the jury will still sense that something doesn't add up and they won't like it if they think the defendant is repeatedly lying to them.

I glance over at the jury box. The woman with the crucifix is frowning as she stares at Jeffrey.

"I think the bartender must have mistaken me for someone else. I only bought one drink. I'm sure he's just confused. They get hundreds of drink orders."

I cover my mouth to hide my smile, but Elizabeth doesn't hide her smirk. She's about to tear the throat off her prey.

"You believe he was confused?" She steps closer to the witness stand. "Just like you were confused about the difference between a teenager's body, a dead dog, and a figment of your imagination?"

"Objection. Argumentative," Ramsey interjects.

"Sustained. Move along, Miss Hardick."

She should have stayed on him about the bartender. The bartender recognized him in a photo lineup. I grip my hands together, looking over at the jury. They're intensely focused on the exchange. Except for the youngest man, who is staring at another jury member with a low-cut shirt, but I'm certain he can be swayed by the others.

This isn't going to lead to a hung jury. Jeffrey Douglas is going to prison and Jenny Dressler is going to get her justice.

At least, I really fucking hope so.

∽

As we all return to our seats after the court recess, the judge adjusts his glasses.

"Will the jury foreperson please stand?" he asks. The oldest man on the jury takes to his feet. "Has the jury reached a unanimous verdict?

"We have, your honor," the juror says.

"Please hand it to Deputy Richards."

I watch the juror give the deputy clerk the verdict form. The clerk hands it to the judge. The judge reads it before handing it back to the clerk.

The deputy clerk clears her throat. "For the crime of vehicular manslaughter, the jury finds the defendant not guilty."

My jaw drops. Chaos erupts.

The judge starts to bang his gavel. The sound of Jenny Dressler's mother crying is excruciating over the chaos of her father shouting and the angry hubbub of the other people who came out to see justice be served.

Jenny's father rushes past me, roaring, trying to get over the bar that separates the galley from the judge's perch.

The bailiff grabs him before he can mount it, shoving him down.

"This is a court of law!" the judge bellows. "Treat it like one or be thrown out!" He slams his gavel again and again.

Finally, the court slowly quiets, the silence only permeated by Mrs. Dressler's muffled crying.

Mr. Dressler raises his hands in defeat. He looks so tired.

"I'm sorry, I'm sorry," he mumbles. The bailiff releases him.

Dressler goes back to his seat next to his wife. He doesn't look at her or the judge or at anyone, really. He just stares into the distance like there's nothing worth seeing anymore.

The last of the proceedings resume. I keep my eyes on the jury as Deputy Richards finishes speaking. They're avoiding looking in the direction of the victim's family and Elizabeth.

After the jury is thanked and excused, Mr. Dressler walks up to Elizabeth, followed closely by his wife, who is still shaking with tears.

"What the hell happened?" Mr. Dressler hisses. "You let that monster free."

Elizabeth takes a deep breath and stops packing her things for a moment to look Mr. Dressler in the eye. Her voice is firm—empathetic but professional. "He's a good-looking man who is a good actor. He knew how to play the jury. I'm sorry, but there's—"

"That's not good enough. I don't want your excuses. You blew it. You could have gone after him much harder and all you did was act like a pretentious ass. You were too confident and you didn't try hard enough."

Elizabeth sighs and runs a hand through her blonde hair. She opens her mouth to speak again, but I cut in. "I'm sorry," I say, butting forward. "I'm deeply sorry for the loss of your daughter, but DA Hardick did what she could. The defense has an easy job—all they need to do is plant doubt in the jury's minds. They only need to convince a couple jury members that he could be innocent and they could persuade the other members if they were charismatic enough. It's not fair. I completely agree. I wish it turned out differently."

He slides his gaze to me like I'm a piece of dog shit stuck to his shoe. "You 'wish' it turned out differently," he repeats slowly. "Your 'wishes' aren't going to put my daughter's killer behind bars, which is the very least of what should happen to him. Save your wishes for a new DA that will actually do her job."

Mr. Dressler looks Elizabeth up and down, disgust written all over his face. Then he storms away, half dragging his wife with him.

I let out a deep breath that I hadn't even realized I was holding in.

"You shouldn't have gotten involved," Elizabeth says to me, gathering her files. She shoves them into her briefcase. "I'm sorry. This isn't the case I should have brought you in on. Take a breath. You need to relax."

I look down at my hands. My fists are clenched so tightly that my nails are digging into my palms.

"I don't understand," I mutter. "He was guilty."

"All we had was circumstantial evidence. We didn't have surveillance footage, we didn't have his car, we didn't have any proof that there wasn't another car on the road that night. I believe he's guilty too, but the jury did their duty. They couldn't say for absolute certainty that he did it, so they had to let him go."

"He's just going to go out and do it again," I protest. "My father said he's suspected in another hit and run, but he was never charged because of a lack of evidence."

"Your father is right. Just keep breathing, Allison. Sometimes the bad guy wins and we can't let that get us down or we'll be too defeated to fight the next one. Come on. I'll take you out for lunch."

I scrape at the nail polish on my thumb. Coral pink. I thought it'd look professional, but now it just feels pointless.

"You don't have to do that," I tell her, looking up. In her heels, she's nearly three inches taller than me and with her dark blonde hair, she could star in a law show.

I feel dull and insignificant next to her. In comparison, a casting director would make me a dead hooker with a crack addiction because the mixture of fluorescent lights and my dark hair always makes my skin look pallid.

"I know my father pulled some strings to let me shadow you, but we don't need to hang out. I'll end up spending the whole time complaining about the case and you'll want to kill me."

"Allison, I'd never kill you. Mostly because your father would have the whole NYPD trying to convict me and I don't have time for that in my life." She zips up her briefcase. "I'm not asking because I want to please your father. I'm asking you because you've sat with me through this whole case and I'm hungry. So, instead of a third night of Chinese food, let's go find a place that serves something decent, and I'll give you some more advice on this prosecuting stuff."

I let my hands drop to my side. "I'm guessing the first piece of advice is to learn to let things go."

"That's the second piece of advice," she says as I follow her out of the courtroom. "The first one is don't piss off the chief of police. And that's why I won't kill his daughter."

∽

Welkin's has a grayish-blue theme—the walls, the tables, the lawyers in their gray and blue suits.

As the hostess leads us to the back patio, I can see my future. I see myself sitting with a stack of documents, fully immersed in the injustice of a high-profile murder.

Or, at least, I dream of that until I see the menu.

"They seem to have forgotten to put the prices on this menu," I say. The sun radiates on half of Elizabeth's face while it barely reaches my hand.

"Don't worry about it. I'm paying," she says, picking up the bar menu.

"People spend too much time telling me to not worry." I grab my menu as a warm breeze tries to steal it from me. It'd likely cost me all the money in my wallet just to replace it. "I'd find that a lot easier to do if there weren't people getting blasted drunk and running teenagers over."

She sets down the menu. "You can't save everyone."

"I don't want to. I just want the people who commit crimes to be punished for those crimes." I take out my bag and yank on the zipper, ripping some of the material that was already threadbare. "I also want to pay for my lunch."

"Allison, you did a lot of legwork for this case. You'd be making me feel better by accepting this small token of gratitude. If you feel that obligated about it, you can do some errands for me later." Elizabeth takes the wallet I put on the table and tosses it back onto my lap. "You're going to need to find a way to relax before you become a prosecutor or you'll end up burning out too fast."

"I'm relaxed." I slouch into my seat, trying to look the part.

She raises an eyebrow. "The whole time we worked on this case, you didn't want a single Friday to yourself. There are much worse cases than this—ones where little children are killed—and I wouldn't blame you if you sat home and drank alone for those. But for these other cases, you need a life outside of it. You can't let the work consume you because then every case will rip you to shreds."

"I don't mind letting it consume me if it means that a victim's family gets justice."

Elizabeth takes a deep breath. "Allison—"

"I just want the families to know that I worked as hard as I could on their case." I sit up again. "I don't want to be the reason someone like Jeffrey walks free. What's the point of being a prosecutor if I don't do that?"

"You have to look at it as a long game."

We lean away from each other as the waitress returns to pour water for us. Elizabeth orders us some wine. After the waitress checks my driver's license and leaves, Elizabeth sips from her glass.

"You have one year left as an undergrad. After that, you'll be a law student. Once your professors know you want to be a prosecutor, they're going to look down on you if they think you're too fragile. Bleeding hearts have a small chance of surviving as defense lawyers. But they'll get slaughtered on our side. Our job is to prosecute. That's it. How deeply you want to fight for justice is admirable, but you can't become emotionally invested in every case. Better still if you don't become invested in any of them. This is a chess game and you need to make it impossible for the defense to move without knocking out their king—the defendant. You need to keep your eye on that goal, not on people's feelings."

The wind charges through the area, rattling the patio umbrellas and scattering the menus and cloth napkins. Elizabeth tries to fix her hair, but it seems pointless to me when the wind keeps coming.

"I'm going to be blunt," I forewarn Elizabeth.

She laughs. "I'm good with that."

I set my hands on top of my bag. "It sounds like you don't consider morality and belief in the law to be part of your job."

"You should fully believe in the law and morality—as long as it helps your case."

The waitress returns with the wine. Elizabeth asks for more time with the menu. I take a sip of the wine as the waitress walks away.

"Allison, Jeffrey Douglas will drink and drive again, and if we're lucky, he'll only hurt someone else, not kill them. I will prosecute him then and with that added DUI on his record, he'll spend a good chunk of his life in prison. In this job, that has to be good enough for you. Anything else will drive you insane."

She smiles at me as she fixes a strand of her hair.

"You could be great at this job, Allison. You've got the drive, you've got the passion, and you've got the commitment. But you know what the most important part is?"

"Criminals continuing to commit crimes?"

She laughs. "That is also true. But the second most important part is that you don't let those criminals live rent-free inside your head. I'll have forgotten Jeffrey Douglas' name within the next two weeks."

"I don't see myself forgetting anytime soon," I say. She lifts her wineglass.

"That's what this is for." She keeps her glass raised. I pick my glass up and clink it against hers. "Here's to Jeffrey Douglas' future demise and to the day we forget his name."

I drink my wine. I plan to forget him, but I just keep imagining his headlights coming straight toward me or toward someone I love. I imagine that he could be drinking right now—just like me—celebrating his win before he gets behind the wheel. I imagine the alcohol also helps him forget names.

But the name he's forgetting is Jenny Dressler's. An innocent girl. Mowed down by a drunken murderer.

If I'm the DA when he enters a courtroom again, I'll make him remember.

I'll make it so that he's saying the name of every person he's hurt while he's lying in his prison cot, begging to die.

3

ALLISON

I imagined that having an EMT as a roommate would come in handy.

If there was an emergency, she could help.

If I was ever lost while driving, I could call her because she'd be familiar with all of the streets.

Best of all, she'd be too tired from her demanding job to care at all about my life.

Yeah right.

"You know I can't show up alone," Julia says, untangling one of her dangly earrings from her curly butterscotch hair. She's wearing a spectacular silver dress that shimmers like water every time she moves. I'm in a white T-shirt and men's sweatpants that are almost too thick to move at all. "This is, like, the one night that Jonathan is working there and I'm not on duty."

I glance around our apartment, wishing it was bigger, so I'd have a place to hide. "Why don't you take Katie?"

"Because Katie has double Ds that men treat like a once-in-a-lifetime meteor shower. The only difference is that they're staring down instead of up."

I glance down at my own boobs. At best, they're shooting stars.

"Your boobs are fine. I love you, Ally, but I know you're just going to sit at the bar, pretend to drink, and not interfere while I convince Jonathan that a bird in his hand is better than two in the bush. And by birds, I mean boobs."

"Why would you let him only touch one of your boobs?"

She puts her hands on her hips. "See, this is what happens when you spend too much time in a courtroom. Your sarcasm scale is off the charts. You need to get out."

"Why do people keep telling me that?" I pick a piece of lint off my shirt. "I'm not a dog you need to take for a walk. We have alcohol here. I have my laptop. Pizza delivery is wildly efficient these days. I'm good."

"Putting a leash on you might help." Julia checks the clock. "You have ten minutes to prove that you're the best roommate in the world. Otherwise, Jonathan will see me and think I'm a sad, pathetic loser, who could only pine for him instead of hanging out with my friends. I'll never be able to step into Black Glacier again."

I stop picking at my shirt. I sit up. "Black Glacier?"

"Yeah." She bounces on the balls of her feet. "It's a bit expensive, but that just means the male selection is top shelf. You've heard of it?"

Yes. At the trial. Jeffrey Douglas mentioned it.

"I think so," I say, concentrating on my shirt again, hoping she won't see my mind racing.

"Someone must have mentioned it to you at the DA's office. They're all well-off, aren't they? They probably go there every night and drink their fancy champagne."

Most women fantasize about male models or billionaires or the perfect destination wedding.

My perfect romance is sitting next to Jeffrey Douglas, lulling him into the belief that he's about to get laid, and when he's about to grab his keys, promising to show me his apartment with a view, I whisper to him that this whole thing was a sting and he's going to prison for a long, long time.

That's not how the law works, but we all have our own dreams.

"If I go with you, will you stop complaining about the DA?" I ask Julia.

She grins. "If everything goes right tonight, I might marry the DA."

"Fine. But I don't think she's into women."

She whoops, giving me a quick hug.

Outside, I can hear police sirens in the distance. It's not unusual around here—last week, I couldn't get into our apartment building because the guy on the floor above us was threatening the police through his door.

But this time, I take it as a good sign. It means justice is coming.

∼

"I can't believe you," Julia mutters as we sit down at the bar.

Black Glacier is more sophisticated than I imagined after picturing Jeffrey Douglas in it. The lightbulbs are all various shades of blue-green. The bar and tables appear to be made of sea glass and there seems to be some kind of mechanism in the floor, so whenever somebody steps on it, a tiny aurora borealis effect is triggered. It's beautiful and ingenious, but it seems like a liability when people are drunk.

It's a personal injury lawyer's dream.

"You can't believe me?" I ask.

She gestures to my clothes. "This."

"I haven't changed."

"Exactly," she says.

"You didn't want to bring Katie because she'd distract Jonathan. I won't distract anyone, which should make you happy. It makes me happy."

She shakes her head at me. "You could meet Prince Charming tonight and yet you look like you took the worst clothes from a frat boy's closet."

I chuckle. "Prince Charming proposed to Cinderella when she was wearing rags," I point out.

She sighs. Then, abruptly, her eyes light up.

"Hey, Jon." She waves at the bartender. "Could I get a lemon drop?"

She turns to me. I smile at Jonathan. He's cute enough, but the sheer amount of product in his hair screams "high-maintenance," too much for me, at least.

"You got it. What about your friend?"

"Could I just get a rum and Coke?" I ask.

After he leaves, Julia turns to me. "What do you think?"

It takes every ounce of willpower I have not to say something snarky about the number of buttons on his shirt he seems to have forgotten. But Julia clearly likes him, so I decide not to be an ass for a change.

"He's cute—" I start to say.

But then I stop.

Because I've spotted someone. The very someone I was desperately hoping I'd see here. Not a gelled-up bartender or a second-year banker trying to blow his bonus check to impress some girls in the next booth over.

It's him. Jeffrey Douglas.

He's here.

I can't believe the worthless asshole is here right after his trial. If he had any semblance of a soul, he'd spend at least a night mourning Jenny Dressler.

But no, looks like it's back to business as usual.

"We should dance," I say suddenly, grabbing Julia's hand. Jonathan drops our drinks off before leaving to serve some other patrons. Julia's eyes follow him like a puppy whose owner is leaving for work. I follow her gaze and curse silently. "He'll notice," I reassure her. "It's a good chance to show him that you're up for a good time."

She picks up her glass and smiles. "I knew you'd get into a good mood as soon as you were here."

I don't bother explaining.

I take my glass and we move onto the dance floor. As we sway together, the swirls of color move under our feet. I keep a close eye on Douglas while I dance. Most of his attention is on his drink, but occasionally his eye wanders to one of the younger women that walk by.

Julia's dress looks even more like water in the blue lighting. She laughs as I pretend to grind up against her.

As I sip from my drink, I can feel the world starting to feel less constricting. Less vile. Julia pulls me closer to her. We continue dancing. One song, two, three. For a moment, I almost forget Jeffrey Douglas exists. But then my eyes land on him again, and the same familiar squeeze of anger takes hold in my stomach.

"I'm gonna go convince Jonathan that I'm suffering from a stress fracture in my ankle," she whispers. "I may need him to drive me home because I'll be too drunk to do it myself. Are you okay by yourself? You have a number to call a cab, right?"

"I'm good," I promise her. "Go get your man."

And I'll go get mine.

She winks before stumbling back to the bar, rubbing her ankle.

I move off the dance floor, finding a seat a couple of stools away from Douglas.

My fantasy scenario runs through my head again. This time through, it seems silly, unrealistic. I'm not a secret agent. I'm not even a police officer.

But I could tell him that I'm watching him. I could make him paranoid that there's somebody who's always ready to call the police. I could set such a hot fire of intense suspicion under his ass that he'd never drink again.

As I'm about to stand up, my phone vibrates in my bag. I struggle to get the zipper to open without tearing the material further. I take out my phone. It's my father.

"Hello?" I answer quickly. It's hard to hear him through the noise of the crowd and the boom of the speakers.

"Hey, Ally," he says. "I heard about the verdict. I'm so sorry. I know you worked hard on it."

"Yeah. It wasn't great," I say, keeping an eye on Jeffrey. He's focused on a woman that barely looks twenty-one.

"I know it's a shitty feeling, but it will—I'm sorry, it's hard to hear anything. Where are you? Are you at a party?"

Even my father is surprised I've joined the outside world.

"I'm at a nightclub," I say. "Julia begged me to join her."

He gives a small noise that's either a sigh or a growl. "I thought Julia would have been a better influence."

"Julia is great, Dad. Don't be mad at her. I'm just her wingwoman."

"Just be careful. Don't accept a drink that you haven't personally seen being made. Don't set your drink down when your eyes aren't on it. Don't go home with—"

"Dad, you've told me all of this before. You know that I know better."

"If you'd seen the cases that I've seen, you'd go to sleep saying all these things over and over," he says. "But it's not just that. Remember that if you want to be DA, your history can become a liability. Don't even be caught around anything illegal. You're also a reflection of me. I know that shouldn't matter, but it does."

"I'd never do anything to make you look bad," I tell him. "You know me. I've never even smoked weed."

"I hope Julia isn't trying to get you to do that, too."

"No, Dad."

"I'm going to head home." I hear his car door slam shut. "You'll call me when you get back to your apartment?"

"Absolutely," I say.

"Good night, Ally. I love you."

"I love you too, Dad."

I set my phone back into my bag and zip it back up. I look down at my drink. I shouldn't have come to the club. I practically came here looking for trouble. As a cop's daughter, I've heard enough criminal cases to know that if you look for trouble, you'll find it.

I take a sip of my drink, but I can't convince myself to leave. I glance over at Jeffrey and watch him order another drink. It creates a wave of rage inside me. If I walk away now, he'll likely drive home while he's completely wasted. What kind of person would I be if I walked away now? Not the person I want or need to be.

I focus on my own drink, which is mostly melted ice now. For a second, it feels like Jeffrey's eyes are on me, but when I look over, he's concentrating on his drink again. I look around. Nobody is watching me.

I wanted to make him paranoid, but it seems like paranoia is contagious.

Unless someone is spying on me, too.

∼

Near the end of the night, I watch Jonathan wrap his arm around Julia and guide her out of the nightclub. There's only one bartender and four patrons left over now, one of which is Jeffrey. I'm resting my head on the bar, irritation searing my thoughts.

A skinny young guy with a goatee leans up against the bar next to me.

"Hey, what's up?" he asks. "You looked lonely over here and I thought—"

"I'm not lonely," I state.

"Oh. Uh, okay. But if you wanted some company, I'd lo—"

"I don't."

"Okay. Bitch." He stomps away from me. I watch the swirls of color burst under his feet with every step.

The bartender stops in front of me. "That has to be the sixth guy you've rejected. A bad day at work?"

"It was a terrible day at work," I say. "It was only four guys though.

Most of them can see from the clothes I'm wearing that I'm not interested in them."

"Optimism isn't the worst sin, but it can be irritating. Do you want another drink?"

"I'm good," I say, sitting up as Jeffrey pulls out a pack of cigarettes. He leaves the bar, heading toward the back of the club. There's an exit back there. He could easily smoke a cigarette and go around the building to get to his car in the front.

I get up, pulling my bag over my shoulder. As it begins to buzz, I unzip it to get my phone. It's my father again. He must be worried that I haven't called yet to say I'm home. I put the phone back in my bag. I'll be calling him soon anyway when I report that Jeffrey is drinking and driving.

The exit door squeaks as I push it open. At first, I don't see Jeffrey, but after the door closes, I notice him leaning close to one of the dumpsters. He nods at me.

"Hey." I try to give him a flirty wave, pretending to stumble a little as I step toward him. "Um, I was just hoping to bum a cigarette from you."

"Sure," he says. He lets the cigarette dangle in his mouth as he taps the pack against his palm. He pulls out one of the cigarettes. I take two more unsteady steps toward him.

Then everything happens fast.

As I reach for the cigarette, he lurches forward, grabbing my arm and yanking me toward him. He drops the cigarettes as he grabs my other arm and shoves me against the wall. The air whooshes out of my lungs. I see stars where my head cracked against the bricks.

"Bitch," he spits out, the cigarette flinging out of his mouth and bouncing off my shirt. "You don't think I remembered you from the courtroom? You don't think I saw you watching me in there? You dumb, bootlicking bitch."

"Let me go!" I struggle against him, but he's a lot stronger than he looks. When I try to kick him, he presses his whole body against me, pinning me against the wall. "My father is the chief of police. I'm friends with the DA. Don't do anything stupid. Just let me go and I'll forget this whole thing."

"You know, that whole time in the courtroom, I imagined being pressed up against you like this," he sneers. His face is right up in mine, breath hot on my cheeks. "It was so *hard* to concentrate on my lawyer and the DA while you were sitting there, so uptight that I knew you'd be the best fuck of my life. I'm thankful that I didn't go to prison because now I can get what I want."

I spit at him.

His jaw stiffens. He spits back at me. It lands on my chin before it drips down to the ground. Still, his hands keep me pressed firmly into the brick wall at my back.

"Just for that, this is going to be ten times worse for you." He moves his hips back to try to pull down my sweatpants.

I stomp on his foot. He jerks backward, loosening his grip. As I turn to run, his hand swings through the air. It hits me so hard across the face that I slam into the dumpster, the metal edge jamming into my ribs before I crumble onto the asphalt.

My bag falls beside me. Inside it, I see the glint of something aluminum.

I pretend to be writhing in pain. I keep one hand on my face as my other hand inches toward my bag.

"Get up," Jeffrey snarls. "Let's see if your high horse protects you from getting fucked next to the goddamn trash."

My hand shoots forward, snatching the pepper spray can from my bag. I pray that it's facing the right way as I press down on the top.

The pepper spray disperses in a cloud of orange. As it hits Jeffrey, his head jerks back. He makes a sound like a mountain lion's scream. He takes several steps back as he tries to use the heel of his palms to rub his eyes, but it only makes things worse for him. Coughs wrack his body as he hunches over, desperate for air.

I scoot back on my butt as his coughing becomes more severe, dragging my bag with me. He's spinning in place, roaring in pain.

I clamber to my feet and take a couple of steps back, toward the exit door. His coughs start to sound strangled. He falls onto his knees, his hands on his throat.

Something is wrong.

He's convulsing on the ground, and foamy drool is issuing from his mouth. His eyes are wide open and a sickening shade of red.

Then, just as suddenly, he stops. Every muscle in his body goes slack.

Oh fuck. Oh fuck, fuck, fuck.

Cautiously, I drop my bag again and step towards him. I reach a hand out to check for a pulse.

But as soon as I'm in range, his eyes fly back open and his arm swings out, hitting against my shoulder before he grabs the front of my shirt. He pulls me closer to him. His coughing sprays his spit onto my face. His other hand grasps my neck, his thumb digging into my throat. It feels like a vise clamped around me, cutting off the air. Stars are swirling again, thick and fast. Black is creeping in at the edge of my vision.

I pry his fingers off my neck, his thumbnail dragging across my throat, and yank his other arm hard enough that he releases my shirt. I take several steps back until I'm pressed up against the wall, gasping for air.

On the ground in front of me, Jeffrey's coughs start to turn into dying rasps.

I dig through my bag and grab my phone. I dial 9. As my finger moves to the 1, my father's number pops onto the screen.

You're also a reflection of me.

Jeffrey falls onto his side. His hands curl into fists. He presses them close to his neck. His face is bright red.

His rasps quiet into whimpers, and then nothing. There is only silence, the distant rumble of cars on the freeway, and my own labored breathing.

Is he dead?

Being the daughter of the chief of police is different than being the daughter of other fathers. As a kid, people assumed I could get away with anything because my father would get me out of trouble, but the truth was that I couldn't be caught around anything illegal because the slightest sign of indiscretion could be turned into a full-blown conspiracy against the police force.

I know how this story will go. The fact that it was accidental won't matter. I've seen how easily prosecutors can twist a story. They won't just convince a jury that I'm a remorseless cold-blooded killer who planned to go to the same nightclub Jeffrey mentioned in the trial and followed him out to the back of the club—they'll spin the story to the media and the city will eat it up.

It'd be nice to believe the justice system will treat me fairly, but I saw today that the law isn't based on facts—it's based on who can tell the best story.

And the best, most sensational story will be that the police chief's daughter is a vigilante that took justice too far.

It will stain my father's career and the city government will force him to step down in order to save face. Even if it's proven to be accidental, the fact that I killed a man will always haunt both of our lives.

Jeffrey is silent, facedown on the asphalt. His hands that were clenched into fists slowly unfurl. I crouch down next to him again. He doesn't try to hit me. I touch his arm. Nothing.

Shit.

I push him onto his back and start to do chest compressions.

He's not dead yet and I can't let him die.

This isn't justice. This isn't what I wanted at all.

4
LEV

The parking lot of Black Glacier is nearly empty.

When Daniil Trofimov approaches me, his size looks like an illusion. He's large enough to make the few cars he passes resemble those toy cars that kids use.

"Hey, boss." Daniil stops a couple of feet in front of me, cracking each one of his knuckles. His eyes sweep the parking lot. He's a great lieutenant, but it's mostly because his size intimidates everyone and he can lead soldiers to do what I need, which is invaluable. "Sorry to bother you, but I figured you'd wanna know."

No kidding, I'd 'wanna know.' The phone call brought me halfway across the city immediately, as few things can that aren't directly business related.

"You're certain it's the chief's daughter?" I ask. He nods. The song from the nightclub changes to something louder, the bass pulsing like a heartbeat.

"What has she been doing since you called?"

"She danced with her friend and then sat at the bar. When I walked out here, she was still at the bar."

"Her father must have sent her." I rub my hand over my throat.

I can only guess at the game that the police chief is playing with me here. Sending his own daughter in to scout me? There's a certain kind of twisted logic in it, I suppose. She's young enough that she could fit in and he wouldn't know that we've researched him enough to know what she looks like.

It's a fucking fishing expedition. They're hoping to find a connection between my nightclub and the Bratva to nail my ass to the wall.

"Do you want me to handle it?" Daniil asks.

"It's an insult," I say.

"I'm sorry, sir—"

"Not you," I cut him off. "The police. They think that they can just send a young woman to act as a lure and we'll make a mistake just because she's got tits. The cops in this city are turning to shit if they thought that would work."

"Do you want me to deal with her?" he asks.

"No."

"Sir, I know the pigs are shit." He starts cracking his knuckles again. "But you know that you've grown your business large enough that it hides everything else. You've done better for us than any other boss. The police wouldn't be suspicious of you at all if it weren't for what your mother did."

I stare at Daniil. He exhales hard enough that it sounds like he's choking before he takes a half-step back, eyes wide with something akin to fear.

"I mean—I didn't mean it like that all. I don't think your mother did anything wrong. Your mother was a wonderful woman. I only meant that if it ... I meant that it's not your fault that the police are suspicious. If everything had started with you, they wouldn't be suspicious at all. I'm sorry, sir. I didn't mean anything by that. Please, sir."

I roll my wrist. There's nobody around. He's a large man, but he has a weak left knee and limited fighting experience. He's used to fighting with a gun. I know he keeps his gun in a holster on his right side, but even if he made the poor decision to try to kill me, I'm close enough to disarm him and use the gun against him. I could claim self-defense. I could just walk away and the rest of the Bratva would clean up the mess for me. The police would never know. Not even Allison Harrington would know about it.

"Leave," I order.

He moves faster than I've ever seen any full-grown man move. I head toward the nightclub.

The police chief's daughter is waiting.

∽

Jonathan sets the whiskey down in front of me. I hand him a twenty-dollar tip. He murmurs his gratitude before walking away. I've only seen him a few times, since I rarely come into Black Glacier, but he's good enough at his job and he has the common sense to not draw attention toward me, which makes him preferable to most of the other bartenders.

Allison Harrington is about twenty feet away. She's directly in my line of view when I look straight ahead. She's different from the photo we got from one of the soldiers. In the photo, she was nearly five years younger and she was heading somewhere with a layer of makeup that made her look like an echo of every other teenager. She was pretty, but in a way that anyone else could be pretty.

Now, she's not wearing any makeup and looks for all the world like a stoner.

And, most irritating of all, she's far too fuckable for any of that to matter.

She has this aura of incandescence, which should be hampered by her black hair, but the contrast only sharpens her allure. There's a fervor in her expression that the photo either didn't show or wasn't there during her teen years. She also seems to have gained some weight since she was sixteen, but it adds a gentle softness to her face and, from what I noticed walking in, a fine-as-fuck ass.

God, if she wasn't the chief's daughter, I'd rip her to shreds. The high would last long enough for me to take her over and over until she was broken.

I swallow down my drink. It's quickly replaced.

I shake off my weakness. I knew walking in here that the police would send a beautiful, sensual woman to try to distract any Bratva member from the fact that she's connected to the department. She must have rejected dozens of men, waiting for one of my men to wander too close.

She'd be worth a fuck, but she's not worth prison.

A beautiful blonde woman with streaks of turquoise in her hair sits down beside me. She orders a mango margarita before turning toward me.

"I'm Natasha," she says. I consider telling her to fuck off, but I need to keep up the façade that I'm just another man in a nightclub. I smile, leaning against the bar to be closer to her.

"Hello, Natasha. I'm Ryan."

I shake her hand before glancing over at Allison. Natasha's eyes follow me. I won't be able to keep an eye on Allison without tipping my hand.

"So, Ryan," Natasha asks. "Have you heard about the thirty-six questions you can ask a person and it will cause the two of you to fall in love?"

"I'm not looking for love," I tell her.

"I'm not either," she says. "But I figure it's a good way to find out if we should fuck tonight."

I raise an eyebrow, pretending to find her bluntness unique. "Okay. What's one of the questions?"

"Hmm. Let's say you have a crystal ball. It can tell you the truth about anything. I mean, anything about you—like who you are, things about your life, your past, your present, your future—what would you want to ask it?"

"If I'm going to be rich someday," I say. Her eyes flicker over my clothing. She must have pegged me as rich. I'll give her points for her ability to spot an expensive suit, but I can see her questioning her decision to talk to me already. Jonathan drops off her margarita. She wraps her fingers around the stem and sips from it.

"Are you going to ask me the same question?" she asks.

"No." I briefly look toward Allison. She's leaning against the bar, her head propped up on her hand. Tired. I could fix that for her. I focus on Natasha again. "If you could sleep anywhere tonight, where would it be?"

"Maybe in my bed. Maybe with you. It depends," she teases and takes another sip of her margarita. She licks some salt from the edge of her mouth. Usually, I'd be all over this kind of woman. Unabashedly sexual, and already dripping with a desperate desire for my approval.

But her antics are bordering on annoying right now. She sets her margarita down. "All right, I have another one. If you could change the way that you were raised, what is one thing that you would change?"

"I'd have given myself a dog," I lie.

We had a dog. His name was Bear. He used to get upset every time my parents kissed. We were never sure why, but my father used to tease him by kissing my mother repeatedly. Bear would bark over and over until my father walked away. As a child, I thought my parents were madly in love and maybe they even were.

If anything, that was the problem.

Marriages should be nothing more than a contract between two people, where it's beneficial for both sides to remain together without any emotions involved.

"Oh, dogs are great." Natasha plucks the lime slice off her glass before taking another sip. "I wish my father had been around more."

I nearly laugh. Daddy issues, a drinking problem, and flaunting enough cleavage for a man to drown in? This girl is a true triple threat.

But nothing she's doing can capture my interest tonight.

As a man stands up from the bar, I see Allison's eyes track him. She stands up and follows him out. I look back at Natasha. She's looking down at her drink, her shoulders slumped.

There is nothing worse than a drunk therapy session.

"Excuse me," I say, standing up. She grabs my arm, her nails painted the same color as her hair dye.

"Wait," she says. "Are you going to come back?"

I look straight at her. "No."

A slow-motion camera might be able to pinpoint the exact moment her heart breaks.

But I pay no attention as I turn and stride away. I move casually across the floor to stay under the radar. I'm not certain what I'm going to do if it turns out that Allison and this man are working together to undermine me.

I just know I can't let them leave my sight.

∼

When I step outside, there's a faint stinging in my eyes and nose. Any unknown substance should be a top priority, but it's Allison that is demanding my full attention.

She's kneeling beside the man, who is flat on his back. She's applying chest compressions, her hair swaying every time she presses down. The man's limp body jolts from her efforts. As his head bounces, his eyes remain open, but there's no reaction to anything that's happening.

I let the exit door slam shut. Allison turns and sees me.

"Do you know how—do you know what stops an allergic reaction?" she asks in a panic, continuing compressions. Her face gleams with her sweat. "I need—can you do mouth-to-mouth? Or I can and you can do chest compressions. Can you do chest compressions?"

"I'm not putting my mouth on a corpse," I tell her. She looks up at me, confusion creasing her forehead.

"He's not—he's not dead. He can't be dead. There's still a chance. He's going to be fine." She shakes her head, her chest compressions becoming harsher. "He can't be."

As she adjusts her legs, I notice a tiny metal can. Pepper spray. He could have been allergic, he could have had asthma, or he could have had some kind of cardiac issue.

They weren't accomplices. For some reason—I could imagine a few—he attacked her and she defended herself.

She's still doing chest compressions, but they're getting slower and slower. It's gradually dawning on her that she's trying to perform a miracle.

And just like that, the answer to all of my problems slides neatly into place.

"You killed someone in my nightclub," I state, the gravity of the situation hitting me quickly. The police will swarm the nightclub. They only need the flimsiest reason to investigate me, and a death in my nightclub while I'm here might as well be a nail in my coffin.

But there's a way to avoid all of that.

"No," she mutters. She stops doing chest compressions. She wipes the sweat away from her face, slicking her hair back. "No. No. This can't be happening."

She's wide-eyed, shaking her head like she's a mental case. There's certainly guilt written all over her, but there's something more, too. Her bag is right next to her. She could have called 911, but if she had called them before I showed up, I'd hear the sirens by now.

I walk over to her bag. I pick it up. It's pathetic. When I pull the zipper, some of the material rips. I find her phone in the bag and hold it out to her.

"Do you need to call someone?" I ask. She slowly turns her head. She looks at her phone. She must see her reflection in it. She shakes her head again before putting her forehead in her hands. I watch her for a few seconds. "You killed a man."

"I didn't mean it," she mumbles. "God, I'm sorry. God."

"Why did you come back here with him?"

"H-he was a bad person. I just wanted to make sure—he didn't do ... I just wanted to keep an eye on him."

My mind jumps to rape. I imagine his hands on her. My grip on her bag tightens involuntarily.

"He touched you," I say. A statement, not a question. She looks up at me, staring up at me with her nose scrunched up.

"How did you ... ?" She stops. "Oh. No. That wasn't the problem. I mean, it was, but it wasn't. He killed a girl after getting drunk. DUI."

She still hasn't called 911. Or her father.

I crouch down next to her. It smells like piss down here, but I can't be certain if it's coming from the asphalt or the body.

"Do you want me to call one of your parents?" I ask. She rests her head against the heel of her palm. She closes her eyes.

"No. They can't know about this."

Reputation is something I understand better than most. A lot of doors were closed to me when I was building Mariya's Revenge; my father's notoriety turned me into a pariah for a lot of people.

But Allison's father is alive, and whether or not he keeps his job is dependent on his reputation. She's worried about contacting anybody because of her father's job—being connected to a murder would give any police chief a bad image and the mayor would likely force him to resign in order to appoint a chief who wasn't closely connected to a felony.

Her body begins to shake.

"Tell me you're not crying," I say. She shakes her head.

"You don't understand," she mumbles. "Everything is over. My father is going to lose his job. Even if I don't go to prison, I'll never be able to get a job. I should have just let him do what he wanted."

"That's pathetic," I tell her.

"You don't understand."

I watch her. The crying is an annoying habit, but even with the tears, she's beautiful. As she chokes down a sob, I'm brought back to a memory.

My mother is crying. My father keeps telling her that she can't tell anyone. When I was older, after I found out that conversation was about the Bratva, I asked him how he could be certain she would keep the secret and stay married to him. He told me that she knew if she turned against him, a jury would inevitably question if she had known he was in the Bratva the whole time and she'd therefore be guilty by association. Commitments are fueled by fear. My mother was fearful of my father's power and violence. My father was fearful that she'd expose him and make him look weak.

I could blackmail Allison. Use her fear to my advantage. I could blackmail the chief, too, but I know the chief is significantly more capable of luring me into a trap. Allison is weak, young, and malleable. Her father is significantly more valuable to me, but there's a way for me to secure the chief's loyalty through her. The tail wagging the dog, so to speak.

"I can deal with the body," I say.

Her head shoots up. "What? Why?"

"Because you're afraid of what a murder investigation will do to you and your family."

"Why would you do that for me?"

"Because I want you to marry me."

~

Silence permeates the space between us.

I stare at her as she stares at me. If I was her husband, it would make me immune to police investigations. Nobody is going to go after the son-in-law of the police chief unless there was enough evidence to convince the whole city I was the Bratva boss—which would never happen.

A laugh bursts out of her. She covers her mouth with her hand. "Are you insane? Are you on something? Were they selling molly in there?"

"Allison Harrington," I say. Her smile vanishes at the sound of her name. "If I marry you, it will force the police to stop trying to investigate me and it will add legitimacy to my business. It's a rational transaction."

"I thought this club was legitimate," she says.

"Cut the bullshit," I say. "I know why you were here. I know that your father wants to bury me and I'm not going to let him do that."

"I was here because of him—"

"You came to my nightclub on the chance that a criminal was here?" I retort.

"No, not exactly, but—"

"You haven't noticed yet, have you?" I ask.

She throws her hands up, letting them smack down onto her thighs. "Noticed what? That you're insane?"

I turn and point upward. Her eyes follow in the direction that I'm pointing to. Three camera lenses point down toward us like sentries' eyes.

I glance back down at her. Her face is stark white.

"I don't even need to go to the police," I say. "I can take this video straight to the media."

"It … it shows that I hurt him in self-defense. It shows that it was just pepper spray."

"It shows you here, not calling 911. How long has it been since he started dying? Certainly long enough that people will wonder what the fuck your father did wrong while raising you. The court of public opinion does not operate on innocent until proven guilty, Allison. All it takes is the shadow of a doubt. You'll never outrun it."

Her fingers sink into her hair. She grips onto it.

"You're a piece of shit," she whispers.

"Sure. I'd consider that a step above murderer."

"I need time," she says. "Give me a day."

"I'm not giving you anything. You either marry me or this city will be screaming for blood over your family's hypocrisy. Let's all hope that every defense lawyer in the city doesn't realize they could use this to claim that any crime your father presided over should be null and void. That would be a significant number of released criminals and it would retraumatize victims' families. And the press ... I shudder to imagine."

I drop her bag near the dumpster. "The offer ends in the next minute. I need to know if I should call the police or call someone to clean up the body.

"If you call the police, I'll just tell them that you threatened to throw me in prison."

I get on my knees. "Those cameras don't have audio. Does it look like I'm begging you to not blackmail me?"

"I hate you," she whispers. "You have no idea what you're asking from me."

"I'm asking your hand in marriage," I counter. "It is a good deal. You should take it."

Her fists clench. "The defense lawyers would never have a case. Those criminals wouldn't walk free."

"It wouldn't be difficult to plant some doubt into people's minds. You sound like Daddy's little girl. You two must be close if he sent you here and you did it. So, I'd bet that you two have talked recently. If you talked to him at all today, it's going to point to the idea that he was involved in killing this man. And an idea is all the public needs to start questioning how corrupt your father is."

She stares at me. Still on my knees, I pretend to propose to her. She smacks my hands down before grabbing one of them.

"I'll marry you," she whispers hoarsely. "Until death do us part. Let's fucking hope that happens soon."

5

ALLISON

I sit in the center of my room, staring at the window. In the apartment below us, I hear Andrew Straub, a four-year-old with an attitude problem, screaming. I have no idea why he's awake at 5:13 a.m., but he's always up before the sun.

My morning is a hazy blur.

5:25 a.m. The sound of car doors slamming shut and speeding toward the center of the city.

5:40 a.m. The sound of a man pissing in the apartment. Julia must have gotten Jonathan to come over.

5:50 a.m. The sound of the creaking floorboard in front of the door. The door softly closing behind someone.

5:55 a.m. I stand up. I pull out the business card that the asshole—Lev Alekseiev—gave me. He wrote his address on the back, telling me to visit at 7 a.m. to talk about our arrangement. The place is on the rich side of the city, just above the reach of the law.

Lev warned me that if I tell anyone about our deal, the security camera footage will be sent to every news station in the city. All night,

I've told myself the facts: it was self-defense, I didn't mean to murder him, and there was a minimal chance that the pepper spray would kill him.

But he did die.

And I'm an accomplice in hiding the crime. Maybe, if I had called the police right after it happened, there could have been minimal repercussions. The moment got away from me. My mind was flooded by the chaos and Lev took advantage of it.

While Lev escorted me back to his office, he called someone to take care of the body. Afterward, he laid down his threats like appetizers—casual but with refinement and if one of them wasn't to my taste, there was another one that would be.

It certainly didn't help that while we talked, he leaned against his desk, making the lines of his body discernible through his white dress shirt. Away from the dead body and in the glow of his office's lighting, I saw his jade eyes, the granite-sharp jawline, and a level of indifference bordering on sociopathic.

And yet when his hand touched my arm, my body wanted nothing to do with the warnings in my thoughts. It just wanted more. Sex, to me, has always been a chore, nothing more. It's never been like this, where a single touch can turn me feral.

As the memory overwhelms me, heat flushes under my skin. I open my door and take the four steps to the kitchen. I fill a glass of water, drinking all of it before setting it in the sink. I need to give Lev a new deal—something he won't be able to resist so I can get out of marrying him.

I could sleep with him.

God, I need to sleep.

Banging on the door. I jump, my heart racing in my chest. The police. He turned me in anyway.

How much will the women in prison hate me for being the daughter of the police chief? I've heard enough stories to know what goes on behind bars. Nothing pretty.

Will Elizabeth prosecute me and charge me with first-degree murder, just to prove to the public and the mayor that she wasn't close to me? Her career will only go as far as her reputation takes her, and she wouldn't think twice about erasing an insignificant black smear like me from her public record.

What if the public decides my father was an accomplice? Reporters can be vicious. Citizens are worse.

Whoever is at the door knocks again, softer now. Julia's bed creaks as she tosses and turns.

I take a deep breath. I concentrate on moving forward, but it's impossible to ignore my legs trying to fail underneath me. As I open the door, I prepare for a police officer to grab me, wrenching my arms behind me to handcuff me.

It's a cop on my doorstep. But not just any cop.

"Ally," my father says. I glance around him. No other policemen.

"What are you doing here?" I ask. His forehead scrunches up.

"It's nice to see you too," he says. "I kept calling you and you never picked up. You said you'd call when you got home. Did you get too drunk and fall asleep?"

The disapproval in his voice drapes over me. If he knew what happened, he'd never be able to look at me or himself again.

"I'm sorry," I say, shaking my head. "I was just tired and the trial was on my mind."

I press my thumb against my lips. I shouldn't have mentioned the trial. Jeffrey Douglas could have been reported missing by now.

"I know that had to be hard on you." He glances past me. "Do you have a visitor or something? Can I come in?"

"Sorry, right. Come in." I step aside and my father walks in. He looks around the apartment like there's going to be a naked man hiding in a corner somewhere. "I'm sorry about not calling, Dad."

"I know you wouldn't have just let me worry," he says. "You're a good daughter. You just need to be more responsible if you're going to be a lawyer."

"I'm not that good of a daughter," I say. He claps his hand on my shoulder, giving it a small squeeze.

"You made a small mistake," he says. "It doesn't mean you're bad. I just want you to think more about your future when you're making decisions. It's not even about calling me. It's being aware of your actions."

He lets his hand fall back to his side.

"I'm sorry," I say, swallowing back the truth like bile. He sighs.

"Honestly, it's not just you," he says. "I'm under a lot of pressure right now. The mayor is breathing down my neck. She doesn't understand what it's like to have everyone constantly questioning you and deciding their own verdicts about who you are."

"What?" I rub my neck, feeling where Jeffrey bruised it. "Why is the mayor questioning you? What happened? Are you being accused of something?"

"No, no, Ally, it's not that." He leans against the counter. "Not directly, at least. There are some allegations of police officers being bought by the Mafia. I'm certain it's bullshit, but it's always bullshit that ends people's careers."

He rubs his temple, his eyes looking down at the laminate counter, but I know his mind is twisted around the idea of losing his job.

"Your career isn't going to end like that," I tell him. "You're going to retire after a long career and everyone is going to talk about how you were the best man for the job. They'll put up a statue of you in front of city hall."

"That's some blind faith you have," he jokes. He grabs me, pulling me into a hug. I hug him back. When he pulls away, he peers at me with the same dark irises as mine. "Are you okay? If you're hungover, eggs can help with that. An egg sandwich is always a good plan."

"I'm fine," I say. "But I have to start getting ready. I have an appointment at Chanson Law School for a tour of the campus."

"I can take you if you want."

"No, no, it's fine," I say. "The last thing I want is for everyone to realize I'm the daughter of the police chief. I love you, Dad, but I want to earn it myself. Not because I'm fifty percent you."

"I hear you, kiddo. Well, good luck with the tour." He squeezes my arm and turns to leave. "Wish me luck with the mayor."

"Good luck," I say as he opens the door. He gives me a quick smile before slipping out, softly closing the door behind him.

In the past, I could count on my hands how many times I'd lied to my father. Now, I've lied so much that I'd break a polygraph. I'd fall apart on the witness stand.

A chill races down my spine.

I head toward the shower, though I'm fairly certain I'll never be clean again.

∼

I expected the house to be large. I was even prepared to see a mansion. But Lev's house is massive. It's white, two stories tall, and the property stretches far enough that he never has to worry about neighbors seeing him. The front-facing rooms have floor-to-ceiling windows with white trimming. The entrance has two columns on either side of it, granite and imposing.

After using the intercom system to talk to a woman and explain who I am, the massive, intricate metal gates to the property swing open. I drive in, parking near a black pick-up truck that's twice the size of my car. He must be compensating for something.

As I approach the front doors, I notice there's wire framing inside the glass. All I can see through it is a long, wide hallway.

I look for a doorbell. There isn't one. As I'm about to knock, I see a small, short, older woman approaching. She opens the door.

"Hello, Miss Allison," she says in a faint Russian accent. She indicates for me to step in. "May I take your bag?"

"No thank you," I say, gripping it tightly. "I'm sorry, I don't know your name …"

"Irina," she says. "Shall I take you to Mr. Alekseiev? He is in the den."

"Yes, please. Thank you."

She starts walking. As I follow her, I'm taken aback by the utter extravagance of the house. There's a chandelier above us, limestone floors, and a spiral staircase with a handrail that's carved to look like writhing snakes.

I nearly walk into Irina. She stops at the first door in the hallway. Even the arched entrances here are elegant.

Irina gestures for me to wait before she steps into the room.

"Mr. Alekseiev, Miss Allison is here," she says.

"Thank you, Irina," Lev's voice says.

She steps out and indicates for me to walk in.

"Thank you, Irina," I tell her.

"It was my pleasure."

She leaves as I walk into the room. There's a large fireplace on the west side, two love seats, and two recliners curved around it. In the center of the furniture is a large glass coffee table. There are various bookshelves around the room and a small bar set up on the east side. The décor makes it appear small and cozy, but I'm pretty sure it's larger than my apartment's kitchen and living room combined.

Lev is sitting in one of the recliners, a lowball glass in his hand. Unlike me, still wearing the shoddy the clothes from yesterday, he's changed. He's wearing a new dress shirt and different pants. It's less formal than what he had on before, but it only means his body is more apparent than ever.

I try to avoid staring by looking at his face, but those eyes have leverage over me. I sit down on the love seat farthest away from him. I pick up a wood carving of a bird, each of its feathers spread out like a fan.

"It's a bird of happiness," he says casually, like we're friends meeting for tea. "An old Russian toy."

I set the bird back down. "You care a lot about your heritage, don't you?"

"My ancestors fought and thrived so that I could live. Why wouldn't I be?"

"I just find it interesting." I shrug before looking straight at him. The intensity in his face almost makes me flinch, but I keep my gaze steady. "Someone who is proud of their Russian history might be easier to manipulate by certain criminal organizations."

I expect him to be angry. To insist he's not connected to the Bratva or that he could never be manipulated. But he smiles. And something about that smile makes me feel less aggressive.

"That's quite the jump," he says. "If I was Italian and proud of my

Italian heritage, would you accuse me of being in the Italian Mafia? Or is your prejudice only for Russians?"

I flush. "I—I didn't mean to—"

"Yes, you did." He leans back into the chair. "If you're going to blow smoke, at least have the courage to stand in the fire."

I raise my chin. "I just want to know how you can afford a house like this. I'm sure Black Glacier makes a nice profit, but not this nice."

"Should I be a little hurt that you didn't look into me at all?" he asks. "You had my full name on my business card."

I cross my arms over my chest. "I knew everything I wanted to know about you from last night."

"Apparently not, if you're still asking questions."

"What would I have found out if I looked into you? Is there a Black Glacier in every city?"

He walks over to his home bar. He picks up a vodka bottle. Mariya's Revenge. It's a top-shelf vodka. I noticed a few bottles of it in the club because the tops of the bottles are shaped like shotgun shells. When Jonathan was asked about it, he told a patron that a shot cost $77.

Lev pours a shot and hands it to me.

"What is this for?" I ask, taking it.

"I want you to tell me what you think of my product."

The shot glass nearly slips between my fingers. "You own Mariya's Revenge?"

"Yes."

I set the shot down. "Why would you need to marry me then? You're rich. You own a successful business."

"'Successful' is an insult. I put Fool's Fire vodka out of business in six months flat."

He's like a blister: self-inflated, under my skin, and rubbing me the wrong way.

He slides his hand into his pocket. My eyes follow the movement, imagining the warmth of his skin, the grip of his fingers, and how it would feel to be between his thigh and his hand.

I snap out of my reverie. When I look back up at him, that alluring smile is back on his face. I could smack it. Or kiss it. Still undecided.

"Anyway," I say. "I think we need to look at our deal again."

"Our arrangement," he corrects.

"I don't care what it's called. You have to know I won't marry you. It's a ridiculous—"

"Proposal?" he asks, an eyebrow raised.

"Proposition."

He takes his hand out of his pocket and clasps them in front of him. "I have this life because I am willing to do what others won't."

"I'm not going to marry you," I repeat.

He takes the shot glass from in front of me, walks back over to the home bar, and starts mixing up a drink.

"It's a little early to be drinking, isn't it?"

"Have you slept since last night? No? Neither have I," he says. "So let the party continue."

I check my shirt, checking if there's any dirt that I've missed on it that gives away my sleepless night. His comment is a reminder that, amongst all of this opulence, I'm the cheapest thing here.

He hands me a drink. It's a rum and Coke. I stare down at it, two ice cubes clinking against each other. I look back at him as he sits back down in his chair.

"You knew what I was drinking," I say. "You were watching me at the club."

I expect him to deny it. He could say he saw it on the surveillance footage. He could say he asked the bartender. He could say it was a lucky guess.

But he just shrugs.

I slam the glass down on the coffee table. Despite the sound of glass hitting glass, he doesn't react. "You were waiting for me to do something illegal, just so you could blackmail me," I accuse.

His eyes flicker over my face, trying to read something in my expression. I hope he sees the full extent of my rage.

"I was waiting for you to do something illegal?" he asks, restrained anger in his tone. "You were waiting to fuck me over."

"Why would I do that? How would I even know that you were there?"

He shakes his head, his hands tensing on his arm rests. "If you weren't there for me, why were you there?"

I take a deep breath. "I was there because my roommate wanted me to go with her. She has a crush on one of the bartenders. If you've seen the surveillance footage, then you've seen me dancing with her. But I saw Jeffrey Douglas, I knew he had committed a hit and run, and I wanted to make sure he didn't do it again. That's why I followed him out. He attacked me. I defended myself."

"You killed him." He runs his hand over his jaw. "That's quite the coincidence that you two were in the same club. I'll check your story."

I open my mouth to snap back at him, but instead, I force myself to just pick my drink back up and take a sip. It's frustratingly good.

He takes a swig of his own drink. I keep him in my periphery. My father told me once that the best chance for me to survive a hostage situation is to convince the abductor that I'm an individual with my own family, friends, fears, and dreams. Convince him of my humanity. But Lev is such a narcissist, he'd never listen to anything about me.

"So, how did you make Mariya's Revenge so successful?" I ask, changing tactics. "It seemed to pop out of nowhere."

"It didn't. I undersold the competition for several years, learned everything I could about marketing, and used my father's nightclub to my advantage."

"Black Glacier?"

"Original Menace," he says.

"Didn't that club burn down?"

"Yes." His face shows nothing again. If I'm looking for humanity, I'm looking in the wrong place.

"Why is it called Mariya's Revenge?"

His stoicism flickers, showing something underneath. It's not quite sadness—maybe shame. But in the next second, it's gone. He drinks. I mimic his movements.

"Please excuse me for a moment." He stands up, setting his drink down on the coffee table. "Stay here until I'm back. We wouldn't want you to accidentally murder Irina."

∼

I take a deep breath. My hands are trembling. I sink them underneath the cushions of the love seat and

take a gulp of my rum and Coke. I didn't mean to upset him, but at least it gives me some time to organize my thoughts and calm my nerves. I need to get into the right headspace before he manipulates me again.

I get up and peek out into the hallway. Somewhere, I hear the faint sound of a vacuum. I step out. As I start to walk down the hallway, I expect one of the floorboards to creak, but the mansion is flawless. I hate it and I want it. Just like I hate and want Lev.

I stop at the entrance of the mansion. The door is right there. It'd be easy to do. A clean, simple break. State my piece and walk away. No more Lev. No more mindfucking. No more of any of this.

But I let go. If the consequences only harmed me, I'd deal with the repercussions, but I can't do that to my father. I can't do that to the victims' families. There's too many pieces of this house of cards and slamming this door shut will cause it all to fall.

I turn around as Lev is descending the stairs. He's carrying a metal ammunition box, the army green contrasting with the yellow lettering. His expression doesn't change as he stops at the bottom of the stairs. He indicates with his head for me to go back into the den.

I glance back at the door, but even as I imagine the cold steel in my palm again, my legs start moving. I sense him walking behind me. The scent of his cologne—smoky and spicy—settles over me, sinking me into irrational neediness. I stumble against the love seat before I sit back down.

He sits in the armchair next to me, our knees nearly touching. I scoot my legs an inch away. His eyes follow the movement, a small smirk playing at his lips. Heat floods my cheeks.

He sets down the ammunition box in front of me and leans forward, his hands pressed together against his lips.

"Open it."

"Why don't you open it?" I retort.

"Because you'll be far more interested in the contents than I am," he says. "I know what's in it."

I fold my arms over my chest, leaning back. I stare at the ammunition box—mostly to avoid looking at him. My mind should be filled with all of the possible things that could be in the box.

Money?

A gun?

Someone's severed head?

But my thoughts keep returning to Lev. His toned arms are visible under his shirt. If my hands slid underneath the fabric, they could explore for hours and still not find every treasure on his muscled torso. Even better, he could explore me and discover parts of me I've never known about.

The ammunition box. I need to concentrate.

I move to the edge of the love seat and fumble with the latch. As I start to get nervous about looking like a fool, I manage to get it undone and lift the top. I reach my hand in and pull out a manila folder.

I flip it open.

I know it's a surveillance photo right away, due to the tell-tale timestamp in the corner. And I know exactly what's going on in the freeze frame.

I'm standing over Jeffrey Douglas' body. Even when I know what happened and why, it looks bad. Very, very bad. The quality of the photo is surprisingly good, but the camera is still too far away to decipher my expression and the way my head is angled towards him makes it look like I'm just watching him die.

Remorseless.

"Flip through the pages," Lev says. "You'll see that Jeffrey Douglas starts exhibiting signs of distress at 2:47 a.m. You don't start genuinely trying to help him until 2:50 a.m. From these photos and the video—which is in here as well—it looks like you wait until he's already dead before you budge an inch."

"That's not what happened and you know it." I shove the photos back at him, desperately trying to keep the panic out of my voice. "He wouldn't let me help him."

"You think a jury is going to believe you when you say you couldn't overpower a suffocating man?" he asks, his brow furrowed in pseudo-confusion. "What about when I give the prosecutor all of my surveillance footage, where it shows you entering the club—and I will tell them you've never been in the club before—and you end up sitting a few seats away from Jeffrey Douglas and then follow him out to the back? Where he dies."

I sip from the rum and Coke, praying he doesn't see that my hand is shaking. "It's a coincidence that we were both there that night."

"Your father has been in the police force long enough that you know juries don't believe in coincidences," he says. "I also have the pepper spray you used with your fingerprints on it. Juries don't believe in coincidences, but they consider forensic evidence to be God's word."

I try to glare at him, but his gaze is devoid of any mercy. It makes me feel like I'm staring at the barrel of a gun.

I need to get rid of this. There's a fire across the room—maybe if I run, I can get it burning before Lev can stop me?

Or just tear it up. Yeah, that'll work.

No, even better—pour my drink over the files. Ruin the DVD and the paper.

I stand up, pretending to prepare to drink from my glass before I hold it up over the ammunition box and pour the drink inside it.

For one brief, tiny moment, I feel like I'm winning.

The liquor splashes into the box—not enough to make it swim like I was picturing, but hopefully enough to do sufficient damage.

Lev watches me, his face betraying nothing.

I shake the last few drops of liquid into it.

"You do what you need to do," I say, a rosy glow of triumph in my chest. "But I hope you know that tainted evidence is worthless evidence."

"I have copies," he says matter-of-factly. My heart drops. "Do you really think I'd be so stupid? I also have two bartenders and members of the security team that will testify that you were stalking Mr. Douglas the whole night while barely drinking and ignoring every man who tried to talk to you."

My grip tightens on the glass. "I'll explain to them what happened."

The green shade of his eyes would look like moss or sea green on anybody else, but there's nothing soft about him. He's a knife, cutting me to pieces.

But I'd rather be in pieces than let him think he has me under his thumb.

"Even if you were acquitted—which I doubt—your reputation and your father's would be tarnished." He leans back into the armchair and tents his fingers together.

He's so relaxed, like this is just another day in the life. Hell, for him, maybe blackmail really is just run-of-the-mill business. But not for me. My heart is trembling, my fingers tap-dancing on my thigh.

"Do you recall Cliff Deforest?" he asks.

I set down the glass, letting it loudly clink against the coffee table, and fall into my seat. "No," I say, my voice a barely audible whisper.

"He was a DEA agent. His brother revealed to Internal Affairs that Cliff regularly stole money from drug dealers. When it was disclosed to the media, the media crucified him and he ended up needing to leave his street because people kept vandalizing his house and sending him death threats. What about Roger Durward? Do you know him?"

"No," I say, my teeth gritted together.

"He was a lieutenant. After his wife said she was attacked by two men, which she claimed is how she lost all of the money from a fundraiser, surveillance cameras showed her in a casino, spending it all on craps. Previously, Roger Durward had gone on the record to say that whoever had attacked his wife would be prosecuted to the fullest extent of the law. After he indicated that he was reluctant to prosecute his wife for various charges, he was forced to resign. He ended up leaving after he also received death threats and couldn't get a job anywhere in the city. His wife still went to prison. Have you heard of Doug Anson? He accepted bribes."

I scowl. "Let me guess—he was run out of town?"

"No. I pay him to get rid of evidence." He smiles. "He's a very charming man. If I need him to testify to anything, he'll gladly do it."

"You're the devil," I accuse, vitriol coursing through me.

"And you're the one who chose to slip into bed with the devil," he replies, the slightest sneer rippling across his face. "Don't try to shift the blame on me. I didn't kill Jeffrey Douglas."

"No, but you've done something that you're trying to hide," I say. "I could have my father investigate you and find out why you were so worried that I was at your club. What skeletons do you have in your closet? It looks like you have a lot to lose."

"Go ahead, sweetheart." He leans his head against his hand. "Your father will be fired as soon as the news breaks about the murder, so the investigation into me will go nowhere and your father will look even worse for going after the person who revealed his little girl's secret."

I grab the ammunition box and fling it toward the fireplace. It smacks against the stone before spilling its sodden contents on the floor. I storm out of the room, the explosions in my brain setting fire to everything except the fact that I want to put my hands around Lev's neck and show him what an actual murder looks like.

I stop at the entrance doors. No matter how badly I want to run out of here, no matter what outburst I try on for size, he's trapped me.

I turn around. He hasn't followed me. He knows he doesn't need to.

I take several deep breaths, pacing around the area. I have to change my mindset. This is for my father. This is for my future. This is for all the victims' families. If I want to be a good person, I need to be willing to make sacrifices.

I return to the den. Lev is still in his armchair, drinking while gazing out the window. The ammunition box and his evidence are still spread out on the floor. He doesn't turn to look at me when I step back in.

"When we're married, you'll need to watch what you drink," I say. He turns to me. "You never know what ingredients could be added to give it a little kick."

"Is that a threat?" he asks with a small smile. "You're eager to rack up that body count."

I pick up my glass off the table, which has been filled up again. He knew I was never going to leave. I take a gulp out of it, enjoying the burning sensation down my throat.

"You're a piece of shit," I bite out. He stands up, takes the glass out of my hand, and leans forward. His lips brush against my cheek.

"But I'm yours," he says.

He stands back and straightens up, eyeing me carefully.

I say nothing.

Lev smooths back his hair. "Let me show you the house."

He starts walking out of the den without waiting for my answer. I follow him out, keeping at least a few feet between us.

The mansion is extravagant, to say the least, but it never descends into a desperate desire to show off his wealth. Many, many parts of his home are expensive—the red-tinted hardwood floors, the skylights, the private courtyard, the cutting-edge technology humming behind every wall—but there's never an attempt to fill up space with unnecessary displays of wealth. There's no gold lions or diamond-encrusted map of NYC.

As much as I hate to admit it, it's refined. But I'm certain it's just like him—enticing façade, but hidden rot under its foundation.

On the second floor, he skips over one of the rooms. The door is closed, so I can't see what it is. I stop in front of it. He turns to see why I'm not following him.

"What's in there?" I ask. "Your doll collection?"

"No. It's my bedroom." Before I can stop him, he opens the door. "You don't need to see it. There's not much inside."

The bed could easily fit three people on it and it has a thick, white comforter—the kind that if you fell back onto it, you'd sink several inches and still feel the layers of softness underneath you. There's only one pillow. The only other notable thing inside is the speakers that are built into the walls.

"I expected a bachelor pad," I admit.

"Is that what you wanted?" he asks. For the briefest second before he looks me in the eye, his eyes flicker up and down my body.

"You just seemed like the type that would have the leopard print silk sheets, the mood lighting, maybe a clap-on disco ball—the tools of seduction, you know?" I say sarcastically.

As I glance back at him, I'm struck by his appearance again. He's not beautiful. At least, that's not quite the right word. Everything about him is too severe—the angles of his jaw, the ruthlessness in his eyes, his movements—to make me think of beauty, but I can feel my pulse in every part of my body when I look at him.

"I don't bring women back to the house," he says. "I'm not running a bed and breakfast."

"Why not? You're such a charming host," I mutter.

He seizes my arm.

It should scare me—he's significantly bigger and stronger than me. Even just looking down at his fingers around my arm, I know that he could snap it easily.

The aggression in his face slips away—not like he's made it disappear, but more like he's tucked it away for later use.

"Let's go back to the den."

He closes his bedroom door. I should be relieved, but as he lets go of my arm—my skin a bright red—I'm stuck with this ache.

I follow him. I don't have a choice anymore.

6
LEV

In the den, I walk straight to the bookshelf. I take down *Russia: From Slavic Tribes to Potential Superpower*. The binding is loose, but the invitation is still easy to find. I take it out and put the book back.

I hold it out for Allison to take. She hesitates before snatching it from me. She reads it. And rereads it.

"What the hell is this?" she demands.

"You should recognize it. You must have gone to it a couple of times."

"No." She's holding the invitation so tightly that she's crinkling the edge. "The Great Blue Foundation gala is for the NYPD and donors. Why do you have this?"

"Because I support our brothers in blue."

"Bullshit," she mutters. "You have to donate a lot to be invited and you were afraid of the police chief's daughter being in your nightclub. You're not funding your own criminal investigation."

"No, but I can make the police a lot more reluctant to investigate me if they know pissing me off will cut off their funds." I sit down on the armrest of the sofa. "The amount of money I've donated to the NYPD could buy enough tanks to destroy all five boroughs."

"How fascist of you," she says. "So, why do you need me?"

"Money doesn't work on some people. They'd rather have the glory or the legacy. I can admire the sentiment, but I'd also prefer to not waste my time or money in courtrooms."

She looks back down at the invitation. "I get it. You have control over everything. You don't need to keep proving that to me."

"I didn't show you this to prove anything to you. I'm allowed to bring one person with me. You're going to be that one person."

Her jaw drops. "The gala is on Wednesday. That's three days away."

"Plenty of time."

"It doesn't matter. I'm not going with you to the gala. You know how pissed off my parents will be if I show up with my brand-new fiancé that they've never met?"

"We're not going to show up as an engaged couple. We'll show up as two people who have been dating for a few—let's say, six—months."

She shakes her head. "My parents will still be pissed. After I tell them that I'm going with you, they're going to want to—"

"You're not going to tell them," I interject. "Your parents won't know that we're arriving together until we show up."

"That's insane," she blurts. "My parents need to know. They're going to have an incredibly hard time believing I've kept a relationship a secret from them for six months. They're going to be hurt if they find out that I just showed up at the gala with a long-term boyfriend that they've never met. We're very close. I don't want them to think I've been keeping such a big secret from them for so long."

"I don't care," I say. "I need your father to find out the same time as all of his NYPD buddies and all of his rich donors. If he finds out beforehand, he could become suspicious and try to punish me for being with his little girl or he could try to do damage control before everyone else in the public eye knows we're together. But once everyone knows, he has to accept it as a reality. This whole situation is about his reputation—he's not going to ruin it because he doesn't like his daughter's boyfriend."

"They'll never trust me again," she says, her voice almost breaking. There's a twinge in my chest, but I brush it away.

"They won't trust you if they find out that you killed someone and tried to hide the murder, either," I say. She turns her head away from me.

"Well, it's always good to know that I have no control over my life," she says.

I pluck the invitation out of her hands and set it on the fireplace mantle.

"Who's your best friend?" I ask.

"What?" Her head whips back around. "Julia. How is that relevant to anything?"

"Arrange for the two of us to have dinner with her. Preferably somewhere that she'll be comfortable. Money isn't a problem. We need at least one person who can say she knew we were dating before the gala. Since the gala is on Wednesday, you should call her now."

"How about you go to hell?" she snaps. "I'm not your employee or your whore. I'm not going to jump to my feet and do whatever you want just because you say it in a demanding tone."

"I can change my tone," I say, taking a step closer to her. Our toes are nearly touching, showing the stark difference between her sneakers and my leather shoes. "But you won't like it."

We stare at each other. Her lips are slightly parted. A strand of her dark hair cuts across her face. Her gaze is steady. If we were on equal footing, she'd be a worthy foe, but she knows I hold all of the power.

She blinks before looking down. She grabs her bag and gets out her phone. She taps on the screen a couple of times before bringing the phone up to her ear and glares at me as she waits for Julia to answer.

It better be Julia she's just called.

I look down at my empty glass, the ice slowly melting. This woman is going to drive me straight to alcoholism. She should understand at this point that she has no power in this situation.

Yet something about her resistance is hot as fuck.

Being the Bratva boss and being rich, people easily bend to my will. The people who don't usually end up dead. But this woman keeps pushing against me, either too dumb to realize that I'd fuck her up as quickly as I'd fuck her raw, or too courageous to properly evaluate the situation.

I look behind me, toward the window. The sun is reaching its highest point. Even on a Sunday, I can't waste time like this. Balancing the Bratva and Mariya's Revenge has always been dependent on me keeping the same schedule and Allison has thrown a wrench in the whole thing.

"Yes. I know. It's insane," Allison says into the phone. She tilts her head back, revealing a sensual collarbone and an appetizing throat. "Okay. Yes. I'm not sure when I'll be back. We'll make something together though, I promise. Okay. I love you too. Be safe on the road."

She gets off the phone.

"We're having dinner at the apartment tomorrow around 6:00," she says.

"She's your roommate?"

"Yes," she says. "Which you would know if you'd bothered to ask me."

"Great. We have plenty of time for that." I stand up. "I need you to change into some running clothes, so we can ask each other some questions. I can have my driver drop you off at your apartment and you can get what you need."

"Why would I need running clothes?"

"Because right now is my running time, but we need to become informed about each other, so you need to come with me."

If looks could kill, I'd be burning in hell right now.

"My clothes are fine," she says. I glance at her sweatpants and shirt. The sweatpants are heavy. She's likely wearing a regular bra under her shirt. It's going to be a pain in the ass for her.

So be it.

"Fine," I say. "Let's go."

∽

Kingston Trail is in Konkiel Park, tucked away on the west side. I keep my breathing steady as I push forward. Allison is somewhere close behind me. She appears a couple of inches to my right side, her breathing labored and her hands clinging to her sweatpants that keep sliding down her hips.

I told her not to wear them and now they're distracting us both.

"It's your turn," I remind her.

"Uh." She sucks in a deep breath. "I don't know. You've shot down half of my questions."

"They're things you don't need to know about me," I tell her. "We just need to know enough about each other that we can convince people we've been dating for the last six months. Ask me something."

"What was your first job?" she asks.

"A waiter. Is rum and Coke your favorite drink?"

"Uh, no," she says. "I just order that now because I'm familiar with it. My father used to love it."

I stop running. She nearly trips, surprised by the abrupt change in pace. She turns to face me.

"You need to tell me more. You can't just tell me that something isn't your favorite drink." I wipe sweat off my face with my arm. "Tell me what your favorite drink is."

"You've barely told me anything. Why am I the one who has to tell you everything?"

"Because you only need to know the basics, so we're not giving different answers to the same question. It's just a precaution for you to know facts about my life, but I need to know everything about you. Julia, your parents, and all these policemen are going to know random pieces of information about you that I should know if I've been dating you for six months. Your parents are also going to be motivated to test my knowledge about you to see if I genuinely care about you, so we need to be prepared. Tell me what your favorite drink is."

"It's ..." She swats a fly off her arm. "It doesn't matter. Nobody there is going to know what my favorite drink is."

"Your parents are going to know what your favorite drink is."

"No. They aren't," she says. "It's stupid. My father used to make me this cinnamon chai tea, but he stopped making it for me when I was in my teens. He must have thought I outgrew it, but I crave it all the time."

"Your favorite drink has no alcohol in it."

"Yes. It's not that crazy." Her hands rest on her hips. She gazes down the length of the trail. My eyes trace down her body. Sweat has sunk through her shirt and I can see the outline of her breasts. They're not as big as the fake tits I normally go for, but they're still worthy of some attention. As her breathing slows to a moderate tempo, she looks back at me. She's caught me staring. I smile at her. She crosses her arms over her chest, which just causes her sweatpants to settle lower on her hips. She adjusts her sweatpants again and turns her back to me.

Most city girls look out of place in the woods, but she looks out of place everywhere. It just makes me want to crack her open wide and figure out exactly how her mind works.

Her body, too.

"It's your turn to ask me something," I say. She looks over her shoulder at me.

"Do you ever get tired of being an ass?" she asks.

"No." I take off running again. After the short rest, she's able to keep up with me now. "We need to decide on a reason for why we didn't tell people we were dating."

"That's easy," she says. "We'll tell them that you wanted me to keep it a secret, so you could keep sleeping with other women."

"No. You're not going to paint your future fiancé as a womanizer. We'll say that I didn't want my negative reputation to affect you."

"Do you mean your womanizing reputation?"

I shake my head. The less she knows, the better. The more time that passes since Jeffrey Douglas' death, the more she will be inclined to stay silent.

"Well, I don't like that," she says, tugging on her sweatpants again.

"I don't care what you like or don't like."

"It's not just my preference. People are going to be able to tell from a mile away that you're an asshole who would never keep something a secret for the sake of another person. We need something different."

I pick up my pace. She runs harder too.

"Fine. We'll say that we kept it a secret because I was too busy to deal with you and the fact that I was too busy meant that we weren't certain if we should commit to each other."

"We were both too busy."

"Fine." I force a smile as we pass a couple jogging in the opposite direction. I look over my shoulder, waiting for them to disappear around the corner. "We also need a story for how we met. I already know you're going to disagree, but my plan was that you spilled coffee on me at a coffee house. You helped me clean it up, we started talking, and we had our first date that night."

"Not a chance in hell," she says, her breathing getting ragged again. God, that sound would be an aphrodisiac in bed.

"I knew you were going to say that." I have to turn my head to talk to her because she's falling behind again. "Why? Because I made you look clumsy?"

"No, that part is completely believable," she says. "The unbelievable part is that the whole scenario sounds like every romance movie in existence. And that makes me a little suspicious. Are you watching a lot of chick flicks? Are you a romantic under all that ego?"

I scowl, but the teasing in her voice is invigorating. There's something simplistic about it—there's no layers or agenda underneath it.

"We have to have another spot where it's normal that we'd encounter each other," she says. "Where do insanely rich people go that average people also go to?"

"The gas station," I say.

"Okay. We met at the gas station. And I went up to you because ... you were being a dick to someone. Statistically, there's a strong chance that happened at some point."

We keep running. She almost trips but manages to keep herself upright and catches up to me. Her arm brushes up against mine as she tries to keep up.

"We met at the gas station," she repeats. "You mistook me for one of your high school classmates. You bought me the bottle of soda I was holding. I had no idea you were rich. Our first few dates were very casual."

If this were an actual business meeting, I'd give her some credit—it's creative without being outlandish.

"Sounds good," I say.

"Can we ... can we please stop for a second?" she pants.

I stop. She stops a few feet ahead of me, leaning forward and trying to catch her breath. Her hand is pressed over her heart. I take a step forward to check on her.

"Do you need to sit down?" I ask. She shakes her head. Her face is covered in sweat, but she pulls it off well. One of the models I fucked a couple of months ago joked that she didn't sweat, she glistened, but she was full of shit. Glisten is too elegant of a word, but as Allison closes her eyes, letting her head fall back as the sun beats down on her, there's an unmistakable authenticity to her.

I could grab her, have her legs wrap around my waist, and fuck her against a tree, then in the fallen leaves. It'd be a perfect end to the run.

She stands up straight, taking a few more deep breaths. She pushes her sweatpants down and carefully pulls them over her shoes and off her legs.

"What the fuck are you doing?" I ask.

"It'll be easier to run without them," she says. "If somebody has a problem with it and calls the police, apparently you can take care of that."

She balls the sweatpants in her arms and takes off running again.

I chase after her. She's in her T-shirt, her underwear, and her shoes. Her ass sways with her movements and her thigh muscles contract and relax with her stride. It's a thing of beauty.

I run slower now. There's significantly less conversation. On some level, she must know I'm watching because she doesn't check to see where I am.

Then the rain begins.

∼

Water drips onto the floor as I close the door. Allison is drenched. Her dark hair appears pitch-black when it's wet and it sticks to her shoulders and arms like latex. Her shirt is clinging to her skin, but more importantly, her underwear seems nearly translucent.

"I'm going to sit down for the next decade," Allison says, walking toward the den. She's carrying her sweatpants in her right hand and her bag on her left arm. The familiar body ache hasn't hit me yet, but Allison is already walking with a slight, wincing limp.

I should head to the bathroom to shower.

I should go to my office to check on the sales of Mariya's Revenge orange-cream flavor vodka.

I should check for movements from the Colosimo family.

But instead, I follow her into the den.

Allison collapses onto one of the couches. I sit down in the armchair. She turns onto her back, her eyes close, and she drapes her arm over them.

"Are you going to be okay?" I ask.

"I'm going to be great if someone kills me and resurrects me," she says. "You run that much every day?"

"No. I try to do it every other day, but it depends on my schedule. On my off days, I do weight training."

"Of course you do," she mutters. "In between the blackmailing, just for the variety."

"If you could have blackmailed me first, you would have. It's the law of the jungle—eat or be eaten."

"I wouldn't do that," she retorts.

"It would be weak and stupid not to."

"You think it's weak and stupid to be moral?" she asks, shifting her arm, so she can peek at me with one eye.

"I think it's weak and stupid to be weak and stupid." I wipe sweat off my forehead. "Do you think that being nice to the world will make the world be nice to you? I'm sure the view from up there on your high horse seems lovely. But here you are, in this den, with me. Your morals won't help you down here."

"Well, you see, Lev …" Allison covers both of her eyes with her arm again. "Normal people have this thing called empathy. It means that when other people feel bad, you feel bad with them."

"That sounds like an impediment in my line of work."

She props herself up on her elbow, her wet hair gliding over her skin, and turns toward me. There's a hint of a smile on her face. I press my fingers near the corner of my mouth, so she can't notice that I'm nearly smiling back.

"What?" I ask.

She shrugs. "I just find it fun to debate with people. It's part of the reason I want to be a lawyer."

"I get it," I say. "I became a vodka manufacturer because I love to drink."

"And you have the nightclub." She stretches, a small noise of satisfaction escaping her lips. I'd love to get that noise out of her over and over. "After I did all that running and interrogating, you have to at least tell me why you thought I was stalking you in that nightclub."

"I'm not convinced that you weren't."

She rolls her eyes before resting her head on the armrest, curling up like a small child. It's a little endearing. Mostly juvenile and signs of a spoiled brat, but still—a little endearing.

She seems happier now than I've seen her so far. I chalk it up to exercise-induced endorphin release. I take in her bare legs, the smoothness traced through with the faint lines of her muscles. As she shifts her legs, I look up to her face. She's looking back at me. I lean back, ready for her to overreact, but she only looks at me. She smiles, slow and reckless.

I want her.

I want to fold her in half and fuck her. I want to pin her down and feel her hips push up against my hips. I want to show her the world without morality or laws, where it's just bodies creating friction.

I move to the edge of the chair. The motion causes her to jerk upward like a frightened deer.

"I should rehydrate," she says, avoiding looking at me.

Allison stands up and immediately crumples to the ground. Her hand slaps hard against the floor to steady herself. I'm off my chair before I realize what I'm doing, my hand on her back.

"Are you okay?" I ask. "I can get you the water."

"No," she mutters, sliding onto her side and rubbing her calf. "It's a stupid cramp. This is a sign from the universe that running is a crime against nature."

"Come on. Let's get you back onto the couch."

Her hand presses on my shoulder as she tries to get up on one leg. My arm wrapped around Allison's petite frame, I help her get back onto the couch and sit down beside her. Her jasmine scent sweeps over me. As I pull my arm away from her, she turns to me. Our faces are so close together, I feel her exhale against my lips.

Her hand touches my chest before her lips do. Her fingers press against my chest as she pushes herself away. Her cheeks are flushed with red.

"I'm sorry," she mumbles. "Um, I'm getting your couch wet. I mean from my clothes. Do you have any clothes I could borrow?"

I scrutinize her. She's turned her face away from me, concentrating on the tree outside the window. She turns back toward me when I don't answer.

"Yes," I say, and stand up without saying anything more. As I leave the den, I hear her behind me, her footsteps soft as she keeps her distance. As we walk up the stairs, I turn enough to see her clinging to her bag like it's a gun that's going to protect her. I keep moving forward, reminding myself that I need her for control over her father and nothing else.

My closet is the room right before my bedroom. I open the door and gesture for Allison to step in.

The closet is octagonal, every wall displaying a different category of clothing. Most of them are very similar name-brand pieces. I have no interest in it, but money makes me look desirable to consumers and women and threatening to my enemies.

I move to the section with my casual clothing. I pick out some sweatpants, a pair of shorts, and a pair of boxers. I toss them to her.

"I don't think any of those will fit, but you can try them on," I say.

She sets her bag down by her feet and pulls on the sweatpants. They don't stay up and the legs cover her feet, creating an illusion that she shrunk. As she pulls them back off, it's hard to ignore the perfect curvature of her ass and thighs. She could murder me with those thighs and I'd still love them.

She tosses the sweatpants back to me, raising her eyebrow when she catches me looking. "Should I change somewhere else?"

"My bedroom is empty," I say. She nearly laughs, a smirk sparking on her face before she turns around, pulling on the shorts. The waistband is also too wide. With her hourglass figure, it seems like they should fit, but her ratio doesn't change the fact that she's a pixie compared to me.

She pulls the shorts off and tries on the boxers. They settle on her hips. She bounces on the balls of her feet. The boxers start to slide down, revealing the top of her underwear.

"I don't know," she says, pulling them back up. I take a gray sweater off a hanger and toss it to her. She catches it.

"That sweater should be long enough to cover your ass."

She pinches the sweatshirt between her knees and peels off her shirt. All the women I've been with in the last five years have had breasts big enough to divide and conquer. Allison's are smaller but combined with her lithe body, it's a territory worthy of a war.

She pulls on the sweater. The hemline ends in the middle of her thighs. She spins around.

"How do I look?"

Like you could kill me and I'd love it.

"It's good enough for now. We should put your clothes in the dryer."

She bounces on the balls of her feet, the sneakers squishing from the water. "What do you think will happen if I leave with your sweater? That I'll steal it? You don't trust me at all?"

I snatch her pants from the floor. "No. The master bathroom is in the room after my bedroom. If you can't figure out how it works, I'll be downstairs. Irina can add your other clothes to the dryer once you're done."

I walk away as she opens her mouth to argue.

With any other woman, I would have just sent her home in her wet clothes.

But Allison is my future wife. And, unlike the others, I haven't fucked her yet.

7
ALLISON

I had only seen the master bathroom in a quick glimpse when Lev gave me a tour before. I wasn't concerned about the bathroom—I was concerned that I wanted to equally murder and sacrifice myself to one of the worst men I'd ever met.

I'm deeply concerned about the bathroom now.

Most of the bathroom is okay, if the definition of 'okay' is heaven on earth. The marble floors, the massive mirror that stretches across the east wall, a jacuzzi, and the black vanities—all breathtaking, all flawless. The walk-in shower is particularly overwhelming.

The outside is simple enough. There's one glass wall, plus an opening on one side, where I can walk through. There is a bright light shining over the shower and thirteen metal contraptions underneath it, which appear to be twelve different water jets and a removable showerhead. The removable showerhead would only reach my shoulder. The water jets are high enough that the water would reach my head, but I can't imagine that they're high enough to reach Lev's head.

There's an electronic touchscreen on the wall beside the shower. I tap on it. Six options pop up.

Waterfall

Massage

Steam

Music

Daily report

Change color

I've never hated rich people more than I have in this moment. I tap Steam. Four of the water jets start producing steam. I watch it curl inside the glass for a minute before I tap it again to stop it. I tap Music. It gives me various genre selections. I tap Waterfall.

Water starts pouring down from the light. Or else, it's not the light, but another shower head. I press Change Color and select turquoise. The light changes color, so the water appears to be a greenish-blue shade. On the screen, it's asking me to choose a temperature. It's set at 100 degrees, so I keep it there.

I pull off the sweater, my bra, and my underwear. When I walk into the water, the water cascades over me. The pressure is almost painful, but as I get used to it, it massages my skin like a real waterfall, except there's a faint woodsy scent. In most houses, I'd imagine it came from somebody's soap, but the scent continues to envelop me with the same intensity, so it must come from the showerhead.

There's a notch in the wall with a bottle of shampoo and a bottle of soap. I spurt out some shampoo and knead it into my hair. It's Lev's scent—that smoky, spicy fragrance that hooks me and makes me feel like the criminal he says I am.

I close my eyes.

I start to imagine things. Like Lev opening the bathroom door. I'd pretend to be outraged by him coming in. I'd probably try to leave the shower, but he'd block me from leaving. His clothes would come off and he'd join me under the waterfall. Our bodies would rub against each other, his mouth hot and open against the side of my neck, his erection pushing against my inner thighs. He'd screw me so hard, I'd only be able to lean against him, his arms keeping me from slipping and cracking my head open.

I open my eyes.

What the hell is wrong with me? Jeffrey Douglas' murder has messed up the synapses in my brain. There's no way I'd normally be attracted to Lev. I've always been attracted to honorable men—the ones who volunteer, the social service workers, the emergency service technicians.

Lev, on the other hand, is a rich, arrogant, controlling prick, who is likely involved in shady business and could have used his millions of dollars for better things than a shower with a touchscreen, twelve jets, and a fucking waterfall setting.

After I've cleansed myself of sweat and dirty thoughts, I step out of the shower. I wander the bathroom, searching through cabinets and shelves for fresh towels. When I don't find any, I take one from the metal bars mounted on the wall, which I assume are the ones that Lev has used.

It's warm.

I pull it around me, the softness and warmth almost as good as the water. I touch the metal bar. It nearly burns my skin.

I could see how Lev decided that being good isn't worth his time. Because being corrupt seems to pay incredibly well.

I open the bathroom door and peek out. He's not lingering in the hallway. I close the door again and get my phone out of my bag. I bring up my browser and search Lev Alekseiev.

Mariya's Revenge Selling New Vodka Flavor

Mariya's Revenge Snatches Top Sales

Mariya's Revenge or Mariya's Revenue? Sweet Flavor, Sweeter Sales

Alekseiev, Mariya's Revenge Owner, Praises the City and the Sinners

For several pages of search results, there is nothing negative about Lev. If he's been involved in any criminal behavior, he's either sued his way out of it being mentioned on the internet or he's kept everyone blackmailed into silence.

As the warmth from the towel fades, I set it back on the bar and slide on the sweater. The smoky and spicy scent takes hold of me again. I try to ignore it, grabbing my bra and underwear, but I know I'm going to be reminded of his body every time I inhale now.

I leave the bathroom. As I descend the stairs, I hear the faint patter of rain and go toward the entrance. At first, through one of the long windows beside the door, it looks like fog has concealed the view of the yard.

It's pounding down so hard that it's causing a mist. I move closer to the window. There's a small section of the road that's visible from the house. I watch a truck drive down, forced to plow through the inches of rain on the road, swerving dangerously as if the tires can't find traction in the downpour.

I won't be able to leave.

It's hard to not believe I did something wrong when I defended myself against Jeffrey Douglas when the universe keeps trying to punish me.

I wander down the hallway, passing by all of his rooms with the hardwood floors, the marble floors, chandeliers, and technology I couldn't dream of living with before this. The dining room has a table with twelve chairs. The table has a glass top with a claw-foot base.

The kitchen has marble countertops and stainless steel appliances without so much as a fingerprint blemishing the shining surfaces.

My heart races each time I enter a new room, expecting to see Lev, but he's not on the first floor. When I reach the kitchen, I stop to listen, waiting to see if I can hear noise up above me. Nothing.

I swallow back the disappointment. I'm not going to go upstairs and look for him. I don't want him to get the idea that he's on my mind.

I return to the hallway and stop at the den. The ammunition box and all of its contents are gone. I move over to the home bar and pour myself a rum and Coke. Grabbing a book, I sit down to read.

∼

The low rumble of voices.

The burning in my thighs.

The sensation of a crater-dry tongue.

I slowly open my eyes. There's a kink in my neck from my neck resting against the armrest. I rub my eyes, sitting up. The book has fallen to the floor. I pick it up, setting it on the end table.

A laugh. I haven't heard Lev laugh, but this one seems too relaxed to belong to him.

I stand up, still feeling the achy tension in my legs. I don't know what I was thinking, agreeing to run with Lev.

Mostly, I wanted to keep him appeased, so he didn't strike out at my father. But another part of me wanted to go wherever he went. I didn't want his mind to be filled with the serenity of a good workout. I wanted him to learn that I was more than the chief's daughter. I didn't want him to forget about me.

I look out into the hallway. It's dim. Either the storm has cast the city in a shadow or several hours have passed. The laugh echoes in the mansion again. I move in the direction where it came from, deeper in the house.

As I get closer, I start to hear voices. One of them is animatedly telling a story.

"—absolutely insane. She looks like she has half a mind to grab her keys and start slashing my face. I've abandoned all hope of reconciliation at this point. She's ready to murder me. She's tiny, but she's full of enough wrath to take down an army. So, I do the only thing I can think of—I tell her that I'm a mole."

I hear the rumble of another voice, but I'm not close enough to understand it. I keep moving forward, my steps softer now that I'm closer.

"I know," the first man says. "She believed me, though, and in her mind, it was better for me to be a backstabbing rat than someone who just abandoned her. The woman would have accepted any other narrative than the truth where I simply didn't care for her."

I see lights now, coming from the dining room area. I stay to the right side of the hall to avoid them seeing me approach. When I reach the doorframe, I press against the wall.

"God never made a bigger mistake than giving people too much confidence and not enough common sense," Lev's voice thrums under my skin.

"Ah well, I worship him every day for it."

The clink of glasses tapping against each other.

"Speaking of arrogant idiots," Lev says. "How is the situation with Duilio?"

Duilio. The word feels familiar.

"Mmm," the other man says. "Nobody has found anything. His men must know by now. They haven't blatantly made any moves, but our men have noticed their usual places are emptier than usual."

"Rats fleeing from the ship or a snake preparing to strike?"

"We can't say either way right now. Lev, I know that it was necessary to do and—"

"Ilya," Lev says. "Hush."

"I'm sorry, Lev. I don't mean to speak out of turn."

"It's not that. I see a shadow. Come out, Allison Harrington."

He enunciates my name like every syllable is a dart, striking the bullseye every time. I look down at my shadow. It's barely visible. It could have easily been mistaken for bad eyesight.

I step out into the doorway. Lev is sitting with another man. The man is around his age, but he reminds me of a time that I don't want to remember—a time of blood loss, pale bodies, and a grief that hit me harder than the car.

"Ilya, this is my future wife, Allison Harrington."

My stomach drops at the blunt reminder this man holds over me. Over my entire future.

"Allison, this is my assistant, Ilya," Lev says, gesturing between the two of us. Ilya, stands up, smiling. He's so pale and sickly looking, but he exudes a genuine warmth.

"It's nice to meet you, Miss Harrington. I don't have anything contagious," he tells me as he outstretches his hand.

"Oh no, I'm sorry. I hope I wasn't staring," I say, shaking his hand. His grasp is soft—not desperate to prove his strength. "I just didn't expect anyone else to be here."

"It's fine, Miss Harrington. I'm used to people staring. We can all just assume that my ancestors survived by convincing everyone we were so sick that nobody should bother coming close enough to kill us. Or maybe they thought we were vampires. Either way, we made it here, so it can't be too bad. Why don't you sit down? We're just enjoying a small meal. I'd love for you to join us."

For the first time, I notice two Styrofoam boxes in front of them. They're both filled with shish kebabs. The scent lures me into the chair between the two men.

I take one of kebab sticks out and, in spite of feeling slightly nauseous after being reminded of my 'engagement,' I bite into one of the meat chunks. The marinade is perfect, balancing a sweet, salty, and savory flavor. As I chew on it, it occurs to me that Ilya wasn't surprised to be introduced to Lev's 'future wife.' But he wasn't congratulatory either.

As I turn to look at him, I see him exchanging a look with Lev. There's faint disapproval in Ilya's eyes, but Lev's gaze is as remorseless as usual. Ilya catches me looking and smiles at me.

"How do you like it?"

"It's great," I say. "I haven't had kebabs in a long time."

"They're actually shashlik," he says. "They're a Russian dish."

"Oh. You're Russian too?" I ask.

"Yes." Ilya glances over at Lev. He must see the same stiffened demeanor as I do. He mutters something to Lev—it sounds Russian and apologetic. Lev must have heard him, but he doesn't acknowledge the comment.

I can't decode their relationship. Lev is Ilya's boss, so Ilya would be Lev's subordinate, but here they are, eating together while joking about something personal and Ilya knows about Lev's 'future wife' without any questions about where I've been this whole time or applauding our engagement or anything normal like that.

Yet, Ilya still seems more than subordinate. He seems subservient.

"I didn't mean to pry about your heritage," I say. "I'm sorry about that. Lev is just weird about it because of something I said earlier. I accused him of being influenced by the Bratva."

Ilya's eyebrows briefly shoot up, but he laughs and relaxes again.

"The Bratva? I'm certain Lev could lead them quite well," Ilya says. He reaches forward, touching my hand, before quickly pulling back. "Miss Harrington, I didn't mean to make you feel like you needed to be apologetic. You don't need to feel sorry around me. I can take care of myself."

His tone is bordering on pleading. He's not only subservient to Lev. He's subservient to me, too.

Why?

I clear my throat. "So, how did you get here through the rain? It's coming down pretty hard."

"The flooding isn't quite as bad as it was," he says. "But I also have a Raptor that Lev bought me, so I'm not worried about it. If you're worried about the rain, I could take you home if you'd like. It's safer in my vehicle than yours."

I glance at Lev in question. His jaw is clenched and there's a flicker of disapproval and possessiveness across his face. I'd be a liar if I said I didn't like it.

I look back at Ilya. "I'd appreciate it so much if you'd do that."

∽

The wipers slice across the windshield, but it's like bailing a boat with a hole in the bucket. The road looks like a river, too, but Ilya seems unperturbed. He might as well be in a car wash.

"Have you worked for Lev for a long time?" I ask, fiddling with my sweatpants' drawstrings. When Lev retrieved my clothes for me, they were still warm. He told me to return the next day. It wasn't a request. That level of arrogance always gets under my skin, but somehow the friction is also addictive.

"About five years," he says. "But I've known him longer."

"How did you two meet?"

"We had some friends in common," he says. His tone isn't harsh, but there's a tension in the arm that's gripping the steering wheel.

I stare out the window, pretending to be lost in thought. I wait until his arm relaxes.

"You two are close."

"Yes," he says.

"So, what crime did he commit?"

He chuckles. "You're a rather peculiar choice. I always thought Lev preferred the ones who stood still and looked pretty. He's always found talkative people annoying."

"That's good to know," I say. "Now I know how to annoy him."

"I wouldn't advise that," Ilya warns. "Why do you want to know what crime he may or may not have committed?"

"I don't trust him."

"Miss Harrington, if you don't trust him, then you don't trust me," he says, his tone turning serious. He looks over at me, sending my heartrate racing since he's not looking at the road. "And if that's true, there's no point in me telling you anything."

"Okay," I say quickly, nodding toward the road. He turns back, his body relaxing again.

"You said the apartment building next to Sylvester's Liquor, right?" he asks.

I nod. I could have lived in a better complex. My father offered to pay for a better place. He showed me crime statistics. He showed me photos of crimes that have happened in the area. But it was the place Julia decided on, I could afford it on the money I'd earned as a tutor, and I didn't want to start my independent life depending on my father's money. So, now Sylvester is my neighbor on one side. The other side is a vacant warehouse, occupied mostly by rats.

Ilya pulls into the driveway. It's a bumpy experience as it's impossible to miss all of the potholes, especially now that they're harder to see in the downpour. He drives past the decrepit cars, two of which are missing their tires. The last one in the row has a smashed window. The broken glass floats in a murky puddle beside it.

"Does Lev know that you live here?" Ilya asks.

"I wouldn't be surprised if he knew exactly what room I sleep in, where I pee, and what I eat every morning."

Ilya snorts. "That's likely true."

He parks in front of the building. The front door is only a few feet away, but the sheets of rain crashing down aren't inviting.

"I'm sorry, I don't have an umbrella," Ilya says.

"It's fine." I jerk open the door. Rain starts whipping into the truck. "Thanks for the ride, Ilya."

I step into a puddle, soaking my sneakers and socks, but I don't stop running until I'm in the building.

Once inside, I bound up the stairs, skipping steps. I nearly run into Mrs. Gillium, a widow in her seventies who is, allegedly, a prostitute. When I get to my apartment, I scramble to unlock the door and lock myself inside.

I stand motionless for several seconds, absorbing the silence of the place, before quickly shucking my soaked clothes and changing into something dry.

I look around my room. Now what? Home feels weird after Lev's mansion. What was once cozy is now weirdly confining. Everything looks shabby, second-hand—mostly because that's exactly what it is, but it never bothered me before. I like my stuff. Or at least, I used to.

Flopping into bed, I open my constitutional law book. I try to focus on the words, but my brain is in shambles. It's like driving through that mess of a parking lot outside my building, but instead of hitting potholes, I keep accidentally running into sensations of Lev.

The sight of him running in front of me, his movements smooth without sacrificing power. A predator, every movement natural and full of purpose.

Or the way I sometimes caught him looking at me. The way his eyes turned me into his prey.

The smell of him. Intoxicating. Overwhelming.

His voice; that deep rumble of unmistakable authority. Power infused in every word.

And most of all—his touch on my skin, the strength in his fingertips, noticeable but restrained, like he was holding back—whether for my benefit or his, I couldn't say for sure.

I reread the paragraph from the constitutional law book.

Civil liberties are the foundation of the U.S. Constitution and the U.S. legal system operates under the unequivocal belief in its supreme law. It is a lawyer's prerogative to work within these ideals and uphold the country's deepest principles.

I sit up, running my fingers through my hair. It's tangled from being wet. I imagine Lev's hands in it. Yanking, teasing, owning.

"Do you think that being nice to the world will make the world be nice to you? Your morals won't help you down here."

Lev's voice echoes in my mind along with a rattling sound. I look around. Wait, no, the rattling sound isn't in my mind. I grab my bag, ripping more of it as I unzip it. My phone's screen is glowing inside it. I pull it out.

A blocked number has sent a text.

Remember, we're meeting up tomorrow morning. 7 a.m. We have to know each other well enough to convince your roommate and everyone at the gala.

Another text pops up as I finish reading.

Bring gym clothes this time.

My fingers start moving before I think about it.

I text back, *no promises.*

I wait to see if he responds, but the tell-tale three dots never appear. I feel my lips twist into a smile despite myself. I lie down, my cell phone resting on my chest. I shouldn't be happy. He's blackmailing me. He's involved in something shady and enough of an asshole that his executive assistant is concerned about upsetting him.

I close my eyes. I play through a new fantasy, where I notice Lev watching me in Black Glacier. There's nobody there but us. He pushes me up against the bar, his cock pressed up against my ass. He doesn't say anything, but when he pushes inside me, there's a crooning noise coming from my mouth.

It's a perfect moment as he starts moving inside me, Lev no longer teasing, just owning me fully, the way I'm desperate to be taken.

Until I see Jeffrey Douglas' decaying body on the other side of the bar.

My eyes snap open, arousal vanishing as swiftly as the steam in Lev's shower disappeared when I turned it off.

I have no idea what happened to his body. Lev never mentioned it.

Did he get the Bratva to help him? Do they know about me? Do I owe them now?

I tuck my hands under my head. I can't close my eyes again. I stare at the wall, hearing the rain drill against the window. I wait for everything to shatter.

But the rain just keeps beating down.

8
LEV

The next day

After finishing my shower, I find Allison in the den, her freshly washed hair twisted into a messy bun. She's playing with a deck of cards. Each card is painted with gold ink, depicting fifty-two "wonders" of the world while the two joker cards depict the galaxy.

Allison's legs are tucked underneath the coffee table as she moves one of the cards. I sit down next to her. She's playing FreeCell.

"Are you winning?" I ask.

"I think I'm proving that I'm not good at thinking long-term." She scoops up all of the cards.

"You didn't need to stop your game for my sake," I say.

"You were being distracting," she says. She sticks her tongue out at me. "Besides, we need to keep quizzing each other, don't we? If anyone is going to see through this scheme, it's Julia."

"How about we do both?" I take the cards from her. "If we played some strip poker, we could learn a lot about each other."

I could lie and say I was just trying to get her off guard. It'd be partially true. But I've fallen asleep, woken up, and showered wanting to experience her, so all that's on my mind is getting her closer to that point.

"I'm sure that would be productive," she says. There's a faint pink tint in her cheeks, but overall, she's less prudish than before. I might break her down yet. "But it might be better if we reveal more of our secrets than our bodies. How about truth poker? Every time one of us loses a hand, they have to truthfully answer a question from the other person."

I keep my eyes on her. She wants me to answer her question about what crime I've committed. It'd be easy to get around. I've committed a smorgasbord of crimes. I could tell her about when I was a child and I stole groceries for my parents. I could tell her that when I was a teenager, I beat a man who grabbed my date between the legs. I could even admit to Black Glacier laundering some Bratva money. It would get her off my back and finally get her on hers.

I hand the cards to her. "You can shuffle."

The first hand is easy. She has nothing. Her lower lip slightly presses up. I can only hope her father won't be able to read her face as well as I can.

I flip over my cards. "Top pair."

She tosses her cards down. Nothing. "Ask me."

"How did you meet Julia?"

I thought this would be a simple question—some dumb sorority sisters or childhood playmates, but her lower lip presses up again. She takes a deep breath.

"It's a long story."

I collect the cards on the table, sliding them under the deck. She fidgets with her ear. Time becomes a test as she waits for me to move on and I wait for her to realize I'm not going to.

"Okay," she says. "Fair is fair. It was about a year ago in November. I was with three of my friends. It was my sophomore year and I'd been friends with these women since the beginning of my freshman year. Um."

She rubs her forehead, avoiding my gaze now. In most people, I'd assume this was a tell, indicating that they were lying, but her eyes are getting glossy. One side of me wants to dig harder into this story, figure out how I can use it to get more control over her father, but the other part of me is uncertain.

"We went to this frat party. It wasn't the first time. We'd been to a few. Far more than I should have been going to as the chief's daughter. And two of my friends were doing drugs. I turned a blind eye to it."

She rubs her neck, pressing against her throat for a second.

"When we got into the car, Lily, my friend … she insisted on driving. She told me she was fine. I believed her. I didn't want her to see me as this uptight chief's daughter, and I believed her. Another car swerved out of its lane—turned out that driver was drunk far more than Lily—and her reflexes were so impaired that she didn't get us out of the way in time. I don't know if you could have done that even if she'd been stone sober. Either way, we crashed. Lily died. The other driver … he got off on some kind of technicality. That's one reason I'm pursuing law. So that never happens to anyone again."

Her voice breaks, her hands cover her face, and she trembles. I move closer to her, not used to being in this position. Offering comfort is not one of my strengths, to say the least. Awkwardly, I wrap my arm around her shoulders, pulling her toward me. At first, she resists, but then she slowly crumples against me, pressing her face against my chest.

The den is filled with her sobs. I try to focus on anything else—

Mariya's Revenge, the Bratva, the Colosimos—because I can't risk letting her emotions affect mine. This is a contract between us. She's nothing to me but a means to an end and a body to fuck.

But I don't let her go.

"I'm sorry," she mumbles. "I'm so sorry."

I'm not certain if she's talking to me or her friends, but I stroke her hair. When she looks up at me, her eyes are a galaxy of emotions. Her hand clings to my arm as she pulls herself upward. Her eyes close as she kisses me. The way her lips slowly move against mine, it's the most sensual kiss I've ever received. I return it, giving her back what she gave me.

Her eyes flicker open. That galaxy of emotions is slightly calmer, but now they seem to quiver in uncertainty. I must be looking at her in the same way. I don't know what the fuck she was just thinking.

She breaks our reverie, looking down at her legs, then sits up a little, moving away from me as she wipes her tears from her face.

"I'm sorry. I haven't answered the question," she says.

"It's fine," I mutter.

"No, um. I came up with this idea. So … Julia was the EMT. She pulled me out of the car. I—I owe her my life."

She covers her hand with her mouth, staring intently at her knee.

"We should actually start heading to my apartment now. The traffic gets busy around this time and if I don't get there soon, she'll start making dinner on her own."

"Okay," I say, though everything seems very fucking far from okay.

∼

When Allison introduces me to Julia, I expect to see a Florence

Nightingale-type—a plain woman, bordering on ugly, the kind of girl whose heart is beautiful, but nothing else.

But I was wrong. Julia is not ugly. Nobody needs to make false claims about her.

She doesn't have the same magnetism as Allison. She's an America's sweetheart level of cute. She doesn't have the strangely angular face of a model or the banality of a prom queen, but she has flowing golden hair and freckles that make her appear more genuine.

"It's nice to meet you, Julia," I say. I shake her hand, placing my other hand over it to convey warmth and investment in the greeting. I glance over at Allison. Her forehead is furrowed as she looks away from our hands.

There's no way she thinks I'd choose Julia over her, right?

"I didn't know what you had here, but I brought some wine." I offer it to Julia. I didn't pay any attention to her while we were shaking hands, but now I see it.

She hates me.

This is a new problem. Usually by the time people hate me, I've already trapped them in their circumstances. I don't need them to like me. But right here, right now, I need Julia to like me and I don't like that. I'm ponying up to the negotiating table in the weak position. Very out of character for me.

"Wow. This is expensive," she says, taking the wine from me. "I could probably sell this for someone to pay their medical bill."

"If that's what you'd like," I say.

"Jules," Allison interjects. "I thought we'd make some pasta. We have all of the ingredients. Lev, why don't you sit down?"

She indicates their living room, which is seven feet from the door and a step away from the kitchen.

"I can help," I say.

"No. You should sit down," Julia says. "Please."

Every instinct tells me to cut her down, but I can't have her running to the chief. I walk over to their tiny bookcase in the corner of the room. Most of the selection is law books. I look out the window. It's facing the parking lot.

The location of her apartment is disappointing. I expected a lot more from the chief's daughter. Either her father doesn't care about her or she's testing his patience.

It's testing my patience, too. It'd take one stray bullet in the parking lot for her to slip away before Julia could save her.

I glance over to the kitchen. Allison is chopping up an onion while Julia is filling a pot with water. Julia steps away from the pot, her hand settling on Allison's shoulder as she leans toward her ear to whisper something. Allison whispers something back. Julia glances at me, notices me watching, and retreats to her pot of water. After she fills the pot, she sets it on the stove.

"Be careful," Julia says to Allison, igniting the fire under the burner. She could be talking about the fire or me.

I get it now. Julia helped save Allison's life and therefore feels more responsibility over her life than an average friend or roommate would. Julia is invested in Allison's life, so my sudden appearance raises her hackles.

I sit down on the couch. I've never met anyone who hated me that I didn't feel indifferent about or despise, but Julia is a first for me. I'm grateful for her suspicion of me. I need to convince her that we're a real, loving couple, but it's nice to know that Allison has someone around that's focused on her well-being.

"Julia." I stand up and face the two of them. Allison is holding onto a colander, her grip tight on the edges. "Could I talk to you for a moment?"

"Sure," Julia says. "Speak."

"I meant without Allison around. Outside."

Julia looks back at Allison. I can only see Allison's face, but there's the slightest shake of her head. Julia turns back to me.

"Sure." She heads toward the door. "I hope you don't smoke."

I follow her out. "Not tonight."

She takes the stairs down, not checking to see if I'm behind her. Once we're outside, she keeps her gaze on the parking lot, her arms folded over her chest. The door slams shut behind us.

"So, what did you want to talk about?" she asks.

"I want you to say what you need to say," I tell her. "And then move on."

She spins around to look at me. "What is that supposed to mean?"

"Allison has chosen me. She's with me. And you can hate me for whatever reason you want, but that fact isn't going to change until Allison changes her mind. So, say what you need to say because the tension between us is not good for Allison."

She tilts her head. "I don't know you. How could I hate you?"

"You're managing it just fine."

She smirks, but her arms remain tightly folded in front of her chest. "You know, after she told me who you are, I looked you up. Why did you change from models to Allison?"

"That sounds like an insult to Allison," I say. "She'd wipe the floor with any of those models any day."

"I don't hate you. I just don't trust you," she says. "If you want me to trust you, you better earn it. Do you know how many houses and penthouses of rich pricks I've been to? The poor neighborhoods get a bad rap but that's just because the rich know how to hide their skeletons."

"You hate me because I'm rich."

She opens up the apartment building door and turns to me. "The fact that that's your takeaway? *That* is your problem. You hear the word *rich* and you skip over the word *skeletons*."

I turn away as the door slams shut. I pull a pack of cigarettes out of my jacket and light up. I inhale until it starts to hurt and let it go. I watch a tweaker dance around his car before banging the front of his body on the hood of the car. He does it two more times before starting to dance around his car again.

When I finish the first cigarette, I start another one. When I've almost burned through that one, the apartment door slams open. First, an old woman toddles through, giving me a wink as she passes by, and then Allison is standing beside me.

"What the hell was that about?" she asks. "Did you threaten her? Blackmail her?"

"I'd think you'd know her well enough that if I tried either of those, she'd cut my balls off," I say. She tries to hide a smile, looking down at her shoes.

"She always gets what she wants. If you weren't down here to threaten her, what did you two talk about? She won't tell me."

"It doesn't matter." I drop the cigarette and crush it with my foot. "The only good news is that she doesn't think we're both frauds. You're a saint and I'm the emblem of rich, corrupt people, who hide skeletons."

"She's not wrong."

I give her a look, but she's already focused on the tweaker. With the sun setting, her features have a faint glow and she couldn't be more flawless. I wasn't lying to Julia about that. The models were aesthetically pleasing when I was fucking them, but unlike them, I could spend a lifetime looking at Allison. Every time I glance back toward her, there's this abrupt loss of breath in my chest. If anything, I should be bitter toward Julia for getting to see her for a year longer than I have.

"We should go back in," she says. Her hand touches my arm. "Try to be nice. She's not just an obstacle. She's my closest friend."

I open the door for her. We walk back in together. When we're in the elevator together, I lean against the handrail. She stands in the center. She's wearing a summer dress—simple, with faded and thinning material. It must be years old, which might be why the material is nearly gauzy. My hands desperately want to trace every curve, savor every inch of exposed skin.

When she moves forward, it's a trial to keep my eyes off her ass. We step back into her apartment, the smell of garlic charging straight into me. Allison pulls me forward. She stops us next to Julia, who is straining the spaghetti.

"Hey, Jules," Allison says, stepping in front of me and leaning over to rest her arms on the counter. Her ass presses against my groin. I don't know if it was her intention, but my whole world has dwindled to the pressure against my cock. If she bounced even slightly, I couldn't be held accountable for my actions. "So, Lev and I were just talking, and we—"

"And smoking," Julie interrupts. "I can smell it."

"He was smoking," Allison retorts. "Which is still legal in the United States. You know I love you, Jules. But the reason I haven't told you about him until now is because of shit like this. I don't need you or my dad to fight my battles for me. I care about him and all I'm asking is for you to give him a chance. That's what tonight is about. Giving him a chance. He wanted me to set this up for all three of us, so he could get to know you because he knows how important you are to me. He's important to me too. So, please, treat me like I have some self-respect and do the same for Lev."

Julia transfers the noodles to the other pot.

"Lev," Julia says. "Could you get the garlic bread out of the freezer? It's under the broccoli."

"Sure." I place my hands on Allison's hips and carefully step away from her. I turn to the refrigerator, open the freezer, and find the garlic bread. Allison steps closer to me to take it from me. As she leans down, I press my hand against her shoulder blades and pretend to kiss near her ear. I whisper, "What the fuck was that?"

"I needed you to keep quiet for one minute," she whispers back. "Don't hate the method when it worked."

Julia keeps her eyes on me, but they feel less like bullets now. By the time dinner is cooked and we're settling down with our plates of spaghetti and garlic bread, Julia seems damn near pleasant.

Julia raises her glass of wine. "To the two of you."

I clink my glass against hers and Allison's. The wine goes down smooth. It makes pretending to be an honorable man much, much easier.

"So," Julia says. "Tell me about yourself, Lev. I already know the professional details, but what are your hobbies? How do you spend your spare time?"

"I rarely have spare time," I say. "It's part of why it took me so long to realize I'd rather spend that spare time with Allison."

I take Allison's hand on the table. I bring it to my lips, kissing her knuckles. She raises an eyebrow at me, but quickly hides it as she gives me a quick kiss on the cheek. She's not the best actress.

"Well, you know she doesn't want to be a housewife, right?" Julia asks.

"I know with how busy you must be, it would be very difficult to keep a relationship when the woman is busy too."

I shrug. "I need a woman that knows she's capable of more and is willing to work hard to get there. That's why I'm in a relationship with Allison. She has the ambition and determination." It's not a lie, for a change. I may only have known Allison a short time, but that's been long enough for me to say she's got a spine made of steel that doesn't match her soft exterior. I like both her outside and inside. A lot.

"That's true." Julia twirls spaghetti onto her fork. It scrapes against the plate. "I have to know one thing."

"Okay," I say.

"If you were to describe Allison, how would you describe her?"

"Jules," Allison cuts in. "That's a ridiculous question."

"It's a valid question," Julia corrects. "I've seen spouses, parents, boyfriends, and girlfriends describe their significant others while we're getting ready to transport their loved ones, while we're in the ambulance, when we get to the hospital. They reveal a lot. You can tell how much they care by what they say. I just want to know what Lev would say about you."

"Julia," Allison says, her voice firmer now. "Stop."

"It's fine," I say to Allison, but my full attention is on Julia. "You want me to talk about how Allison is a good person, that she has the strongest moral compass on earth. Isn't that right? That's what you want me to say?"

Allison is frozen in place, but Julia leans back into her chair, unperturbed.

"Are you saying she's not a moral person?"

"On the contrary. She's exceedingly moral. And she has the spine to back up her morals," I reply calmly, thinking of how Allison gave herself over to me, a complete stranger, in order to protect her father. Of how angry she was at Jeffrey Douglas getting off scot-free. The way she wanted to see justice done. She's not so unlike me when it comes down to the core. That unnerves me for some reason. "If I were to describe her, I'd use one word. Tough."

Julia nearly smiles. "You do care. Good."

I look over at Allison. She's gazing back at me, her eyes slightly widened and her lips parted. An edge of desire cuts through me. I need the woman. Badly. And I don't like needing anybody. It gives her an upper hand over me that I can only hope she doesn't figure out.She quickly looks away from me, grabbing onto her wine glass and taking a gulp of it. She'll read into my statement just like Julia did, thinking it means more than it means and she'll punish herself for it.

I stand up, reaching for the wine bottle. Her eyes follow my hand. I stop. The car crash. A drunk driver.

I let my hand fall to the table, empty.

⁓

When Allison and I walk out of her apartment building, I keep my arm around her waist. I nuzzle my face against her hair, inhaling her faint jasmine scent. The scent runs through my veins like a drug.

"How long do you think she'll watch us?" I ask near her ear.

"Jules? She's probably just polishing off what's left of the wine."

I lean against my car. "You told Julia you'd be right back."

"I did," she agrees.

"You don't think it would sell the story better if you came back to my place?"

"It might," she says. "But I'd also lose my status as a highly moral person if I went home with you."

I narrow my eyes. "You're not a virgin."

"No." She smirks at me. "Or yes. You might never know."

A challenge if I ever heard one.

"You should come closer," I say. "In case Julia is watching."

She steps closer to me. I grab her hips, pulling her taut against me. I kiss the edge of her lips, just barely feeling the minty tang of the lip balm she put on a few minutes earlier. She leans into my kiss at first, but takes a quick step back as I pull away.

"We were very lucky," she says. "I thought she was going to figure everything out."

"It has nothing to do with luck. Just good bullshitting skills." As I turn to go toward my car door, I hear something boom like thunder.

I whip around, looking at Allison. She's staring at the sky, expecting to see an incoming storm, but that wasn't thunder. My hand is already on my Glock, hidden in my IWB holster. By the time I turn around and pull it out, I only see empty crosshairs in the sight.

There's a flicker of movement in my periphery. A stocky man is running away from me, the glint of a gun in his hand.

I raise my Glock. As soon as he's in my sight, I pull the trigger.

I should have been more patient, aimed slightly more to the left, because it only hits him in the shoulder. His body lurches forward, slamming into the asphalt.

I turn, checking on Allison. She's crouching near the hood of my car.

"You all right?" I call out. She shakes her head. I walk over to her. She flinches away from me as I kneel down next to her. I scowl. "Are you okay or not?"

"You've had that gun on you this whole time," she says.

"Yes."

"And you just shot that man."

"Correct. Were you hurt at all?"

She shakes her head. Her eyes focus on something past the car. I turn.

The man is getting back on his feet. As I raise my gun, he takes off running again. The man is stocky but surprisingly fast. He gets onto a motorcycle and pulls away. I raise my gun again, then lower it. Julia could be watching through the window.

"Get in the car," I order Allison, putting my Glock back in its holster. By the time I've turned on the car and slammed the door shut, she's put on her seat belt. Her seat must have glass on it, but she doesn't complain. I speed out of the parking spot, the car fishtailing as I tear after the motorcycle.

I pass two cars. The bike turns down a more desolate section of town —I used to pass through it when I was a teenager running wild around the city. I pass a sedan and make the turn. The bike and my car are the only ones on this road. It's one of those neighborhoods where nobody ever hears anything and nobody ever sees anything.

I gain on him, little by little, until we're close.

When I'm near enough, I ram my foot against the gas pedal, yanking the wheel to the left. As I'm parallel with the bike, I jerk the wheel back to the right. The man instinctively veers away from me. Too hard, though, too sharp. The bike can't handle it.

My tires screech in protest of my aggressive driving, but it's lost amidst the reverberating storm of noise as the bike crashes. We drift to a squealing stop and I shift the car into park. In the distance, I see the torn-up grass and a motorcycle lying about twelve feet away from a man. He isn't moving.

I open my door and pull my gun out as I walk over to the man. His pants are soaked with blood and there's a growing puddle of blood on his right arm.

"Look at you," I remark, keeping my gun down for now. "If you didn't see tonight ending this way, you should have done your research."

Black hair, dark eyes, olive skin tone, a prominent but narrow nose—predominantly Italian.

The Colosimo Mafia. Cowardly shits.

That's all I need to know.

I raise the gun.

Allison nearly collides straight into me. She stops herself, steadying her balance with her hands on my left arm.

"Don't," she says. "Don't kill him. Please, Lev, don't."

"He tried to kill me and he could have killed you," I try to shake off her hands, but they grip my arm tightly. "That's more than enough reason for me to pay him back with better aim."

"Lev, please, I—you know, I understand better than most. And it didn't make me feel any better. Just put the gun down. I can call my dad. I can explain what happened."

I shake my head, turning toward her. "You think if you call your father, he's going to just clean this up with a nice little bow and I won't pay the price for being here?"

"I don't—I didn't mean he'd clean it up. But he'd understand. You were caught up in the moment. He tried to kill us. I—"

Her face changes, the tension slipping away as her eyes widen and her eyebrows shoot up. In my periphery, there's a glint of silver.

I turn, my Glock raised.

I shoot three times. The man's gun clatters to the pavement.

I turn back to Allison. Her hand is over her heart, but she's fine. Outwardly, at least.

Heaving a sigh, I walk over to the man to check him over. There's no wallet or anything. The fact that he came after me is a bad sign. It likely means the Colosimo Mafia has already repaired itself from the death of the don and is fully intent on retaliating.

I glance back at Allison. The shock must be wearing off because she's trembling and looking at me like I'm a ticking pipe bomb.

I'll have to call someone to take care of this, but right now, I need to deal with Allison. I walk back toward her, putting my arm around her shoulders. I expect her to flinch away, but she doesn't react. She lets me guide her back to the car like a marionette. Given how stubborn she is, that tells me plenty about her state of shock.

I wipe the glass off her seat and keep a hand on her elbow as I help her into the passenger side. As I walk back over to my side, I can feel the glass shards in my palm. I pull out the two larger fragments, edges slick with blood, and toss them into the storm drain.

I couldn't care less that Duilio or Siro are dead. I don't care about their grieving widows, their orphaned children, the idea that they could have changed—I couldn't give less of a flying fuck if they spent millions of dollars on homeless shelters and now hundreds of homeless people are dying in the cold.

I care only that they wanted me dead and that they were in my way. It was a problem with two outcomes: I end up on top or I end up six feet deep. There are no other possibilities.

But, seeing it on Allison's face, it feels more personal. I still don't care that the gunman is dead, but I understand how someone else could. I understand how they'd picture a child waking up to find out his or her father is dead. I understand how someone would say that he happened to be on the losing side, through no fault of his own. That he was just doing his job, following orders like a good soldier. That I deserve the exact same fate for all my sins.

But I don't. Because, unlike this man, I don't leave my target breathing.

As my heartrate slows down, a sharp pain radiates from my side. I glance down.

Blood.

9

ALLISON

In Lev's car, we slip onto the back roads. I feel the breeze through the broken window, but it barely registers against my skin. My bag is still hanging off my shoulder and chafing against my skin, but I can't seem to figure out how to move my arms or hands to do anything about it.

I twitch my fingers. They work.

Not paralyzed. Not dead.

I've witnessed two men killed in front of me and it felt like I was a ghost in both situations. I had no control over the situation. Everything happened around me and I was left just standing there, useless and guilty.

Heat rushes under my skin. I curl my hand into a fist. Prosecutors don't freeze when a defendant becomes volatile. They demand answers. They see a weakness and strike.

I flex my hand again. I pull my bag off my shoulder and set it on my lap. I grip the strap, squeezing it in my hands.

"What the hell? What the fuck?" I say, the words coming out slowly, then picking up speed. "What just happened? Who was that?"

"I have no idea," he says, his eyes focused on the road.

"You have no idea who you just killed—you have no idea, and yet you had a gun on you this whole time when we were just having dinner in my apartment. You have no idea, but you just killed that man and acted like it was nothing. You have no idea. Tell me something, Lev. Give me something. I deserve that much at least."

"I saved your life and you're making demands?" he asks. "Just take a breath, Allison. Just breathe."

"You spent all this time accusing me of being a murderer, but you killed that man and you're not showing the slightest remorse. You're a sociopath." I shake my head, looking out the window as we turn onto a sketchy road. We pass by a group of men standing at the corner. They eye the car with some interest but disregard it when they notice the broken window. "If you don't tell me what's going on, I'll tell my father what happened."

"And he'll find out what you did. He'll start suspecting we're accomplices," he says. "Or, unlike his daughter, maybe he'll be happy that I saved your life. Ally, it's—"

"Call me Allison. We're not that close."

"Allison. It's better if you don't know anything. You don't need to know. I'll make it so it doesn't affect you again."

He takes his cell phone out of his pocket. As he finds a number on his screen and brings the phone up to his ear, the thought that he's breaking the law sneaks to the front of my mind, which is ridiculous in the context of the rest of the night.

"Hey," he says. "There was a situation in front of Allison's apartment and another on Dover Street. I don't need the clean-up crew. But it was them. They've already recuperated."

I glance over at him, trying to read the space between the lines. As he looks back at me, I let my gaze slide down. That's when I notice it.

Crimson.

Just the slightest bit, peeking outside of his sports jacket. I reach forward, pulling the flap of his jacket back. The bloodstain looks like a continent against the white of his shirt. It's darker in the center than the outside and the cloth is sticking to his skin.

Lev takes his hand off the wheel, his legs keeping the wheel steady, and pushes away my hand, continuing to talk on the phone.

"You were shot," I hiss.

"We'll talk about it later. I'll deal with it," he says to whoever is on the other end of the call. Hanging up, he sets down the phone and turns to me. "It's fine, Allison. It's just a superficial wound. The shot grazed me. You should check yourself. Adrenaline can fool your body into thinking you're not hurt."

I run my hands down my body, checking for wet spots or signs of pain. Nothing. I look over at Lev. I almost expect him to be checking me out, but his body is tense and his forehead is furrowed.

"I'm fine," I say.

"Check again."

As I run my hand over the back of my thighs, he presses a button for his mansion gates to open up. I pull off my seat belt while he parks.

My brain is on fire, each piece of information and emotion adding a new flame. Jeffrey Douglas died as a result of my actions. Lev kept a gun with him during a simple dinner. This strange man wanted to kill Lev. He could have killed me. Lev killed him without hesitation or remorse. And we left another crime scene.

My life isn't this. I don't manufacture relationships for selfish personal gain. I don't get into car chases. I don't watch people get killed and get in the car with the murderer like nothing happened.

The bodies are piling up. There's going to be a point where I can't see over them.

I jerk my door open and take off running.

I pass by a massive mountain of a man standing by the door. I barely give him a second thought, yanking open the front door and running inside. I get to the end of the hallway, ending up in the dining room. I take my cell phone out of my bag. My hands are trembling as I find my father's number. I tap it.

Lev grabs me so abruptly that I can barely register where he came from. He wrenches the phone from my hand, ending the call before it hits two seconds. He throws the phone onto the table. It bounces once before sliding to a stop.

I smack him. I shove him. The tension under my skin is enough to break me and I need to break someone else to release it. When I try to hit him again, he grabs my wrists. His fingers easily overlap mine—just another reminder of how much bigger he is than me.

"You should have made your first hit count," he growls.

In his eyes, I see the killer—I thought he was hard and emotionless, but I see the frozen rage now, just needing a flame.

I wait for him to shove me away from him, to hit me, to make me feel his complete control over our situation. He keeps his gaze on me but slowly loosens his grip on my wrists until he lets them go.

"You need to remember what's at stake—your career, your father's career, your whole family's reputation, and all those victims' loved ones. That man was trying to kill us. I did what I needed to do to protect us."

I rub my wrists. "Then tell the police that."

"I'd rather die."

"Fine," I say. I reach around him to get my phone, but he grabs my shoulder and shoves me back.

"You're not getting that back any time soon."

I swing my hand up, hitting him across the face. He barely winces. He grabs my arms, yanking me around him, and shoving me up against the wall. He steps up, our bodies almost touching as he pins my arms against the wall.

"Take a goddamn breath," he commands. I lunge at his face, not sure what I'll do if we connect—bite him, maybe?—and he pulls away just in time. His lip curls up, anger flashing in his eyes. I'm certain he's going to hit me. I'm certain that this is the point where he changes from the manipulative sociopath to the brutal monster who needs someone to lash out at.

He kisses me. It's an open-mouth kiss, a bruising kiss. It's brutal and my body arches against his to meet the brutality. When he pulls away, my body is flush against his. With every breath, I try to get my body to relax, but my body is thrumming and desperate for more.

I take a deep breath. "You can't hold Jeffrey's death over me now. We're both killers, so you can't tell me—"

He kisses me again. The kiss is like grief, going through stages. First, denial as I start to push against him. Then, anger as he pushes himself against me hard enough that it takes some of my breath. His mouth demands my mouth's attention, punishing me for my resistance, and I love it. As I start to kiss him back, my hands on his waist, my fingertips brushing against his gun, we switch to the bargaining stage. I promise him passion as long as he gives it back to me in the same degree. His hands are off my arms, moving to my hips as he agrees to my terms.

We're both killers now.

I put my hands on his shoulders and push him away. There's a starving look in his eyes and he seems ready to pounce on me, but he sways for a second before raising his hands in compliance.

Stage four: depression.

"I need some time," I mutter, moving around him. I grab my bag. He leans against the wall.

"I can't let you leave right now," he says. "Your life could still be in danger. Just stay until after the gala."

"You mean until you get what you want?"

"I didn't get what I wanted," he says.

I bow my head, fiddling with the straps of my bag. "I need to be able to leave. I still need a dress for the gala."

"I'll get you one," he says.

"You can't keep me a prisoner in your house," I tell him. He rubs his bottom lip. He's a blade, all sharp edges, solid, and smooth. He could slice me in half and both my halves would want him.

He walks over to the table and picks up my phone. He holds it out to me. When I try to grab it, he flicks it out of my reach.

"Your father doesn't need to know anything. It will only hurt people," he warns. I snatch the phone out of his hand, turn from him, and walk away.

As I walk down the hallway, I expect him to call out to me. When I open the front door, I expect to have the Titan-sized man guarding the door to drag me back inside. Nothing happens.

When I get into my car, I touch my mouth. I try to get the warmth and tenderness to sink past my lips and linger, but as I drive down the road, it fades away.

∽

I haven't been driving long before I notice the car following me. Any other day, I probably wouldn't have noticed. But any other day I wouldn't be a murderer engaged to another murderer. I wouldn't have the blood from my fiancé's minor wound on my shirt—a wound sustained when he killed a man. Given the circumstances, it seems pretty clear the car behind me is keeping pace.

My law textbooks come to mind. Stalking didn't become a crime until 1990 when the first law was passed in California after several high-profile stalking cases ended in murders. Stalking was defined in 2005 as a crime where a person incites fear for the safety of another person or persons or causes them a significant amount of emotional distress.

That seems to fit the current situation like a glove.

I peer at my rearview mirror. The black car is still there.

It remains a car or two behind me except for one street, but I have to turn several times to get to my apartment and it turns with me.

I veer sharply into my apartment's parking lot. It's not quite as smooth as Lev's driving, but the black car doesn't make the same turn. It gives me enough time to park, lock the car, and run into the apartment. I sprint up the stairs. It's late enough that I don't pass anybody. I lock myself in the apartment, then run to the window facing the parking lot.

The black car is pulling in. It parks near the two cars that are missing tires. I stare at it. Nobody gets out.

I take my cell phone out of my bag, staring at it. I could call my father, tell him about the car. But if it is the police, it could cause them to become more suspicious of me—they'll twist it in front of a jury, saying it's a sign of a guilty conscience.

Except it won't be a twist because I am guilty and my conscience is a stack of bricks on my shoulders.

"Hey. Where did you go before?"

I whirl around. Julia raises her hands to show she's unarmed.

"Whoa. Are you okay?" she asks. "You look like you've taken enough meth to take on—wait, you didn't do meth, did you?"

"No," I scowl. I turn back to the window. I can't see if the person is still in the car. The windows are tinted.

Julia steps up beside me. "What are we looking at? That's a nice car. It isn't Lev's, is it?"

"No," I say. "I think it was following me."

"Why would a car be following you?" she asks.

I shake my head. "I don't know. But I'm going to find out."

I drop my bag on our couch. Fear is beating hard in my chest. But I know if I'm marrying Lev, I'm going to need to be able to stand up to him. And Lev can shoot a man without flinching, so the least that I can do is confront some sociopath in a public place.

By the time I'm almost to the car, I see the silhouette of the man inside the car. He barely fits in the driver's seat. As I grab the handle of the driver's door, lurching it open, I recognize him.

It's the same man who was guarding Lev's mansion. The mountain man.

"What the hell," I snarl. "Why were you following me?"

The man shrugs, less volatile than I would have expected. "Lev told me to watch out for you."

"Why wouldn't he just tell me that?"

The man pauses, checking over his shoulder. "It's not my business to know, Miss Harrington. There's another, um, person watching out for you on the other side of the building. It's not just me. But I will have to tell the boss that you came out here to talk to me. It wasn't a very smart thing to do."

I slam my palm against the roof of the car. "While you're at it, tell Lev that I told him to go screw himself."

I turn around, rage slamming down with every footstep away from him. When I'm nearly back to the apartment, I turn back around and head back to the car.

"Never mind. Don't tell him anything," I say. "I'm going to tell him myself."

I take my phone out, walking a few steps away from Lev's guard dog. It rings twice.

"Hello, Allison," Lev answers, irritatingly calm. "I'm going to assume that you have some complaints."

"Complaints? Oh no. Never. I love thinking that I'm being stalked by a psychopath my whole drive home and then finding out that he's working for you. I might turn it into my new hobby."

"If it's any reassurance, I can't prove that he's a psychopath."

"Well, we have proof that you're a sociopath," I snap. "Why wouldn't you just tell me? Did you want to scare me? Is there some lesson in this? Do you want me to be paranoid everywhere I go?"

"It's nothing like that. You didn't take my first option, so I altered my plan. This is the second option."

I grit my teeth as Julia comes out of the apartment.

"What was it?" she asks. "Is everything okay?"

I nod, covering my phone's mouthpiece. "It's fine. Lev just thought we might need someone to watch out for us. Like we're little children."

"Oh." She smiles. "Cool."

"It's not cool at all," I say.

Lev clears his throat. "Could you put me on the phone with Julia? We both want what's best for you while you're on a suicide mission."

I remove my finger from the speaker.

"No," I say. "Julia, he didn't even tell me he was going to do this."

"That's a bit shitty," she admits. "But he must have seen the neighborhood we're in and thought you needed someone watching out for us. It's a little overbearing, but I'd rather have someone watching out for me than risking getting stabbed by Blake."

Blake is the meth-head that lives on the first floor. Julia has saved his life twice and she's not overly enthusiastic about the guy.

"Allison," Lev says. "Why does it sound like you're outside right now? Go back to your apartment. Lock the door."

I hang up on him.

~

When I slide back into bed, it already feels like a dream—one of those dreams where your brain tells you that something is your childhood home, the courthouse, or your bed, but it doesn't resemble any of those at all. Everything has changed so much since I went to sleep last night that it might as well be a different bed.

It's too quiet in this room.

And empty.

My heartrate should be slowing down, but it patters along like the mice in the walls. I stare up at the water-stained ceiling, the shapes reminding me of Lev's wound.

And the thought of blood reminds me of the man he killed.

In the quiet, the truth sneaks into the room. Seeing the man be killed in front of me was more traumatizing than seeing Jeffrey slowly die because I was less than a second away from dying, too. We were nearly in opposite positions. And it was all because of my own naiveté. It was because of my black and white morality. Lev was right

—my morality didn't help me at all. I made Lev hesitate, and it almost got us killed.

But Lev saved my life.

I grip my hair, pulling it up into a bun, imagining tying it up, but instead, the prickle of pain in my scalp only makes me think of Lev. I need his hands in my hair, his body pressed against mine until my thoughts dissipate.

The kiss. It was war and peace and all those tense times in between.

I take my phone off its charger. I find Lev in received calls and tap on the number.

I could blame it on being sleep-deprived.

I could blame it on trauma.

I could blame it on how long it's been since I've been in a relationship.

But those are all mitigating circumstances and I'm still guilty.

He answers on the first ring. "Hello, Allison."

"I just wanted to know if you cleaned out your wound," I say. There's a pause. It seems to stretch the distance between us.

"Yes. Thank you for calling to check."

"Well. It's evidence," I say.

"Is that the only reason you called?" he asks.

"No," I say. "I also don't have the money to buy a dress for the gala."

"I can provide you with any funds you may need."

"Oh. Okay." I tug on my hair. "But …"

I let the word drift off. I don't have any dispute with what he said, so I don't know why I keep talking.

I wait for him to fill the silence. He doesn't.

"But I've only shopped at, you know, cheap places. Department stores. If I'm your date, I'd assume I need something more elegant. I don't know where to buy those things."

Silence. The seconds creep by.

"If there was a question in that statement, I missed it," he says.

"You're an asshole," I say.

"Also not a question."

"Well, I—I was just thinking that you could show me some places to shop at." I rub my thighs, the burning sensation from running coming back. "You wouldn't even need to take me anywhere. You could just give me addresses. But from what I've seen in the movies, I don't think they'll help me without someone rich by my side, so if you came with me … I could pay you back by doing housekeeping or something like that."

"Okay."

"Okay?" I ask. "After all that, you're just going to say okay?"

"I own one of the most profitable vodka companies in the United States, Allison. I don't have time for people who talk around what they want or people too hesitant to ask for what they need. The meek won't inherit the earth."

"I'm not meek."

"Of course not," he says. "You would never give up what you wanted because you were too frightened at the idea of chasing it. Good night, Allison."

"Wait." I yank my blanket off, sitting up. "You don't get to say that and just hang up."

"You called me," he said, an edge of irritation in his voice. "Tell me why."

The command hits me like a verdict. Guilty.

"You saved my life," I say.

"Yes."

"Thank you."

"You're welcome," he says.

"And I can't sleep," I add.

"Don't think about what happened tonight. Just forget about it."

"The problem is that I'm not thinking about that," I say. I lie down again. I close my eyes, the words that I should and shouldn't say colliding in my head.

"Tell me," he says. That dream-like sensation returns. If he asks about it tomorrow, I could pretend they were the words of a woman in a state of shock.

"I'm thinking about what would have happened after the kiss."

There's the softest intake of breath. "Nothing. Because you're a saint."

"What if I wasn't?" I ask. There's a sound of his body shifting against soft material—possibly his bed.

"I would have bent you over the table and fucked you."

I slide my hand under my pajama shorts and underwear. My fingers dance around my clit.

"I don't think so," I say.

"Oh?"

"No. I would have wanted to thank you for saving my life."

There are more sounds of him moving on his bed. "Oh?"

"But you'd have to help me."

"How would I do that?"

"Because I've never ... um, I've never gone down on someone before."

There's a small laugh, but it's not degrading. It's like he thinks I'm cute. I press my fingers against my clit, my hips rising to meet my hand.

"I could help you with that," he says, his voice sounding more strained. "I would tell you to get on your knees. To unbutton my pants. To take my cock out."

My slit is slick with wetness. I've always taken forever to become aroused, to the point that the only man I've slept with—a high school boyfriend—always fucked me dry. My body has never reacted this way.

"I'd be ... impressed," I say, my voice hitching. "I wouldn't be certain if I could do it."

"I would show you. I'd tell you to work on the head first. Just press your tongue against the tip. Look at me while you're kissing and tasting me."

"Mmm." I rub harder, pushing two fingers inside me. My grip on my phone is tight enough that my fingers ache. "I'd love the way you had your hand in my hair."

"I would guide you to my balls. You'd take each one into your mouth. Your tongue would feel like paradise."

His breathing is quickening. I can picture him, his cock in his hand, getting himself off on just the thought of me. My heart is beating so fast, I might die here with my hand in my underwear and I wouldn't mind.

"I'd take you in my mouth," I whisper. It almost turns into a moan. "I'd try to take as much as I could."

"I wouldn't stop you."

His voice is low, barely audible.

"Lev—" My hand is rubbing so hard against my clit, I'm certain I'm going to be bruised in the morning. "I'd take you in as deep as I could. I'd let my tongue roll under you. When I pulled back, I'd let my tongue play with the tip of your cock before taking you back in."

"I wouldn't be able to take your teasing. I'd take your hair in my hands. I would guide you as far as you could take. I wouldn't be able to control myself. You would look so damn good. I just wouldn't be able to stop myself."

My pussy throbs harder than my heart, faster and faster, until the orgasm hits me like a storm. Incoherent noises slip out of me. My body arches off the bed as wave after wave of pleasure slams me. I'm taken away by a tsunami of unrestrained bliss.

Lev makes a noise between a growl and a groan. It's almost enough to get me off again. I listen to his labored breathing, a provocative lullaby.

I close my eyes. My heart slows down. Sleep starts to take hold of me. At some point, Lev tells me to have sweet dreams.

And I do.

10

ALLISON

The Harrington bloodline is made of fighters. My grandfather, my uncle, and my dad all served in the Marines. My grandfather was a state trooper and my dad is the chief of police. My uncle is a firefighter. My mother was a nurse before becoming a homemaker.

We were made to be on the frontlines.

So, I can practically feel the disappointment of generations past when I'm terrified as I drive up to Lev's mansion. If I were afraid because he'd killed someone, it would be a sensible reaction. But after my hormones got the best of me last night, I've strongly considered leaving the city and never returning.

If the universe cared about me, Lev would be hidden away in his mansion and I'd have time to calm my nerves. But he's outside, taking paper bags out of the back of a cherry-red car. The vehicle that was a casualty last night is nowhere in sight.

He turns as I park, a paper bag in each arm. His sturdy frame makes my legs a bit unsteady as I step out of my car. The way he holds the bags near his waist focuses my attention on his groin. I force myself to concentrate on a willow tree in his yard instead.

"I assumed you'd be here later," he says.

"It's 7:00," I say. "That's our time."

"Yes, but it was a late night," he says.

I flush. "I don't need much sleep."

"Close the trunk," he says. I shut the trunk and follow him into the mansion. As he walks to the back of the house, I focus on the walls, the floor, the recessed lighting—anything other than his body. There's a memory of tasting him which doesn't exist but desperately wants to.

He sets the bags down on the kitchen counter. He starts taking items out of the bag—milk, powdered milk, sweetened condensed milk.

"I didn't think you'd be the type to get your own groceries," I say.

"I usually don't." He moves to the other bag. He pulls out cinnamon sticks, powdered cinnamon, nutmeg, and black cardamom. "But I wanted to get some specific items and I didn't want to risk someone missing something or getting the wrong product."

He takes out a honey bottle shaped like a honeypot. He pulls out four tea tins and folds up the paper bags, setting them between two canisters on the counter.

I check the tea tins. They're different brands of chai tea.

"You remembered what I told you about the cinnamon chai tea." I touch my cheeks as heat rushes into them again. "That's incredibly kind of you."

"It's for our con," he says matter-of-factly, like I'm the idiot for not realizing that. He puts the various types of milk into the refrigerator. "Just a part of the plan. Nothing more."

"I've known a lot of people for over six months—I've known Julia over a year—and she doesn't even know about the chai tea. We could have invented any story." I shrug. "It's just nice that you remembered what I said to you."

"That was the point of questioning each other."

As he moves to grab the tea tins, his elbow bumps into my arm. His hand immediately caresses where we collided, an automatic apologetic gesture, before continuing what he's doing. It's the smallest detail, one he probably barely even notices himself doing, but it's a kindness I doubt he's ever granted anybody else.

Except me.

A song starts to play—crunching guitars and heavy bass. He stops putting the spices away and takes his cell phone out of his pocket. When he taps on the screen and puts it up to his ear, the song ends.

"Ilya," he says. His eyes shift back and forth as he listens. He quickly glances at me before handing me the black cardamom and walking down the hall.

The indication is clear: do not leave the kitchen.

But thoughts of the Harrington bloodline are still top of mind. I'm a frontline girl. Not a wallflower relegated to the sidelines.

So I wait just a few seconds before following him down the hallway.

I stop right before the den's entrance.

"They're desperate," Lev's voice retorts. "The Colosimos know they can't overpower us. Duilio was competent enough—with some help—but his son is being controlled by his emotions and letting it cloud his judgment. He'd rather let the family die in his rage than forfeit and rebuild strong enough to strike back later."

The Colosimos.

I know who the Colosimos are. When I was little, the Colosimo Mafia was the boogeyman in Manhattan, the Bronx, Brooklyn, Queens, and Staten Island. My dad used to be haunted by the violence they committed. There was one incident where the girlfriend of a Mafia member was raped and worked with the police to arrest the rapist. Dad believed they must have begun to suspect that she was feeding the police information about them—which, as far as he knew, was not the case. The girlfriend's neighbors reported hearing screams from her house. When the police arrived at her residence, they found her dead with several gashes, broken bones, mutilated, with a rat stapled to a section of her body that was not disclosed to the media.

Several streets where there was a heavy Mafia presence didn't report a single crime for over two years.

The fear of the Colosimos faded, but not because of time. Less than five years ago, the top players in the Colosimo family began showing up murdered and whispers of a Russian Bratva taking over the Colosimo territory began filling the streets. People were grateful—only because it meant that, if they were killed, it would be quick instead of the torture that the Colosimos preferred. The Bratva wasn't any more innocent than the Colosimos but they weren't cats that played with their food.

They were Dobermans that went for the throat and ripped it out.

Lev is Russian and proud of his Russian heritage. He lives with a suspicious amount of luxury. His first thought when he saw a dead body at his club was to use it to his advantage. Someone tried to kill him. He killed someone without showing the slightest remorse. He kept a gun on him in the most innocuous situation.

He's a Doberman—no room remains for doubt.

I need to protect my throat. I slip quietly away from the den.

∼

Fifteen minutes later, Lev returns to the kitchen and we head to the car, not discussing his phone call. Sitting in the passenger side of Lev's car feels like a terrible metaphor. I'm just riding along. I have no control over what direction we go. I could bail now, but I'd only hurt myself and other people who are behind me.

I fiddle with my bag. It's nearly ready to fall apart.

He glances over at me. "You're going to need a new bag for the gala."

I nod. "Sure. Are you in the Bratva?"

His hand twitches on the wheel, the car swerving slightly. It's enough to send a chill down my spine.

"How is that related to your bag?" he asks.

"It's not. I just need to know the truth."

"You need to be focusing on the gala," he says. "That's what's important right now."

"No. It's not." I turn, so my body is fully facing him, the seat belt digging into my shoulder. "We're going to be married, so I have the right to know the truth about my husband."

He raises his eyebrow. "That may be the first time you've accepted what's going to happen. Good."

"Don't get too happy about it. I still want an answer to my question."

He keeps his eyes on the road, only shifting them to check for other cars. I stare at him, waiting. In the window behind him, I can see we're entering a sophisticated part of the city, where there's less traffic and the architecture is clean and modern. The silence blisters in my ears, tension building in my chest.

He's just going to ignore me. He's not going to answer, which answers my question in its own way, but it's also a reminder that I'm even more powerless in this relationship than I had thought. I could run to my father about my suspicions, but before he could find anything to arrest Lev, I'd be found with a bullet in my head.

I also led him straight to Julia. I couldn't force her to go into hiding with me when her job is everything to her.

He stops at a red light and turns to me. "Yes."

He locks eyes with me. He must see the fear in mine, no matter how hard I try to blink it away.

"Are you actually ... in it or do you only help them through your business?"

"It's better if you don't know any more than that." He presses on the gas. My body lurches forward. I hadn't even noticed the change in the light or the traffic, but we don't crash and die, which could be a blessing, or maybe not so much. Maybe that'd be the easy way out. "You're the one who worships the law. If you don't know anything, you have plausible deniability and since we're not married yet, we're not protected by spousal privilege. That would mean if you took the stand, you'd either have to tell the truth on the stand or perjure yourself. Neither option would end well for you."

"You suddenly care about the law now?" I turn back toward the road and press my fingers against my temple. "I find that hard to believe."

"Then don't believe it."

I watch a pair of young women laughing with each other as they carry shopping bags. They cling to each other's arms as they try to not fall from laughing so hard.

If I'd ignored Jeffrey Douglas, my life could have remained that simple. It's just another moment where my moral compass led me straight to my own ruin.

"Once we're married," I say, "you'll have to tell me the truth."

"It's your trial," he says. His foot is jiggling now. I've never seen him nervous.

"Maybe you're antsy because you're lying to me."

"No. I'm not antsy. I'm usually working out right now, so I have a lot of pent-up energy."

"Oh."

I'd forgotten about his exercise regimen. It should have occurred to me that he'd always have a busy schedule and my request would interrupt it. It's hard to relate the man who is taking time to go shopping with me with the man I saw kill someone yesterday. The man I now know for sure is part of the Bratva—fairly high up, I suspect.

My bag vibrates. I pull out my phone. It's a text from my mother.

Haven't heard from you in a while :) text me so I know you're alive. Love you!!

I text back. *Everything is going good. I love you.*

I put my phone back in my bag. I glance at Lev. His leg is no longer jiggling.

"Who's texting you?" he asks.

"It's not my father, if that's what you're worried about," I say. "It's just my mom checking up on me. You can read it when we park if you want."

"It's fine."

I swallow, the tension in the car making me feel claustrophobic.

"Do you ever hear from your mother?" I ask. He shakes his head but doesn't say anything more as he parks the car.

I look out the window. The sign in front of the shop says *Renovate*.

～

Renovate Boutique is designed like a beehive. The center room is hexagonal with several displays showing dresses, shoes, bags, and jewelry. The walls are covered with hanging dresses, each wall showing different colors like a spectrum. There are several rooms surrounding the center room, which from what I've seen in one of the dressing rooms, are all hexagonal too.

The sales assistant, Louisa, puts dresses in my arms like they're babies. While I told her my preferences, she seems insistent on basing my choices on my body frame, skin tone, and hair color. Her latest one is a short dress that resembles a rose with its color and layers.

I glance at Lev. He's sitting on one of their sofas while intently focused on his phone. He could be intentionally ignoring me or merely plotting someone's death. It's completely possible that he's doing both.

I go back into the dressing room. Three sides of the room have massive mirrors that cover their walls. There's also a stool, where I set my clothes after I undress again. I'm a little less self-conscious compared to the first three times I've changed but there's still a feeling that I'm not like the other women who walk in here—the thin, tall, ex-model arm candy of rich husbands. I couldn't even get the first dress over my hips. These dresses are for women who don't need a police chief father in order to find their way to Lev's bed.

I pull the dress up, taking a breath as I manage to sneak it past my hips.

So Lev is part of the Bratva. He's capable of killing people. In all likelihood, that man he killed in front of me was not the first man he ever killed. He didn't hesitate at all when the man was completely defenseless. The only reason he didn't shoot him right away was because I interrupted him. If he's willing to kill a defenseless man, is he willing to kill anyone? Everyone? Or is it only people who try to hurt him?

I take the dress off. It pinches at my waist and I hate the prom-esque look of it. I get dressed again and take the dress out to Louisa.

"It's just not right," I tell her. "I'm sorry. I don't mean to be so picky."

"That's fine." Louisa waves away my concern. "This one might be better for you. With your pale skin and your hourglass body, it will make you look gorgeous. I believe that, one hundred percent."

I take the dress from her, but I'm focused on Lev, who is talking to someone now, his lip curled up in a small snarl. I try to hear what he's saying, but he's keeping his voice quiet. His lips form a few curses.

Louisa's eyes are on me, waiting for me to try on her dress. I retreat to the dressing room and shed my clothing again.

Can I be that critical of Lev for the murder he committed after what I did? They were both in self-defense. And, in the murder he committed, he was protecting me. It was a life for a life and I can't be ungrateful that the life that was spared was mine. If he'd hesitated for a second—if he was inexperienced in killing—a mortician could be dressing me instead of me dressing myself.

I pull the dress up. It fits. I check myself in the mirror.

My throat swells. My legs fill with lead.

It's a simple white dress. The ruffles on the skirt make it look like a waterfall.

It's not exactly like the dress I was wearing on the night of the car crash—the stitching is a lot more intricate on this one and the other one had a top that resembled a corset while this one is looser—but I can see myself in that dress that night. I remember putting it on and believing it was going to be just another fun night.

I remember the blood staining it. Being certain some of the blood wasn't mine.

I crouch down. I lean my forehead against the mirror. My breath steams the glass, though it feels like it's getting trapped in my chest.

I see the other car coming closer and closer. I start to scream, but it's not soon enough for Lily to swerve.

Sweat drips onto the mirror. My chest feels like it's cracking open—maybe because we hit the sign so hard that the seat belt left bruises I could still see long after they faded.

I open my eyes. Julia is crawling into the car, her words soothing, though they're not making sense to me. There's a drop of blood clinging to the edge of my eyelid. It's obscuring my view. I turn to look forward. I see Lily in the rearview mirror. Her head is lolling back.

I can't see her clearly, but I know she's dead.

I'm shaking.

Julia is talking to me.

Lev is talking to me.

His arm is around me, pulling me away from the mirror. He must be kneeling because I feel his legs on either side of me. His hands rub my arms, moving over me like his touch might skim off the ache.

"Is she okay?" Louisa's voice asks.

"She will be," Lev says. "We need a moment."

"Of course, absolutely. Take as much time as you need."

High heels click away. Lev caresses my hair. There's a sense of tranquility that sinks from my scalp to the rest of my body. I rest my head on his chest. My breathing calms; the memories scatter. I listen to his heartbeat.

Even as a child, I never felt truly secure. I was anxious, worried about my dad getting hurt while working. But with Lev comforting me, all of that washes away. I still care about everybody, but it doesn't grip me to the point that it's constantly on my mind.

It makes no sense because he has brought an immense amount of stress in my life and I don't think I can trust him. The lingering threat of what he could do to me and everyone I love is how he keeps me under his thumb.

"You're someone I would never hurt," Lev says, as if reading my mind.

I have no reason to believe him, but he says it with the same conviction as when he told me he was in the Bratva. Still, I have to wonder who else he would hurt. It's not me that I'm most worried about. I dug my own grave.

It's the rest of the people I love. My dad, my mother, and Julia—they're all innocent.

He must see the conflict in my face and kisses me lightly on the lips. It's lacking any sensuality or implication. In the logical part of my brain, I know he meant it as a gesture of comfort. It was a way to calm me. But the other part of my brain is filled with ricocheting intensity and needs an outlet.

My hands grasp both sides of his face. I kiss him like a crashing wave. He lets me have full control for a second or two, receiving all of my grief. When his hands sink into my hair, gripping onto it, we become combatants. We clash against each other, our lips exploding against each other.

When he pulls the dress away from my chest, it tears. I stand up, yanking it off the rest of the way and tearing more of it. He stands up. He unbuckles his belt, pulls it out, and lets it drop to the floor. His eyes stay on me, hungry and demanding, as he pulls down his pants.

His erection is barely restrained by his boxer briefs. I touch my mouth, recalling our phone conversation, and stand up, my legs almost shaking.

He steps up to me, his hands cradling my head as he kisses me. The kiss is rushed but still punctuated with intensity. His erection presses up against me.

I pull down my underwear. As I bend over to get it off my ankles, my face comes close enough to his erection that I have half a mind to go through our phone-call scenario. I stand up straight again, a faint pulse between my legs.

As I look down at myself, I see the flaws again. The small breasts, the stomach without the visible abs, and the layer of fat on my hips. Lev mentioned that he'd slept with models. In comparison, I'm a consolation prize, or worse.

I keep my head down, thinking of ways to talk my way out of this. All those models must be much more experienced than I am too. He wouldn't have slept with them if they weren't.

There's movement in front of me. Lev's shirt has been dropped on the floor. I glance up at him.

He wasn't lying about the weight training. His chest is a testament to what weight training can do. His body must be pure muscle, every part of his chest and waist firm and defined, run through with rippling veins.

His wound from last night is slightly red but there are also some rough stitches holding it together. It's not the only mark on his body—there are at least a dozen scars, in various sizes and states of fading.

It could mean a million different bad things and I don't care about any of them right now.

He pulls down his boxer briefs and kicks them off.

I imagined his cock on the phone. Of course, I did. I imagined it to be larger than average with a decent thickness.

I underestimated him.

"Take the stool. Put it up against the mirror in front of you and remain facing the mirror," he commands.

The stool has an iron frame, but the cushion seems comfortable enough. I pull it in front of me and look into the mirror. I see the two of us. He has to be at least eight inches taller than me. His body looks like a mountain, sturdy and carved of stone, ready to swallow me in its depths.

"Kneel," he orders. I get onto the stool. I have no idea what he's planning. The pulse between my thighs is getting stronger and begging for attention.

I watch him in the mirror, approaching me. His cock presses under my ass. I open my legs the smallest bit.

His hands grasp my hips. His cock rubs against my wetness. A small groan slips out of me. He presses his hand against my spine, forcing me to bend forward. My face is less than an inch away from the mirror. The head of his cock presses against my entrance. I reach back toward him, but before my hand reaches him, he plunges into me.

It's like a spark of electricity shoots through me, ending straight where his cock ends. Blood is as hot as fire as it burns through me. It's like closed gates were opened inside my body and the only tension is my desperate need for more of him. It's natural and extraordinary.

He keeps a tight grip on my hips as he pulls out. When he thrusts back in, it's the same flood of sensations. He keeps a slower pace, teasing me when he pulls out and fulfilling me as he thrusts back into me.

I look up, seeing us in the mirror. His left hand moves up, cupping one of my breasts. I place my hand over his as he massages my breasts. He starts to thrust faster, rapidly increasing in speed. I have to press my hand against the mirror to stop myself from hitting my head against it. As I continue watching us, he locks eyes with me. He kisses the side of my neck before nuzzling his face against the curve of it.

When he looks up again, there's the slightest smirk on his face. He slows down his thrusts again. His right hand slides down from my hip to the front of my pussy. His fingers circles around it. My body twitches as he comes closer and closer to my clit. When he's close enough that I'm swaying my hips to get that bit of pressure from his fingers, he flattens his hand. He taps my clit with his open hand. It sends a jolt through me. Before I can recover, his hand rests over the front of my pussy and every time he thrusts into me, my clit jostles against his hand.

For the first time, powerlessness is a blessing.

Lev presses his forehead against my shoulder. His thrusts start getting faster. His breathing becomes more labored. I bite my lip as I realize small moans are slipping out of me. There's heat and throbbing building up in my pussy. It's intimidating, but I know I'd chase after whatever is coming no matter what.

It hits me a lot harder than when I got myself off. My whole body goes stiff as my pussy rapidly squeezes Lev's cock. An eruption of ecstasy hits me, reverberating in every part of my body. It's almost surpassed when Lev growls and I feel his hot pleasure fill me.

He slowly pulls out. I nearly fall off the stool, but he catches me and lays me down on the floor. There's so much that should be consuming me, eating me from the inside, but as he kisses me, the world could burn and I'd let it. The courtrooms could be destroyed and all the judges could lose their jobs—I'd be fine with it. There's no such thing as desire right now except for how much I want to be here with Lev.

In this moment, it's the only justice that matters.

11
LEV

After we have sex, I leave the building to smoke. When I return, Louisa gushes about Allison spotting the perfect dress.

The dress is wrapped up in a box, so I never see it. I shouldn't care. In my tax bracket, I've seen every kind of dress, from rich old widows in an abundance of frills to young gold diggers outfitted in sheer material. More to the point, I've seen plenty of dresses crumpled on the floor with a naked woman standing over them and they all look unimportant in those moments.

So why do I care about this one?

Why does the thought of Allison stepping out of her room in something I've never seen before thrill me so much?

I can't explain it. So I ignore it.

Back at my estate a short while later, Allison sprawls on the couch.

I set her cards on her chest. "Thank you." She smiles lazily at me. It's so carefree, so satisfied, I can't help but smile back.

"We could still implement a mix of interrogation poker and strip poker," I say. "We could both end up winners."

"It would also distract us and the gala is tomorrow night. Focus, sir," she drawls, wiggling her eyebrows with the last word. She must know it should irk me, her joking disrespectful—and yet, it doesn't.

She peeks at her cards and sets them back on her chest. I give myself two cards and flip over three more onto the table.

"We have plenty of time. We're doing things my way. So here's the new set of rules," I say. "You can fold, but it means you have to take off a piece of clothing. You can raise, but if you lose, you'll have to take off two pieces of clothing. But if you raise and you win, I'll answer two questions."

"You are very confident in the cards you haven't seen," she laughs.

"At some point, I'll end up on top—in every way."

She squirms. "I'm not going to raise."

I check my cards. Hmm. I flip over another card. Her eyes light up for the briefest moment before she starts to fiddle with her bra strap.

"Do you want to raise?" I ask. She glances at me, a smirk growing on her face.

"Yeah. I do. Two pieces of clothing, Lev."

I flip the last card. Life is too good to me.

"Well," she says, dropping her cards on the table. "I hope you like three of a kind."

"I do," I say. I lay my cards down. "But I like a straight better."

"Son of a gun." She sits up. "How do you do that? It's a game of luck!"

"You can convince yourself of that if you like, but you still need to take two pieces of clothing off."

Allison hesitates, a shy half smile lingering on her face as she surveys what's available. She isn't wearing socks—she never put them back on after the shower she took when we got back from the store. It leaves her clothing options rather limited.

"You know what?" she says suddenly, straightening up and beaming. "This is good. I'm going to go in with a whole new tactic."

She pulls off her shirt. I raise an eyebrow as she unhooks her bra and tosses it to me. Her breasts sway with her movement. It's hard to not imagine my mouth on them, my hand cupping them both as I'm fucking her from behind. Just a finger brush against the nipple to feel it stiffen under my touch.

My face must be an open book, because it takes only a moment for her smile to widen. She's glowing with pride at turning the tables on me. All I can do is laugh and shift around to try to hide the growing steel between my legs. I can't let her know just how dramatic of an effect her body has on me.

"It looks like my tactic is working," she says confidently. "Deal again."

I shuffle the cards, but I keep my eyes on her. She smiles at me. She knows she has me. God, I could fuck her over and over. I could fuck her so hard, it would destroy that ten thousand dollar couch and I'd just move on to fucking up the next piece of furniture.

"I think you've shuffled enough," she mentions, her finger trailing between her breasts.

"You're far too confident," I say. I lean forward to place the two cards between her breasts. I let my hand linger as I feel her sharp inhale.

"Don't hate the player, hate the game," she says. "Specifically, the person who invented the new rules."

I pull my hand back and place two cards in front of me.

"Let's get you naked," I say. I flip over three cards. "Raise?"

"Nah."

I check my cards before flipping the next card.

"Raise?" I ask again.

"Nope."

I flip the last card and look up at her. It's hard to focus on her face.

"I'm not going to raise," she says. I lay down my cards.

"Two pair," I say.

"Mmm." Her eyes crinkle as she smiles wider.

"You have a better hand."

"You don't know that," she argues.

"You're smiling like you won the lottery. You weren't smiling that much in the beginning, so you either have a better two pair or three of a kind. I'm going to go with the latter."

"Three ladies!" she says, laying down her queen. "I should have raised. That means I have to make this question a good one."

"Go ahead."

She contemplates me, her eyes skimming over mine like she can see right through me—see all my thoughts clanging against each other.

"Tell me about your parents."

"That's not a question."

"Okay. What was your childhood like?"

As much as I want to, I can't pass on the question. It would violate our agreement on the game's rules. "Chaotic."

I gather up the cards, pushing them together until they're stacked.

She reaches forward, her breasts baiting me. She snatches her bra from my lap and starts putting it back on. We lock eyes.

"If you don't play by the rules, then I'm not going to," she says.

"I answered the question. If you wanted a different answer, you should have asked a different question."

She finishes clasping the back of her bra. She fixes the straps. "And I took off my clothes. Now I'm putting them back on. I'm certain my father won't find it strange at all that I don't know what your parents do."

She picks up her shirt. The fear yanks at me again like a parachute being pulled. I'm not this cowardly.

"They're both dead," I whisper. "You can spin any love story about them that you want to."

"Did they die because of…"

She trails off. The word *Bratva* stings the room. I stare at her, watching her features change from angelic to human—downright untrustworthily human.

I see my parents in her face—two backstabbers who were born to destroy each other.

I shuffle the cards but I don't answer her question. There are two sides to every story. In this case, both sides are ugly.

My ringtone starts to play. I pull it out of my pocket.

"Ilya," I answer.

"Members of the Colosimo family have taken the VIP tables at Black Glacier."

There's a small edge in his voice, but he's mostly calm.

"I'll be there," I say.

I set the cards down and stand up. I have to give Duilio's son credit for the strategy. It would be reckless for me to attack them without knowing what they want and even more reckless to attack them in my own club. It's intimidation with a low risk of retaliation.

"You're leaving?" Allison asks. I focus on her, almost forgetting she was there for the briefest moment.

"Business," I say. I bend down, cupping her face. I crush my mouth against hers, punishing her for that teasing glimpse of her body. Her fingertips touch my waist, scrambling to bring me forward. I move my hand down, slipping it under her shirt and grasping her breast. I give it a quick squeeze as my mouth moves toward her ear. "You deserve a lot worse than that."

I pull away. Her eyes are glazed with neediness and her mouth is tinged pink.

I turn and walk out of the den. As I feel her lip balm on my mouth, I try to play over the last few seconds. I hadn't decided to kiss her. It was instinctual. This city—my city—is a jungle, and out here, instinct can be life-saving or fatal. In this case, I don't see it saving my life.

As I get into the car—a gleaming Cadillac that has been hibernating in the garage—my thoughts trail back to my parents. I loved my mother. I don't blame her for anything. But she's still a reminder that Allison can only be a sexual partner.

Anything more is risky. Show her too much of the man behind the curtain, and I invite danger into my own home. A woman who needs more from me than I can give …

And my blood on the ground when she inevitably stabs me in the back.

∼

If Mariya's Revenge is my pride and joy, Black Glacier is my shame and misery.

I keep it open for the Bratva, but the police are suspicious of any nightclubs under the Alekseiev name because of my father. If I could drop it, I would, but it's so profitable that the police would be too suspicious if I tried to cut my ties to the place.

When I walk into the club, it's moderately busy. Tuesday nights are one of our slowest, but there's still enough people inside to guarantee a great profit margin, keep a bartender busy, and give any man here decent odds of getting his dick wet.

On a raised platform, five VIP tables overlook most of the club. The men there are unmistakably Italian—the dark hair, dark eyes, olive complexion—and a poor gene pool that gives them a rapidly receding hairline.

I walk up to the section. Duilio's son isn't difficult to pick out. Everyone else either keeps their gaze down around him or keeps their hand gestures restrained. In appearance, he doesn't resemble his father. He's slim with a casual demeanor that could fit in at a country club. Whereas Duilio looked at everyone with an air of self-importance, his son observes everyone with a lazy curiosity—until he sees me approaching. Then he sits up, his focus as sharp as a sniper's.

He stands up when I'm less than a foot away. My arm instinctively reaches back for my gun, but I let it relax as his eyes follow my movement. His actions may betray his emotional immaturity, but not even an idiotic child would make the mistake of trying to kill me in a club with my men scattered amongst the crowd.

"Mr. Alekseiev." Duilio's son gestures to the chair beside the one he just vacated. "I'd be honored if you joined me."

I take the chair, pulling it out. I'm not enthusiastic about having my back facing an open area, but I'm not about to show my caution in front of the Colosimo Mafia.

The Italian sits down beside me. He gestures for the two other men at the table to leave. After they are gone, he turns to me.

"So, Mr. Alekseiev," he says, his voice slick with fake courtesy. "Do you mind if I call you Lev?"

"I'd prefer if you didn't call me at all," I say.

He nods. "Fair enough, Mr. Alekseiev. I'm Marco Colosimo, but I suppose you already know that."

"I didn't know your first name." I turn my body, so I can check what's happening behind me without seeming paranoid. His men are lingering nearby, but don't appear to be preparing for an attack. "Your father never mentioned it."

It's meant as a small cut and from the look on his face, it cuts even deeper than I expected.

"Well, it's not like the two of you met up with each other to talk casually," he says. "I am sure you think that my men meeting here is some kind of power move—"

"I agree," I say. "It's not a power move. At least your father had the balls to not wait around for me, hoping to God that I'd notice him. He contacted me directly. None of this bullshit."

He forces a smile. "I'm glad we agree. I simply wanted to be somewhere that we could talk. After all, we have a lot to talk about."

"We don't have anything to talk about."

"You were in talks with my father when you killed him." His jaw tenses at the last few words. "Perhaps we can finish that conversation."

There isn't a second I would ever believe that Marco cares about forming a truce and collaborating to take down the Calvino Mafia.

"Finish it then," I say.

"First, I'd like to tell you something." He picks up his glass, swirling the pale brown liquor inside. "I hated my father. People care about the bruises, but it's the disappointment and shaming that sink in deeper. I've heard that's something you might understand."

"I have no complaints about my father," I say, opening my hands to show my apathy.

"Not anymore, no," he says. "And, now, I suppose, neither do I. From what I've heard, we had similar mothers as well. Of course, mine died from cancer, which isn't comparable to your tragedy, but—"

"Why don't you keep the rumors pertaining to my personal history in your diary and out of this discussion?" I try to keep the anger out of my voice, but it creeps in. He raises his eyebrow, hearing it. It's a mistake. It's fine for me to be annoyed about dealing with him, but getting angry about my parents can only be seen as a weak spot.

"I understand, Mr. Alekseiev," he says. "My point, though, is that— despite my hatred for my father— family is still everything. I want you to know, in Jesus' name and on my mother's grave, you're going to suffer for what you did."

His tone doesn't change as he talks. He's in better control of his emotions than I thought, which is a problem. Emotions can be exploited. Cold logic is much harder to manipulate.

I lean forward. "I could shatter that glass in your hand and slice open your carotid artery. I could take my gun, shove it down your throat, and blow your spine out of your body before anyone else got a single shot off. With one gesture, every Bratva man in here would shoot you and all of your men and spray every patron in here with your DNA, and every fucking civilian in the joint would testify that they didn't see a motherfucking thing. Junior, if you make a threat, you better be certain you have the upper hand or you're going to be surprised at how goddamn easy it is for me to kill you."

Marco doesn't blink. "Go ahead," he says. "But you're a rational man. Even if you managed to kill me, it would only lead to investigations into Black Glacier. Even if I left now and you or your men killed me, my credit card information will show that the last place I went to was Black Glacier and I'm sure the police would love to include this club in their investigation."

He slides the glass over in my direction, taunting me.

"Mr. Alekseiev, at least a few people here know who I am. One person might know who you are and if they don't, they'll find out if my dead body is discovered. Even if they don't know, we paid for the best tables here. We're practically on a stage. Everyone is watching and they're wondering what our connection is, so if I die, you will be the first one questioned."

I indicate for Daniil to step forward. Marco refocuses on him. I hand Daniil the glass. "Get Marco three shots of Mariya's Revenge."

"Yes, sir." Daniil leaves with the glass. I turn back to Marco.

"You have the same problem," I say. "If you kill me, everyone has seen us together and everyone knows the Colosimos still resent my men for showing the city that you're just unstable thugs."

"The city doesn't know who you truly are, though, does it, Mr. Alekseiev?" he taunts. "Besides, I have no plan to kill you in the short-term. I said I'd make you suffer and I meant that. These things take time."

He glances around the club. Daniil returns with the three shots and sets them between the two of us. He retreats. Marco and I don't reach for the shots.

"I'm not going to kill you yet," Marco says. "But I'm threatening your kingdom. You're threatening me with prison time, which would be a relaxing vacation for a man of my means and connections. You should remember that I'm not the face of any major legitimate businesses, so I have nothing to lose—you made sure of that. I'm going to tear you apart like it's your autopsy. And I'm telling you this now because I know you'll look back at this moment and know that

I'm everything you think you are and that's going to be the other thing that kills you, Lev."

He takes a shot and downs it. He stands up. As he passes by me, he bumps the glass against my arm.

"It's great to meet the owner," he says, his voice carrying over the sound of the music. As he continues to stride down toward the bar, I see several people turning to look at me.

I fight the impulse to go after him. He's a worthwhile contender, but he's wrong. I'm not going to let him go to prison. I'm going to kill him myself. As soon as I have the police chief in my pocket, I'm going to stick each of Marco Colosimo's body parts in a different section of the city like skulls on a spike.

And each one of them will be painted red with the same warning:

Do. Not. Fuck. With. Me.

∼

Getting drunk is a game for undergrads, easy women, and people who never grew up. But as I step into my house, my body feels heavy and my thoughts weightless, floating away.

I wander through the house. I imagine Allison in every room—drinking in the den, eating in the kitchen, showering in the bathroom, napping in my bedroom—but she's not in any of them. There's no reason that she would be, but she infiltrates every room.

I'm not the kind of man. I don't let shit bother me, but she's so deeply under my skin that it's aggravating every part of my life.

I stop in my personal gym. The warmth from the liquor is changing into heat from rage. I jump onto the treadmill, selecting nine miles per hour. I run for fifteen minutes but the frustration digs into me farther. I pound out thirty pull-ups. The aggression continues to grind against my brain. I start wrapping my hands for the boxing bag.

My cell phone beeps. I take my time reaching it.

Allison Harrington: *Is everything okay?*

It's such a small thing. The tension in my shoulders and jaw eases. I tap her number on the screen and bring the phone up to my ear, letting out a slow breath.

"Hello," she says. She sounds like she's underwater or ill. "Did you fix whatever you needed to?"

"Not exactly." I walk over to the gym's mirrors in front of the dumbbells and kettlebells. I replay our sex in the dressing room. "But it's not important. Are you ready for the gala tomorrow?"

"I mean, I will be if I get enough sleep."

I glance at my phone. 2:29 a.m. *Shit.* My phone must have just been reminding me that I had a text and I hadn't noticed it before.

"I apologize. I didn't realize it was so late."

"Wow. You aren't used to apologizing, are you?" She laughs. I press my ear harder against the phone, taking in her joy. "It's fine, Lev."

Her voice sounds nice when she's just woken up. I imagine her, curled up on her bed, her hair splayed over her pillow, wearing some kind of thin shirt that can't conceal her nipples.

I should have checked to see what her bed looked like when I was at her apartment.

I could relax if we fucked again, but phone sex would be a decent substitution.

"So, is everything okay?" she asks again. Her words slur slightly together, sticky with sleep. It takes me a few seconds to understand what she said.

I'm certain I could coax her into telling me her deepest fantasies and get her desperate to have me fuck her again. But the sound of her tired voice works its own magic on me.

"Tell me about your court cases," I say softly.

She laughs. "You want to know about what I did with the DA?" she asks. "It was mostly the one case, but I helped out other people in the office. There was one interesting case, involving a house covered in cat prints."

Her voice is a lull in a storm as she goes on, talking about this and that. The actual things she says are less important than the fact that she's the one saying them and I'm the one listening. It's like playing a game where the outcome doesn't matter—all that matters is the back and forth between us. Her exhaustion seems to have taken down all of her emotional walls. She is simple, raw, vulnerable, even as she says nothing that she wouldn't tell a stranger on the street.

After the first ten minutes, she talks less and less. She becomes quiet except for the sound of her breathing. I could stay on the phone and listen to it for another few minutes, but I know that would be irrational.

"Good night, Allison," I whisper.

"Good night, Lev."

I end the call and sit there for a moment. I rub my face, trying to pull my thoughts away from Allison. Sitting there, it feels like I'm in the depths of an illness. I'm not myself. I shouldn't have cared whether or not she was tired. I shouldn't have called her at all. Tenderness is a virus and being around her has infected me.

I massage my shoulder. I need to redirect my focus to my work. Fear is the father of love and there's no fear when I focus on my company. Not only am I certain in its longevity, but I'm also certain that even if the end comes, I'll see it coming from miles away.

I can't say the same about people.

12

ALLISON

Irina answers the door when I arrive at Lev's house.

"Welcome, Miss Harrington," she gestures inside. She's holding an ibuprofen bottle. She catches me looking at it. "Mr. Alekseiev is being stubborn. Maybe you could convince him to take some medication?"

She offers the bottle to me. I take it. "Did he hurt himself?"

"No, not exactly," she says, picking up a rag and dusting spray off the floor. "It's not my place to say anything. Mr. Alekseiev is in the den. It was nice to see you again, Miss Harrington."

She sprays the handrail of the spiral staircase before wiping it down. I pass her and head into the den.

I've found myself discovering new parts of Lev—his criminal connections, his concealed kindness, his body—but I'm not expecting to find him in his den, lying on the couch with his clothes rumpled, his arm covering his eyes, and the strong scent of alcohol lingering on him.

Irina's evasiveness makes a lot more sense to me now.

"Do you need some ibuprofen?" I ask.

He shifts his arm. "No. You're early."

"No, I'm not," I say. "It's nearly 4:00."

He grabs his phone, the screen lighting up his face. "Shit."

I set the ibuprofen on the end table. "It's not the best time to start indulging in any addictions."

"It has nothing to do with addiction. It's a migraine." He sets his phone down. "Everything will be fine."

I sit down on the couch's armrest. It's strange to feel comfortable in my blackmailer's house, but that's exactly how I feel. Like I'm at home.

Lev sits up, rolling his neck, and winces. "We need to talk about the gala."

"I think we've quizzed each other enough. Unless you're ready to confess more."

"It's not about quizzing each other. It's about the engagement."

That part always slips my mind. All this time it's felt like we're preparing for some adult version of the prom. The bad parts are easy to forget.

"We're going to announce our engagement the morning after the gala," he says.

"Why wouldn't we do it at the gala?"

"Less risk," he says. "We'll pretend that I proposed the night of the gala after a very romantic night together."

The doorbell rings. Lev barely glances in the direction of the door before he closes his eyes again, rubbing his temples.

"Is that Ilya?" I ask.

"Close," he says. "Did you want to see Ilya?"

There's an edge in his voice I haven't heard before. I don't see him as a jealous type, but I can't figure out what other emotion it could be.

"No, I just haven't seen anyone else visit."

A woman enters the room, carrying a large bag over her shoulder. She's almost fairy-like in her beauty. Her blonde hair flows down her head like sunlight, her skin is flawless, and everything about her is the definition of dainty.

She's gorgeous and I hate her for being in Lev's den right now.

Lev gestures to her. "Allison, this is Sophie. She's Ilya's wife. She's going to help you get ready for the gala."

"Oh, Ilya's wife. Great." I hold out my hand, hoping she can't see my embarrassed blush, and she shakes it. Her hand feels incredibly fragile. "Thank you so much. I'm not great at makeup or anything like that."

"You should have seen what she was wearing at the club," Lev says. I give him a dirty look, but he just smirks at me.

"I'm sure he remembers every detail of what you were wearing, Allison," Sophie says. She wraps her small arm around me. "You brought your dress, right?"

"Yes. It's in my car. I'll get it."

After I get my dress—still in the box—I retreat with Sophie upstairs. She's brought expensive shampoos and conditioners for me to use. As I shower, enveloped in the warm, musky scent of her shampoo, I contemplate what kind of information I might get out of Sophie. Ilya must know some details about Lev's Bratva connections, but that doesn't mean Sophie will. She seems too delicate to be involved in any of this.

When I finish my shower, I put on the dress. Sophia combs my hair with a gentle touch. I watch myself in the mirror as we talk about the gala, my family, and her relationship with Ilya.

"He is truly the sweetest man," she says. "He's the only man I've ever been with that I know I can trust no matter what."

"Oh?" I ask. "So, you know everything about him?"

She slides a bobby pin into my hair. "I know what I need to know."

"Does that mean you know a lot about Lev?" I ask.

In the mirror, I see Sophie's face skip through several emotions. Her lips press together for several seconds before she looks up at me. "Could I give you some unsolicited marital advice, Allison?"

"Sure," I say, though I'd strongly prefer court-admissible criminal evidence.

"I married Ilya because I knew he'd always value me and that's what I needed. I didn't want men who treated me like something that was fragile or like a ball and chain," she says. "And what Ilya needed was someone who was willing to accept the messy parts of his life. He couldn't give it up and I wasn't going to force him to choose between me and those messy things. You have something inside you that you need. It could just be companionship. But you need someone who is willing to fulfill that need and someone whose need can be fulfilled by you."

"You know I don't have a choice in this," I say. She finishes my hair.

"Let's do your makeup now," she says. She opens her various makeup sets and starts applying foundation. Initially, I think she's just going to ignore what I said. We sit in awkward silence for a while as she works.

But when she's nearly finished, she looks me in the eye.

"Do you think, if you had a choice, you'd never return here?" she asks.

She doesn't wait for my answer as she starts putting away her makeup kits.

"I can't wait for Lev to see you. He's going to fall on his knees and worship you."

I laugh bitterly. "Maybe you don't know him that well after all," I grumble.

Sophie winks with a weird kind of all-knowing confidence. "You'd be surprised."

After she's done packing her things, she helps me down the stairs. I'm not used to the heels, but after walking down the hallway and getting tips from Sophie, it becomes a bit easier. Sophie enters the den first.

"Lev, are you ready to see your date?" she asks.

He makes some noise that could be a no or a yes.

"Allison, come in," Sophie calls to me.

I step inside. Lev is by the home bar, drinking from a glass. He must have showered in the downstairs bathroom and changed while I was getting ready. His hair is combed back and he's wearing a dark gray suit, fitted to show the sharp lines of his torso and the width of his shoulders. His hand is shoved into his pocket, with a diamond-encrusted watch winking from his wrist. The black shirt underneath the suit jacket is the perfect complement to his skin. It takes everything I have not to pounce on him and run my tongue along his jawline, to undo the buttons of his shirt one by one and let my fingers explore what's beneath …

He looks so damn good that I finally understand why Julia goes out of her way to pursue certain men. Lev turns male beauty into a religion that I'd put my faith in.

He turns to look at me. His green eyes soften suddenly from their usual severity. The tension that seems to encompass his body leaves him. It's like someone sucked the air from the room.

"Oh."

~

The Tide & Shore Hotel sits on a hill, the driveway curling around it and splitting to lead either to the parking lot or the beach. As Lev and I walk up to it, his hand skims against my back. The dress I'm wearing is black and backless. It ties together behind my neck, with lace that covers my shoulders and extends past my knees. There's a black skirt underneath it, but it only reaches partway down my thighs. If I had been going to the gala solely to support my father, I'd have chosen something more conservative, but knowing I'd be by Lev's side the whole night, I selected something to hold his attention. It must be working; Lev has kept his hand on some part of me ever since we got into his car.

In the lobby of the hotel, an older man wearing a dress uniform is standing behind a table covered with a white cloth. He checks the licenses of two people at the table against the clipboard in his hand before smiling at both of them.

"Welcome, Mr. and Mrs. Sadler. Thank you for honoring our men in blue. The red tables are for our donors. Please enjoy the music and the hors d'oeuvres before the dinner starts."

Lev's hand grazes against my ass as we step up to the table and he pulls his wallet out of his back pocket. The man smiles at us.

"Welcome to the Great Blue Foundation gala. May I see your IDs?" the man asks.

As I fumble with my new clutch, Lev gives the man his driver's license. The man glances at it. He stiffens. His eyes shift back and forth between the license and Lev. Lev keeps his eyes locked on him, his expression passive. It reminds me of when we first met and I thought he was apathetic about everything.

The man hands the license back to Lev, careful not to let their fingers touch. He stares at Lev for another second before turning to me.

"Ma'am?" the man says. I offer my license. He barely looks at it before his eyebrows shoot up. "Oh, Miss Harrington. I apologize, but you're not on the list. Does your father know—"

"She's my plus one," Lev interrupts.

The man frowns, glancing between the two of us.

"I see," he says. "Well, welcome, Miss Harrington. Please enjoy the hors d'oeuvres before the dinner starts."

He hands me back my license. Lev's hand drifts to the small of my back. I lean toward him, our bodies bumping together, as he pushes open one of the doors to the ballroom. He steps aside to let me in, then follows behind me. His fingertips briefly touch my hips before he slips his arm around my waist. In the wake of his touch is a light, simmering tingle dancing on my skin—just like always.

At least a hundred people are spread out in the ballroom. Two lines of tables are on either side of the room while the center is empty except for a marble dance floor and a bar in between two massive speakers at the front of the room. On the right, the tables are covered with blue cloth and have vases filled with bluebells. White stars flicker on the cloth from the table lamps. On the left, it's the same setup, but the tables are red and the vases are filled with small red roses.

"Very patriotic," Lev remarks.

"He recognized your name?" I ask. When he doesn't answer, I look over at him. He's looking up at the blue fairy lights that crawl over the ceiling. "Lev?"

He glances back down at me, forcing a smile. "Unfortunately, my father and I share the same last name and he was less than friendly with the police. I'm guilty by association."

"You are guilty, period," I say.

"Semantics. And they wouldn't know that if it wasn't for him."

He pulls a bit away from me. It would be barely noticeable to anyone else, but I feel the slight absence of body heat and miss it instantly. I turn my focus to each person in the ballroom, trying to forget all of the guilt between us and attempting to find my parents hidden among the crowd.

A group of people moves away from the bar. Talking to the bartender are two people, polar opposites. The man, with his dark gray hair and his broad frame, stands tall, posture rigid with years of ingrained discipline. The woman, with her dyed blonde hair and tiny frame, leans against the bar, laughing at a joke that no one else is laughing at.

My parents.

They're slanted away from me, but I can't shake the feeling that I've been caught. I am the worst kind of person—I let a man die in front of me, I lusted for a murderer, I dreamed up an extravagant con to fool my parents and all their friends, and I'm going to marry a man who is involved with one of the most powerful crime syndicates the city has suffered under.

I'd disown me if I were them.

"Take a breath," Lev says. His body is pressed against mine, his hands on my hips. He told me the same thing the night he killed that man on the motorcycle. I try to force in a breath, but the thought of that man, his limp body on the side of the road; the memory of the celebratory ambience in Black Glacier before I followed Jeffrey Douglas, collides in my head.

The breath gets caught in my throat. I press my hand against my chest, bending down to try to get it out.

Lev is saying something, but I'm too far under to hear him. He guides me away from the middle of the room. I barely notice. I try to think of something else, but the loud music pounds in my head just like the music at Black Glacier did.

I can smell the pepper spray.

I can feel the fear. Like it's only been buried under my façade this whole time. It never went away. It just waited until I was vulnerable.

Lev's hands are in my hair. When his lips touch my mouth, the smell of the pepper spray fades, replaced by his scent of smoke and spice. When he pulls my hips tight against his, his lips moving against mine recklessly, the fear is burned away by the contradiction of need and satisfaction. His fingers trail down my spine and there is nothing in the world except where his fingers touch.

He steps away from me and my breathing slowly becomes more natural. His hair isn't as neat as it had been. I don't recall my hands being anywhere near his head, but they must have been.

His hand cups my cheek. "You're okay now?"

I nod. He looks sideways. An older couple is staring at us.

"Hey," he says. Like a pair of deer frightened by a gunshot, they scurry away and don't look back.

Lev turns back to me. "We need to talk to your parents. You don't want them to find out from the man checking IDs or that couple."

I nod several times, but I don't move.

"Allison," he says. His hand brushes down my arm. "It will be quick. We came late on purpose. The dinner is going to start soon."

"People already know we're together," I say. "So, let's just leave. You got what you wanted."

"What I wanted is for your father to be fully aware of the situation," he says. His hand drops. Anxiety floods back into my body. I reach toward him, but he takes a step back. "There are two options. Either I kiss you right in the middle of this room like we just fucked, or you go over and tell your parents. Both options will get their full attention."

Hate is a strong word, but entirely accurate in this moment.

I walk alone down the center of the room. With Lev by my side, the heels had begun to feel empowering and sensual, but without him, they feel unfamiliar and cumbersome.

When I turn my head, Lev is a few feet behind me and his eyes flit up from my ass. He shrugs, guilty but unashamed. I refrain from flipping him off.

I need to remember that, no matter how sweet or caring he acts, this is all he wants. I'm a pawn in his massive game of chess.

As I'm nearly in front of my parents, my mother turns. For a couple of seconds, she doesn't recognize me. The location, the dress, the hair, the makeup—it all turns me into a stranger. The recognition slowly dawns on her.

"Ally!" she nearly yells, though I'm right beside her. She throws her arms around me, hugging me tightly. My father turns around. "I didn't know you were coming! Why didn't you tell us? This is so great. I feel like I haven't heard from you in years."

"I, um, I wanted to surprise you," I say. My father pulls me into a hug.

"It's good to see you," he says. "You look beautiful. How did you get in? Did Michael just let you in?"

"No, uh ..." I bend the clutch in my hands. "I've ... there's something I need to tell both of you. Something important."

I could tell the truth right now. Lev isn't within earshot. My father would arrest him without evidence and jam him as far up the ass of the correctional system as humanly possible.

But it would end up costing him everything and it would break his heart to know that he was one of the reasons I decided to go into this deal. It would cost everybody an irrevocable amount of pain and Lev would, more likely than not, eventually walk free with an effusive apology from the city government.

And then he'd probably come for me.

My mother puts her hand on my arm. "Go ahead, Ally. What is it?"

"I've been in a relationship," I say, letting the lie simmer on my tongue. "For the last six months."

My father looks over at my mother, observing to see if she knew about this. My mother tilts her head.

"That's ... that's good, Ally," she says. "Why would you hide that from us?"

"It's a bit complicated." I twist my clutch harder. "But ... he's here."

I turn. Lev is already approaching us. I keep my eyes on his face to avoid looking at my parents. He looks so impossibly good.

"Mom, Dad, this is Lev," I say. As I turn to glance back at them, Lev's arm slides around my waist and I see my father's face. I watch it change from faint recognition to confusion to disbelief, then straight to livid with 'do not pass go; do not collect two hundred dollars'-type speed. Blood rushes so quickly to his face that I have no idea how he manages to remain upright.

"It's wonderful to finally meet you, Mr. and Mrs. Harrington." Lev holds his hand out. My mother shakes it, but my father purposefully turns away from him and toward me.

"I need to talk to you privately, Ally," he says. I reach for Lev's hand that's around my waist without thinking. When my father's eyes follow my movement, my hand retreats back to my clutch.

"Don't you want to all talk together?" I ask.

"It's fine," Lev says, his arm disappearing from my waist. As much as I hate to admit it, I miss it. "Your mother and I can get a drink and get to know each other."

"Or you can step back," my father says.

"Peter," my mother chastises. "Don't be a jerk. This is your daughter's boyfriend. Let's not make a scene. How did the two of you meet, Ally?"

The look that my father gives Lev could turn lions into kittens, but Lev looks back at him without any indication that he's noticed my father's anger.

"As strange as it sounds, we met at the gas station," Lev says. He smiles at me as if remembering the moment. I imagine the real memory is playing in his head—my body leaning over Jeffrey Douglas' as I perform CPR, trying to tell him that a corpse isn't dead. "She came up to me, acting like she knew me from a long time ago. After about a minute, I realized she thought I was one of her old classmates."

I nod, touching my temples like it can erase the image of Jeffrey Douglas choking.

"It was super embarrassing," I tell my parents. "I kept apologizing, but he was very cool about it. He bought me the soda that I had been planning to get."

Lev's hand settles on my back again. His thumb strokes against my spine. It's enough to center my thoughts, banishing the memories of that night to shadowy parts of my mind.

"And you happened to be in a gas station?" my father asks Lev.

"Why wouldn't he be in a gas station?" my mother asks. My father runs his fingers down his tie.

"Mr. Alekseiev is rich," he says. "Rich enough that he doesn't need to get his own gas."

"He's rich?" My mother appraises Lev again.

"I'm well off, but I still get my own gas. Chalk it up to a quirk of personality," Lev says. "When we met, I was getting gas and, at the time, I was still smoking and needed a lighter, so I went inside. Simple as that. I quit now, though." He winks at my mother, dripping with charm.

"You know that Ally wants to be a prosecutor, correct?" my father cuts in the moment Lev stops talking. He takes a step closer to Lev.

My mother takes an unsteady step back. She tries to catch my eye, but I'm too aware of how easily violence could break out between these two, so I keep my eyes on both of them. "District attorney in fact, one day."

"Yes," Lev says. "I'm looking forward to it. I know that Ally is passionate enough about justice and doing right by the victims' families that she'll put in all of her time and effort to convict them. She will be an amazing DA one day. I'm certain the city will be safer with her in that position."

"Well, that's so nice of you," my mother says. My father shakes his head. A caterer stops beside us.

"Good evening, ladies and gentlemen," he says. "Would any of you like to try the cheddar, apple, and arugula flatbread?"

"Sure," I say a bit too quickly. I take two pieces. Impulsively, I give one of them to Lev. As I take a bite out of mine, I see my father watching my hand pass off the flatbread to Lev. It might as well have been a kiss.

"I'm sorry," I mutter, though I'm not completely certain why. Lev briefly squeezes my hip. It could be a reassurance or a reminder to keep the con up.

My whole world becomes two men's reactions—my father's frustration and Lev's arm around me.

"Ally, we need to talk privately for a moment," my father says firmly. As he opens his mouth to speak again, the sound of a microphone being tapped fills the ballroom. We all turn to see an older man in the center of the dance floor.

"Everyone, thank you so much for coming," the man on the mic announces. "I'm certain you're all starving and we'll have plenty of time to honor our wonderful law enforcement officers after we've eaten, so we're going to start the dinner now. You'll notice that every table has six names on it and we'd be immensely grateful if you could take a table with your name on it. Thank you so much, everyone. Let's eat."

Lev takes my hand. "Mr. and Mrs. Harrington. It was a pleasure to meet you. We'll talk again after the dinner."

As he guides me toward the red tables, I turn to see my parents. My father's face is turning a ruddy pink while my mother is whispering to him, her hand on his chest.

I try to think that it could have been worse. But then again, the night isn't over yet.

∼

The dinner is flank steak with blue cheese, fried potatoes, and roasted veggies. The steak nearly melts in my mouth, incredibly tender and saturated with flavor. It's almost good enough to make me forget that my life is falling apart around me.

Lev seems to barely notice how good the food is, seeming more focused on drinking than eating. He's managed to keep up appearances as we talk to our four other tablemates—all generous donors like everyone else on the red side—but I can feel that his mind is elsewhere. His movements are slower and less deliberate than usual.

"Ally."

I turn to see my father behind me and stand up, nearly tripping in my shoes.

"Dad," I say. "Hi."

"We need to talk for a moment," he says. "Come outside with me."

He starts walking away without waiting for my response. I turn to Lev. He takes a gulp of his drink, watching me over the edge of the glass.

"Should I go?" I ask him.

"He's going to question you at some point," he says. He smiles at Mr. Campbell and his secretary, who have switched their focus to our conversation. "Her father hates me," he says to them, shrugging. "Unfortunately for me, he's the chief of police, so if I'm arrested later, you'll know why."

Mr. Campbell laughs and his secretary follows suit.

I leave the ballroom. My father isn't anywhere in the lobby, so I continue out the front doors. He's lingering at the edge of the sidewalk—a man no longer certain where the boundary is.

"How could you go for someone like him?" my father demands as soon as I step up next to him. I open my mouth, prepared with a lie, but he spins around, his hand cutting through the air between us. "No, honestly, I don't care about that. You need to end it now."

He's nearly shaking with anger. Lev and I had prepared ourselves, armed to the teeth with lies, but I wasn't ready to see my father so upset.

I focus on the sidewalk edge. "You can't decide these things for me anymore."

"This isn't a request, Ally. I'm telling you this because I care about you. He's not a good person. You're going to end it."

He knows.

I form the words in my head—the "I love him" speech, the "I'm not a little girl" speech, the waterworks, if necessary. But that's not what comes out.

"I don't care what type of person he is," my mouth enunciates. "He's important to me. I'm sorry if that hurts you."

He stares at me. I keep my gaze down as the seconds pass by.

"What is going on with you?" he says. "You keep this a secret from us, you bring him here without telling us, and now you're blatantly disrespecting me?"

I turn around. "I can't talk to you until you've calmed down—"

My father blocks me from going back to the hotel. "He's deeply involved in the Bratva."

My breath gets caught in my chest, which is lucky because my anxiety must resemble shock as my father nods at me.

"We don't have any proof, but we're certain he's powerful within the Russian Bratva. I don't know what his plan is by dating you, but I don't need to know anything. You just need to get into a car right now and leave. I've already called a car service."

"I'm not—I can't leave," I say. It looks like Lev's proposal scenario might not play out like we thought and I don't know what will happen to our deal if his plan doesn't work—likely Jeffrey Douglas' death will come out and the fallout will be dire.

"Why not?" my father demands.

I wish I could say that my only motivation is covering up Douglas' death, but another side of me sees us married and it's not the worst circumstance. It paints me in a bad light. Ethical Ally, shacking up with a criminal. What a shitty person I must be, willing to let every heart break to pursue my lust.

"Because I don't believe you," I lie. I see the shock on his face. It gives me enough of an advantage to open the hotel door and slip back in. I rush back into the ballroom, the dress feeling restrictive now.

I go to a corner, trying to catch my breath. The backs of my ankles hurt from my shoes rubbing against them, but the pain grounds me. I close my eyes tight, resting my forehead against the wall.

Get up. Let's see if your high horse protects you, Jeffrey's voice whispers in my ear. I have no moral standing anymore. I traded it all for a hot touch and a filthy night with a beast.

I let my clutch fall to my feet. I picture it being my bag instead and witnessing the pepper spray fall out. I recall grabbing it, thoughtlessly spraying Jeffrey in the face.

I see his head jolt back. I hear his screams, like metal scraping metal. He rubs his eyes, but it only makes it worse. He's coughing. He's choking. He's falling onto his knees. His hands are clenched. His face is red. His hands are limp. All color fades from his skin.

His dead hand is on me. It's grabbing me, trying to pull me down to hell with him. I try to shake it off, but it grabs me harder. It pulls me toward him.

But his chest is Lev's chest, which I could recognize anywhere.

I open my eyes. Lev's face comes into focus. He's holding me so tight that my ribs can barely move, but instead of feeling suffocating, it calms me down. He kisses below my ear, his mouth lingering there like a secret.

When he lets me go, the past becomes something that is trying to test me and I no longer feel the need to be put on trial by it. He takes my hand and leads me to the dance floor.

There's so much I need to tell him, but right now, the silence between us is an acquittal I desperately need.

13

LEV

Every time I look at Allison, I'm gripped by fear. It's fear that I've never known before. I'm afraid that she's an illusion and my hands will pass right through her. I'm afraid that she will see she has as much clout as me as in this deal and walk away from it. I'm afraid that she's going to get hurt or even killed. I'm afraid that one day she'll use that power over me to stab a knife into my back.

With my arm around her waist while we dance, she brings out an uncivil side of my mind. The way a few strands of her hair have fallen from her bun and are brushing against her cheek. The way her body feels under my hands with every one of her steps. The way her feet always miss the third beat. The soft smile on her face. It mostly makes me want to tear off her clothes and fuck her on one of these tables, but another part of me would be equally fine with just taking her away from the crowd and drinking in my den.

I want her to be mine in every way.

"I'm sorry about my father," she mentions. "He's usually levelheaded."

"He didn't kill me, which was one of my concerns," I say. I pull her closer, so we can keep our voices low.

"He knows about your connections." She brushes a strand of hair away from her face. "Your, uh, your other business."

"I get it," I say. "I knew he would. That was why you couldn't tell him beforehand. This whole black tie affair is less for him than it is for all of his colleagues and the people who keep the police force well-funded."

Her fingers touch my elbow. Of all the touches I've received from women before, this one is the hottest. This one stirs me the most. It brings my cock to rigid attention.

"I thought you'd be more worried about your plan," she says.

"He doesn't want to be seen as an overprotective father that will arrest someone because they're dating his daughter." I put my mouth closer to her ear. "That's the whole plan."

She nods, her chin brushing against my shoulder. I brush my lips against her temple.

"You should stop worrying about it," I say. "Just focus on getting everyone else to believe we're in love."

She pulls slightly away and gives me a quick look, her eyes reminding me of the ocean at night—dark, turbulent, inscrutable. I can see she's hurt by what I said. If she's starting to fall for me, it could be good for my plan but dangerous for me. It's a thin line to walk.

"Of course," she whispers. "I get it. It's a good plan."

I pull her closer, not quite ready to let her succumb to her shame and sadness. My cock brushes against her thigh. I slide my leg between her legs, nudging them open a little farther. She raises an eyebrow at me, but we continue moving close to each other.

"Tell me," I say.

"Tell you what?"

"How you think two people in love would act."

"Well," she muses. "The man would cradle her face, tell her that she was the most amazing woman he ever met, and carry her to the car when she's too drunk to walk. He also wouldn't blackmail her or try to seduce her in the middle of a gala."

"I'm not that kind of man and you're not that kind of drunk," I say.

"We could change both of those things."

"I'd rather not."

She moves her hands up to my arms. I prefer her hands to be lower, but she's looking up at me again, which makes it a decent compromise.

"Then how do you think two people in love would act?" she asks.

I move closer to her ear again, my cheek brushing against hers. "They'd be fucking constantly."

I feel her shiver. "That seems time-consuming."

I kiss her cheek before pulling away again. "Love doesn't need to make sense."

It's hard to hold back my desire for her now. I've imagined her in every position in this room—pressed up against the wall, bent over the table, on top of the bar, her head between my legs. The only reason I haven't done it is because I'm aware that her father could walk back into the ballroom and it would guarantee a shot in my head.

But as Allison looks at me, her pussy rocking up against my thigh and desire singing in the darkness of her pupils, I'd almost be willing to take a bullet if it means I could fuck her now.

I lean down, kissing her. Her mouth crumples against mine for a second before she kisses me back just as intensely. I grip her hips as her thumbs press harder into my skin. I could never be close enough to her until I'm inside her. She's everything to me right now.

There's a vibration between us. At first, I conclude it's a strange reaction from our bodies, but as it continues, I pull away. I pat the sides of my jacket, finding my phone. Allison looks at me, her expression dazed for several seconds before she bows her head, turning away from me.

Fuck.

It's Ilya. I consider ignoring it, giving Allison all of my attention, but I know it's a mistake to trade Bratva time for a woman's affection. It won't lead to anything but my own prison sentence.

I walk off the dance floor, feeling everyone's eyes on me as I put the phone up to my ear. Allison and I must have had an audience.

"Ilya," I answer. "What's going on?"

"It's not good," Ilya says. "Our newest recruit, Rodion. He's dead."

"The Colosimos," I say.

"They haven't taken credit, but it wasn't a good scene," he says. "He was mutilated. Missing body parts. His wife called us after she called the police, so we couldn't clean up."

"Keep your eyes open. We'll retaliate once we know more," I say. He doesn't say anything. "Ilya?"

"Yes," he says. "Good."

I hang up. I know what he's thinking—I'm going soft. Allison is whittling me down to someone who will take a hit without hitting back. But the last time the Colosimos retaliated, Allison almost got killed. If it were just me, I'd lead with a scorched earth tactic, but I can't risk the chief's daughter, especially now that everyone important knows we're dating.

I turn. Allison is at the bar, ordering a drink. I need to tell her about the Colosimos. I need her to be more prepared than Rodion's wife if something happens to me.

And God, I need to fuck her.

∼

We leave the ballroom not long after. I need an escape and tell Ally we need to talk. I can feel her father watching us with a death glare, but he doesn't intervene. I wouldn't be surprised if he follows us down to the ocean where we're now standing, but I don't hear his footsteps on the rough mix of sand and stone.

Ally picks up a small piece of driftwood. She tosses it out into the ocean where it disappears under a wave. I wait for it to resurface, but it never returns.

"What did you want to talk about?" she asks. She's barefoot, her shoes in her hand. The city lights are a faint glow in the distance, transforming her into a silhouette, but when she moves closer toward me, the illumination from the hotel creates a shrine of light around her. It looks damn near like a halo.

"One of my men died tonight," I say, pressing two fingers against the edge of a circle of large stone bricks. Inside, a teepee of sticks waits to be burned. "Killed by the Colosimos."

"That's terrible." She veers closer, pulling herself up onto the stone bricks, and sits, setting her shoes down beside her. Her knees nearly brush up against me. "Were you close?"

I shake my head. "I don't get close to anyone in the Bratva. I'm not telling you this to get your pity or sympathy. I need you to know because his wife fucked up. She called the police before she called us. The police can't prove anything on a phone call, but it paints us in a bad light. Gets them looking in the right places. It also means that we had no time to cover up anything we needed to cover up before the police got there."

Her knee taps against my waist. "If you want me to intervene in the police's investigation, I can't do that."

"Getting you involved would only give the police a scent to locate me through," I say. "No. I'm telling you because if I get killed, you need to know how to handle it and I know you're not the type to blindly accept directions, so I'm giving you context. The Bratva is at war with the Colosimos. The man on the motorcycle was a member of their Mafia. If I'm killed, you need to burn down my office. Everything important is in there. If the police ask—"

"You want me to commit arson?" she interrupts.

"If they find out my connections to the Bratva, they're going to assume you were complicit. The information about Jeffrey Douglas' murder is hidden in the office as well, so arson will be the least of your problems." I put my hand on her knee, which has started jiggling uncontrollably. It stops. "And you can convince them that whoever killed me was the one who set the fire."

Her hands grip the edge of the firepit. When I try to take her hand, she tucks it under her thigh.

"Why can't someone else do this?" she asks.

"Because it would look suspicious if someone else showed up at my house after I was killed. Their motives would be immediately questioned. The easy way to avoid that is to have someone who would have a good reason to be in my house—like my wife."

Her mouth forms around the word 'wife.' She tucks her other hand under her thigh. "Why can't you just tell me where the important things are, so I can get rid of them? Burning down your whole office seems excessive."

I trace my finger around her knee, seeking an answer that she won't despise me for, but I always end up with the same explanation.

"If you knew where information was that could be manipulated to implicate the Bratva, you would use it against me," I say. "It's well-hidden but it's not fireproof. The best option I see is for you to burn everything down."

She nods, more receptive to the truth than I thought. Almost suspiciously accepting of it.

"But this is all really unlikely, right?" she asks. "You killed that man after he tried to kill us twice. You're not going to die."

"I'd imagine the Colosimos first sent someone who needed to prove himself—an amateur. He was too eager to shoot and that's why he missed a shot that should have been easy." My hand subconsciously reaches for my bullet wound. "It only takes a man with a little bit of patience. I have a public life as the owner of Mariya's Revenge. If someone wants to kill me, they just need to wait for the right opportunity. And not miss their first shot."

She sweeps back some of her hair, a shiver slipping through her. "I mean, as long as I inherit all of your money, it's good." She offers a nervous, half-hearted laugh.

"You're not taking this seriously."

She looks up at me suddenly. Her eyes are cold and her jaw is rigid, but there's an emotion that's less steady underneath her anger. "You don't get to threaten me into marrying you, fuck me, and then talk about getting killed. Don't drag me into your life and then tell me that you're going to die and leave me stranded."

I stare at her. In her own way, she's right. I'm the tide, pulling her into the darkest parts of the ocean and telling her she may need to swim on her own soon. It's cruel, but it's also necessary. Part of the territory.

"Ilya will help you," I tell her. "You just need to—"

Her laugh cuts me off. She starts pulling bobby pins out of her hair. Her hair comes out slowly, then all at once. She shakes her head, letting the pieces fall where they may.

"You are impossible," she says. "I can follow instructions. You think that I'm worried about living in your mansion and burning your office down?"

"That's what you were talking about."

She pushes off the firepit, her knees hitting against my abdomen as she slides down. Her body pushes against mine as she turns, walking back toward the ocean. She stops where her feet sink into the wet sand. The waves wash over her feet. I follow her, trying to see what she sees, but we're staring at two different perspectives.

When I put my hand on her back, I feel her take a deep breath and let it out slowly. I kiss her cheek, her neck, the curve of her neck, and her shoulder. She leans against me, her body melting. I wrap my arms around her waist. Her thumbs hook around my hands.

When she spins around, her elbow hits against my chest. She takes a quick step back, the ocean waves crashing higher up on her legs now.

"I'm going back in," she says. "To be clear, that means I'm done with this conversation."

As she goes over to her shoes, puts them on, and then starts to walk back toward the glow of the Tide & Shore, I see a lone person walking away from the hotel. For a second I think it's her father, following us at last, but he's not dressed up like the other guests. He's wearing a white button-up shirt and dark pants, but they're stiffer than most dress clothes and they're nowhere near the price tag of anyone else's attire here.

My gun is in my car. I couldn't be certain if there was going to be a metal detector and I couldn't risk someone at the gala noticing it when I was in a room full of police officers.

The dark metal in his hand is barely visible in the shadow cast by his body. My hands are clenched. I'll end him slowly, just like the Colosimos kill people, so the next man they send after me will do it knowing the consequences.

My blood is racing, boiling. The fight is in my veins, ready to erupt. Ready to make this would-be killer suffer.

But the man isn't Italian. His arms swing casually and he doesn't notice Ally until she's about twelve feet away from him. His eyes trace her body up and down. As she passes by him, he turns to check out her ass. The light hits the metal in his hand.

He isn't carrying a gun or a knife. It's a lighter.

He turns back around and sees me. He takes a quick step back as his face turns bright red.

"I'm sorry, mate," he says. "I didn't mean to, uh, stare. I'm just, uh, I'm just here to start the fire before everyone comes out."

He stops walking when we're less than three feet away from each other. His knees are slightly bent, his eyes shooting back toward the hotel—a prey animal prepared to escape. With all the simmering tension under my skin, it would be so fucking enjoyable to send this man running with his tail between his legs, flexing my power, and not dwelling on the fact that Ally seems immune to my authority.

But instead, I let him sidle past me, hurrying up his steps until he's at the firepit. I consider going to the parking lot and getting my Glock, but I know it'd be an irrational choice. If the Colosimos sent someone here, it would be a suicide mission or, worse, a mission that would get them caught and interrogated by the police. The last thing the Colosimos want is police attention.

The hotel employee lights the firepit, standing by it as the flames grasp the bottom of the sticks, growing as the wind passes by and feeds it.

I take my cigarettes out from the interior pocket in my jacket. I walk up to the firepit and pop out a cigarette. I light it using the small, flickering flames.

I smoke through three cigarettes as the employee chatters about the chemistry of fireworks and how his job is part of his long-term plan to become the CEO of a Fortune 500 company. I try to be patient through the various nervous speeches, but he doesn't seem to mind my lack of contribution to the conversation.

As I throw my cigarette carton into the fire, noise starts up behind me.

The donors and law enforcement stream out of the hotel. They remind me of angry townsfolk, but instead of pitchforks and torches, they cling to their purses and cell phones. They're smiling, but underneath the pretense, there's a tribalistic, anger-fueled self-righteousness. If the police get lucky and charge me for my crimes, they'll point their fingers and scream for my head, but I slipped into business so easily because I needed the same traits in a legitimate business as a crime syndicate. Keep your knife behind your back until it's needed and be willing to destroy before you're destroyed. There is no compassion, only profit.

Ally is on the left edge of the crowd. She's talking to a man with blond hair and enough hair gel to fill an oil tanker.

Jealousy isn't an emotion I experience. It's based in fear and I am not a man who scares easily. Everything I've ever wanted, I've taken.

But after that employee's reaction to her and seeing her gaze straight at this man like anything he's saying could be vaguely important, I know I need to play my part better. Someone who has been dating Ally for the last six months wouldn't let these men keep looking at her and monopolizing her attention.

He'd want her so immensely, he'd take her for his own.

I walk up to her. The blond stops talking but Ally barely notices until

I've wrapped my arm under her arms and slipped my arm under her knees, scooping her up. One of her shoes flips off as she yelps, grabbing onto the front of my shirt.

"What—" she starts.

"Sorry," I say, cutting her off to talk to the man. "I need to build a castle with my girlfriend."

I stride back to the beach with Ally in my arms. She glares at me.

"What the hell was that?" she asks. "Is this your version of flirting?"

I drop her feet in the sand. She stumbles. I grab her arm, but she lets herself drop onto the sand. Her fingers wrap around my wrist as she smiles and yanks me down with her.

I collide into her, my hand slamming near her hip and our mouths close enough that I can smell the alcohol on her breath. My lips press against hers, forcing her lips open. The vigilant part of my mind can hear the crowd rumbling with disgust and intrigue over us, but as her hands slip under my waistband—where the Glock would have been if I'd taken it with me—nothing matters but the warmth under me.

I pull back, caressing the side of her face. As I look straight at her, all I can think is how badly I want her to surrender herself to me and how badly I want to surrender myself to her.

I settle down beside her as the crowd surrounds the firepit. She keeps an arm behind me while I keep my hand on her thigh. She jumps at the sound of a bang. My body tenses, my pulse taking off like a rocket, but as I see the hotel employee with an opened bottle of champagne, the bubbles flowing out onto his hand, and Ally rests her head on my chest, my pulse slows and all of the memories of guns dim from my mind. I wrap my arm around her waist as glasses of champagne are handed out.

The older man who announced that dinner was going to be served—Police Commissioner Keith Holman, appointed by Mayor Coleman nearly two years ago, a husband and father of three children, and who occasionally makes surreptitious nighttime visits to the apartment of patrol officer Karen Brost—raises his champagne glass. Everyone follows suit.

"Here is a toast to all of our brothers in blue and to all of you who spend your hard-earned money to ensure the safety of this city." His words are a bit soft at the edges and his eyes are glazed. My research into him never mentioned alcoholism, but it's easier to hide than most people think. "Here's to a future where all of our children are safe, where our officers are safe, and where we can live our lives without fear. Let's raise our glasses to a better future and for everyone who contributes to that."

Several people holler and clap. Everyone raises their glass higher in celebration before clinking their glasses against everyone's glasses beside them. Since Ally and I are the only ones on the ground, we clink our glasses with each other. She puts her hand on my arm before I can take a sip and gives me a quick kiss.

"I don't regret it," she whispers. She drinks her champagne before I can ask her what she means. As we set our glasses down, there's a whistling sound before the first firework goes off. Bright blue fills the skyline. Several more whistling echoes follow as fireworks start going off in quick succession. Red, white, and blue are common color bursts, but occasionally they throw in orange, green, or turquoise.

Ally moves closer to me, her arms wrapped around my waist. I scan the crowd, but I don't see her parents. I bow my head against her hair and kiss near her ear. She turns, looking up at me, a genuine smile bursting on her face.

"You're an amazing woman," I tell her. "And I will carry you when you're too drunk to walk to the car."

She laughs. "Ah of course, you'd use my own words against me."

"It doesn't mean two people in love wouldn't also be fucking constantly."

"You might be right," she says, tapping her finger against my nose. I pretend to bite at her finger. She giggles. "Because I've wanted to be under you all night."

She leans back, lying down on the sand. Her eyes are closed, her chest rising and falling with every breath.

I slip my hand into my pocket. I pull out the small wooden box, a sun and a brown bear carved into it. I flick it open and take out the ring. According to the lapidary, it's a princess-cut engagement ring. All I know is that the price tag would convince anybody that I'm highly invested in this relationship.

As I take her hand, a smile curves onto her lips but she doesn't open her eyes. I slide the ring onto her finger. Her eyes open and she sits up.

"I thought we were going to wait until morning to do this," she says, staring at the ring.

"I changed my mind," I say. "I wanted all these other men to know you're claimed, so there's no confusion later."

"Other men?" she asks.

"Your father. The other policemen. The blond fucker I kidnapped you from," I say.

She smiles before kissing me, soft and filled with promise. "You're cute when you're jealous."

"I'm not jealous," I say. "I just think other people should know what's mine."

"Jealous," she repeats, laughing.

I kiss her, harsh enough that she falls onto her back. When she reaches for me, the ring scrapes against my skin, but the sting only makes me want her more.

⁓

In the parking lot, Ally is drunk as hell and I've called Ilya to pick us up. Under normal circumstances, I'd drive and be fully capable, but I know it's something Ally can't handle since the crash.

She abruptly steps away from me. She reaches back like she didn't realize what she'd done. Her fingertips brush against my arm.

"It's my parents. I'm gonna say goodbye."

I grab her arm before she can leave. She gives me a questioning look. I take her hand, slide off her ring, and pocket it.

"I don't think you want to have a brawl in the middle of the parking lot. You can tell them later," I say. She gazes at me, that defiant look complementing her face. She reaches toward my breast pocket like she's going to take the ring back out. Instead, she dives forward, kissing my cheek.

She walks across the parking lot and greets her father, her hand touching his arm in a reassuring gesture. I can't see his face, but his body relaxes after five or six seconds. Her mother, on the sidelines, catches me watching. I straighten up as she starts walking over. I force a smile as she stops, turning, so we're both facing her husband and her daughter.

"You'll have to excuse my husband," she says. "She's our only child."

"I understand," I say.

"And it was very surprising to find out that she's been secretly dating someone."

"You're both very important to her," I say. "We just weren't certain how we felt about each other until a couple of months ago. By then, she didn't want to hurt you and we let it go on without clearing the air. I apologize for that."

"I see," her mother says. "And what happened a couple of months ago?"

I watch Ally and her father hug. When they pull apart, she has a huge smile on her face. She nearly stumbles in her heels as she takes a step back, but she's nearly bouncing now as she talks, her hands moving with her words.

"It's hard to explain," I say. "I just saw her and … I knew that if she left me, I'd just be going through the motions for the rest of my life. I hadn't realized it before her, but I've spent my life putting a checkmark next to every one of my accomplishments and believing that material success was happiness. I don't know anymore. I might want more."

Her mother nods. "You love her. She brings something into your life. From the way I've seen her look at you, I think you do the same for her and that's all you can ask from a partner."

When I called Sophie to help Ally get ready, she broached the topic of relationships. She talked about how marriages work because both people get what they need out of it. She said there's compromise, but the relationship doesn't survive on compromise like a contract does—it survives on two people who want to give what the other person needs. I dealt with her lecture because I didn't want her to back out of helping Ally, but if I hadn't needed her help, I would have told her that my marriage with Ally was a contract.

And now Ally's mother is saying nearly the same thing as Sophie. But she also thinks I love Ally, so this whole discussion is comprised of fables.

"So, your relationship is like that with your husband?" I ask.

"Oh yes. He can be boneheaded and sometimes he says the first thing that pops into his head. But sometimes that's a good thing." She smiles. "Just be good to Ally."

"Because her father will kill me if I'm not. I know," I say.

She shakes her head. "No, you should be good to Ally because she is fair. If you're good to her, she'll be good to you."

Ally's father is waving her mother over. She holds out her hand. I shake it.

"It was nice to meet you, Lev," she says. "Hopefully, we'll see each other again soon."

"Yes, we will," I say. As she walks toward her husband, he raises his arm and she tucks right in underneath it. The chief is a thorn in my side, but his love for his wife is undeniable. His relationship is more genuine than anything I've ever had.

My parents used to be like that—the couple that everyone wanted to be part of. Or, at least, they were like that until my father started gaining power and all the dominoes fell.

Ally skips over to me. She opens up her arms and I let her collide straight into me. I wrap my arms around her. When we kiss, I try not to think about power—the kind that corrupts, the kind that other people have over you, and the kind that detonates when it's in the center of two people who refuse to surrender it.

14

ALLISON

As Lev and I kiss, he cradles my head. It's easy to forget everything he told me earlier when his body heat anchors me to this spot in the parking lot. We're both drunk and I love it because the rest of the world has become blurred and time becomes inconsequential.

My shoulder jabs against the ring in his pocket. He pulls it back out. I hold my hand out. Instead of sliding the ring on again, he takes my hand, flips it over, and sets the ring on my palm.

I slide it on. It's twisted—a ring that costs more than a year of my rent from a man that only wants to marry me because of my father—but with the way that I've felt about Lev lately, it also feels like a memento for something that will inevitably go up in flames.

He tilts my chin up. I close my eyes as he kisses me again. It's all pretend, but it's nice to live in a fantasy. It's nice to believe that Cinderella could inherit the prince, the wealth, and the kingdom without anyone suffering, without knowing it's all about perception, and without having to worry that once the wedding bells stop chiming, the prince might transform into a beast.

Through the chatter of everyone saying goodbye, my father's voice rises above them. He almost sounds like the rest of the drunks shouting, but there's an angry edge to it, crashing through the rest of the voices like a judge's gavel.

"He's a goddamn thug. I can't believe you'd fall for his lies, too. He's making a fool out of both of you," he says, his voice getting louder as he approaches. "I just can't let it go."

My father's face is a deep shade of red as he storms up to Lev and me. I step in front of Lev, but Lev puts his hand on my arm, pushing me aside and moving up to meet my father's anger. I stumble but grab Lev's shirt to catch myself. My father's eyes follow my arm to Lev's shirt. I let my hand drop. He glares at Lev, his anger pulsing out of him.

"I don't know what bullshit you told my wife," my father snarls. "But you're going to regret trying to mess with my family."

Deputy Chief Ronald Rauch hurries over to the three of us. He puts his hand on my father's shoulder.

"Pete, this isn't the time or place," he says. "We all get personal about our families, but you need to take a breath. Just go home. We've all had a bit to drink and we don't want to make any mistakes."

"Think about your reputation, Chief," Lev says to my father. My father takes a step forward, despite Rauch's hand trying to keep him back.

"I don't think you're someone who should be talking about reputations."

I put my hand on Lev's arm, trying to get him to take a step back. Several seconds pass, the two men staring each other down.

"Lev," I urge. "Please."

Lev scowls but moves an inch back. I rest my hand on his chest, partially as a gesture of solidarity, partially to keep him from stepping forward again.

"Dad, listen to Mr. Rauch," I say. When I look at my father, he isn't looking at Lev. He isn't even looking directly at me. He's looking at my hand.

My hand with the engagement ring on it.

He nearly lunges forward, but Rauch grabs him, restraining him.

"People have their phones out," Rauch hisses into his ear. "You can't flip out here. You think the media will care about how much money we raised if the chief starts a brawl?"

"I don't care," my father grunts, but he stops struggling against Rauch. Rauch releases him. My father takes several deep breaths, shaking his head. He's trembling with anger. He turns to me. "I thought I raised you to be smarter than this. You're being reckless. I didn't raise a foolish woman who would fall all over a man just because he's rich. I'm so disappointed in you."

"You damn well know Ally is incredibly smart," Lev cuts in. "And I'd appreciate if you didn't refer to my fiancée in such a demeaning way. She's going to put you in her shadow sooner rather than later, *Officer*."

"You shut the fuck up," my father snarls. My mother has walked up behind him. She tries to put a reassuring hand on his back, but he moves away from her like he's repulsed by all of us.

"Dad," I start, taking a step toward him.

He shakes his head, pointing his finger at me again. "I can't talk to you right now. Linda, let's go."

He stomps toward his car. My mother gives me a quick smile but follows him without saying anything. Rauch gives us all a wary look before turning toward the rest of the parking lot, where some donors and policemen have stopped to witness the scene. A few of them have their phones held out in front of them.

"Thanks, folks!" Rauch calls out. "We're sorry about that. Remember, never mix alcohol with the new boyfriend! Have a good night, y'all!"

Lev wraps his arm around my waist. I nearly stumble twice as he guides me to the car. He opens the door for me and helps me into the seat, but I barely notice. As he gets into the driver's seat, I start shaking. My face floods with heat. Tears start to gather on the rims of my eyes.

"Ally," Lev says. That's all it takes. The waterworks are unleashed. Lev puts his hand on my back, rubbing between my shoulders. "It's okay. It'll be fine. I promise. Everything will be good soon enough."

I want to believe him, but I know that he means that everything will be good soon for him.

For him, marrying me is the secret code to ensure his freedom.

For me, it's the end of all of my important relationships.

They'll all be overwhelmed by lies soon and at the center of it will be a man who knows me well enough to stop for chai tea on the way home, but not well enough to know that I'm not that smart and I am being foolish. Otherwise, I wouldn't be relieved when he doesn't drop me off at my apartment. I wouldn't feel his hand on my knee and consider letting my world burn while I isolate myself with him forever.

∼

As I sit in Lev's den, I feel inadequate. Poor. Everything around me is worth more than I could ever dream of making.

My father has never before said he was disappointed in me. He wasn't like those emotionally distant fathers, who kept their feelings under wraps. He told me he was proud during every significant step of my life. If he was disappointed, he might convey it in subtle ways, but he never felt it strongly enough to say it, to hurt me like that.

Lev sits down beside me. He took his jacket off in the car, but for once, I barely notice his hardened body underneath his shirt. His hands are clasped in front of him. There's a half-inch of space between us, but it might as well be miles.

"Do you want me to make your chai tea?" he asks softly.

I shake my head, letting it drop in my hands. "That's just going to remind me of my father more."

He nods, frustrated. I know he feels useless. This isn't something that can be solved with money or muscle. It's out of his element.

His knee starts to jiggle. I remember that he did it in his car when we were driving to get my dress. He told me it wasn't anxiety, but pent-up energy from not working out. I did the same thing when he was telling me what to do if he was killed. I'm taking on his mannerisms —and worse, his ideals.

He stands up and walks over to the home bar. I keep my head bowed. I listen to the clink of glasses, the clatter of ice, and the sound of liquor being poured.

When Lev appears in front of me with the glass of liquor—whiskey, maybe—I'm still surprised. It's like my brain has splintered, no longer caring to make connections because all those connections point me in the wrong direction.

I sip from the glass. Lev sits back down beside me, nursing his own drink. He's barely still for a moment before he shifts his weight, his knee starting to bounce again.

"My parents," he says, "used to have this perfect relationship."

He's staring straight in front of him, his hands loosely holding his tumbler. I hold my breath, my mind playing through all the possible scenarios that he could be remembering.

He takes another sip of his whiskey. He doesn't say anything more. I set my drink down, laying my head against his arm as I pull my legs onto the couch.

As much as my world is burning into ashes, it's not the worst possible place to end up.

"I need to ask something," I say.

"Ask it."

"How deeply are you involved in the Bratva?"

He lets out a slow breath. "Why are you asking this now?"

"I saw how my father and the guy at the door reacted to you. You said the man on the motorcycle was one of the Colosimo men and you must be irreplaceable to be able to kill him without getting in trouble for it. He could have had information."

"He was going to kill you. I had to kill him."

"And the Bratva wouldn't have cared about me dying. You could have used my death to get the Colosimos in trouble."

"You're more useful alive."

"Lev," I say. "I already know. You're high up on the chain. You're high-ranking. You're one of the leaders. If you weren't important to the Bratva, they wouldn't let you keep all this money. But they'll turn on you, Lev. You talk about dying at the hands of the Colosimos, but at least they'll tell you that they're coming for you. I've heard what the Bratva can do and the Bratva will kill you without any forewarning."

"That won't happen."

"You can't know that."

"I can know that," he says. "I know that because I'm not just high-ranking, I'm the highest rank. I'm not just one of the leaders; I am the leader. The Bratva won't turn against me because I am the Bratva."

I sit up, moving away from him, my back pressed against the armrest. "No. No, you're not. If you were the leader of the Bratva, you wouldn't have been able to walk into the gala. You wouldn't be able to run

Mariya's Revenge and the Bratva at the same time. People would figure it out."

"People have." He shrugs. "Thanks to my parents. Think, Ally. Do you see me answering to anybody? Do you think I got on the phone and begged some man to forgive me for killing that Colosimo man? Do you think I would have struck a deal to marry you if I thought someone above me could disapprove of it? No. I make my own choices."

Even as I open my mouth, I know it's true. I close my mouth, trying to find a flaw in his logic, but he's right. I've let denial lead me this whole time.

Lev stands up. He walks past me as he leaves the room. He left his glass on the coffee table. I stare at it.

Should I leave? Is he getting a gun to kill me, now that I know the truth?

I walk over to the fireplace and pick up the fire poker, testing the weight in my hand. If he has a gun, it will be difficult to hit him hard enough before he gets a shot off—God knows he's a good shot—but it could be my only chance.

But he said he's never hurt me.

I grip the fire poker tighter. I could never trust his word. Now isn't any different.

As I hear his footsteps, I raise the fire poker like a baseball bat. Every muscle in my body is tense, tight, coiled, ready to spring. My life depends on it.

His steps grow louder. Closer.

He's at the door.

I readjust my grip. I'll only have one chance to swing.

He walks in with the metal ammunition box. I freeze. He barely glances at the fire poker.

"If you put that back, Irina would appreciate it," he says, putting the box on the coffee table.

I tighten my grip on the fire poker. "Are you going to tell everyone about Jeffrey Douglas?"

"Are you going to bludgeon me to death?" he retorts. "No. I'm giving you all of the surveillance footage and evidence I had collected to use against you."

"You're giving it to me?"

"Yes."

"Why? That's your leverage."

He leans against the back of the couch. "I proposed to you impulsively, based on the fear that your father had sent you to spy on me. I don't operate out of fear, Allison. Ever. It was a mistake to make and the mistake has only been compounded all along. By giving you back your own leverage, I'm giving myself control back too."

"Are you breaking up with me?" I cut in. I sound angry, but that fear he's talking about is in the center of my chest. I must be suffering from severe Stockholm Syndrome, but I don't care what the name is. I need more time before I'm locked out of his life. And I don't like hearing that everything we are is a mistake.

"No," he says. "I don't want you to be forced to live by fear either. So I'm giving you the leverage I had."

"You're messing with me. You have to have copies of all of these things. You told me you had copies."

"And they're in there." He leans toward me. "I had no time to prepare to do this. I don't need to use mind games. You can go to the police if you'd like. I'll beat the case, but maybe it'll make you feel better."

He rubs his forehead. When he looks at me again, there's a pain in his eyes I hadn't seen before.

"I don't want you to live in fear of me. My parents lived in fear of each other and I'm not going to go down that road. At this point, you're a complication and I don't need it. You can go to your parents, admit that they were right, and live the rest of your life perfectly happy."

He's not looking me in the eye. His words should feed into my feelings of inadequacy, but all those hard feelings fade and all I feel is the need to be closer to him. I'm not ready to live the rest of my life yet.

Without giving myself time to overthink things, I undo my dress' knot behind my neck and let the fabric fall. I couldn't wear a bra under the dress without the band being visible, so when Lev looks at me, I have his full attention. I slide off the couch, pulling the dress down to the floor. It puddles at my feet. The feeling of silk on my skin is pleasant, but the look that Lev is giving me is thrilling and threatening all at once.

I settle back on the couch, naked except for silk underwear. Lev's eyes are predatory, skimming over my body like he's plotting how to conquer every part of me. My pussy pulses at the thought.

He pounces, his hands on my shoulders as he pins me to the couch. He crushes his mouth against mine, his hands sliding over my body with an insatiable hunger. I try to kiss him back, but he's a famished predator; I can only receive his need and give myself over to him completely.

He yanks his shirt open, a couple of the buttons snapping off. He whips it onto the floor before returning to his starved kissing. His hands move down to his belt, grinding near my clit as he works the buckle and unfastens his jeans. I arch my back, needing more contact.

He lifts himself off me, climbing off the couch to kick off his shoes and pull down his pants. His size surprises me again. I've seen it before, but either my memory is fuzzy from the alcohol or it just seems bigger in front of me.

His hand strokes his cock, his eyes scouring my body. My body is nearly shaking, from need and fear.

"Lie over the armrest," he orders. I don't think twice about it as I do what he says. I settle over the armrest, my stomach comfortably on the thickest part of it.

He moves over toward my head. His cock dips in front of my eyes. As I raise my chin, stretching to reach it, he grabs under my arms and pulls me farther up, so the upper half my body is dangling over the couch. I put my hands down to prevent myself from falling.

"No," he says. "Keep your hands behind your back."

I unsteadily cross my wrists behind my back.

The couch shifts and I feel Lev's legs settle outside of mine. His cock taps against my ass twice before circling around my slit. One warm hand settles over my wrists, clasping around them. His grip slowly tightens. His cock presses against my entrance.

He slams into me. At first, there's hot pain shooting through me. I cry out, but as he presses his weight against me, burying himself in me, the pain sharpens the desire, like it has deepened what I'm capable of feeling.

He keeps his weight on me, a slight ache in my wrists from it. I feel his warm breath against my hair. I squirm against him, trying to get some more friction. His body quivers over me as he gives a breath of laughter.

"What is it about you?" he mutters. "I try to get rid of you, try to get rid of your control over me, and you make me lose control again."

I try to move my hands. He tightens his grip.

"Are you afraid?" he asks.

The answer is yes.

I'm afraid my relationship with my parents is over.

I'm afraid of the future.

I'm afraid of the Bratva.

I'm afraid of getting a call and hearing that he's dead.

And underneath him, yes, there's fear, but in this position, I trust him completely. It's fear, but as long he's there, it's thrilling fear. It's conquerable.

His grip on my wrists starts to loosen and his weight starts to lift. He starts to pull out. Uncertainty starts to enter the room.

"No," I answer his question.

The moment I speak, he thrusts back into me, jabbing my clit against the armrest. I wince, but as he picks up his pace, the friction sends strikes of lightning up my body.

He releases my wrists. I try to put my hands underneath me against the side of the armrest, but every time he bears down, my hands slip. I grip onto the edge of the couch cushion as I keep sliding forward.

His hands slide under my breasts, giving them a squeeze before he pulls me back a bit. It prevents the blood from rushing to my head like before but my clit isn't hitting the armrest like before. I move my hand underneath me, barely brushing against my clit before he pulls my arm out, pinning it down on the couch cushion.

As I feel the peak approaching, he stops. He pulls out, the emptiness inside me more present than ever. I turn my head to look at him. Beads of sweat curve around his forehead as he grabs my shoulders, flipping me over easily. He spreads my legs open, my right leg draping over the couch. He slams back into me, but instead of returning to his previous rhythm, his pelvis grinds against my clit.

His hands cradle my face and he looks directly at me as the climax rips into me. He must know he needs to hold me together because the ecstasy shatters inside me. Riptide after riptide of pleasure floods me, pulling me under.

Lev groans, deep and gruff, as my pleasure triggers his orgasm. His cock spasms inside me, filling me with his heat.

He rests his forehead on my clavicle. When he lifts his head again, his expression is softer than I've ever seen it. He raises himself up, kissing my forehead once and my lips twice.

He pulls himself off me slowly and picks up his shirt, wiping the sweat off his face. I move onto my side. This is how it ends. He's had his last fuck, gotten it out of his system.

"Did you want to fuck me in as many positions as possible?" I ask softly. "Is that why you stopped and moved me?"

He carefully folds his shirt, not looking at me. "I just wanted to be able to see your face for once."

He sets the shirt down. He crouches down near the couch, so we're closer to being eye to eye.

"We're going to shower," he tells me. "We're going to sleep. And I'm going to keep you until the day I die."

They're not quite wedding vows, but as he scoops me up in his arms, our skin sticking to each other, I know he means every word.

I don't know whether to cry tears of joy, or scream and run like my life depends on it.

15

LEV

I've always slept erratically. When I was a child, I'd see the shadows of my parents through the crack of the door, intertwining to become one shadow. When I was a teenager, I kept the door closed, but I could still hear the screaming, the pleading, the sound of flesh striking flesh. The night before I left the house, my mother was trying to muffle her crying. My father had raised us from poverty to middle class, so when he told me if I proved myself as a foot soldier, I'd become a Bratva boss one day, I was eager to leave the house to prove my tenacity. I told myself I'd return one day and find a remedy for the poison in our home.

But my mother did that on her own and that's when my regrets began filling up the barrel chamber.

I wake twice in the nighttime, which is a significant decrease. Every time, I turn to see Ally. Her body is a range of hills and valleys, each crying out for my touch, my kiss. The first time I wake up, I settle my hand on her hip. The second time, I move my hand over her breast, her heart beating under my palm.

When I wake up the third time, I check my phone. Three notifications.

Ilya: No leads yet.

1 missed call

Ilya: 4 14 6 2 10 23 70 32 23 7

I stare up at the ceiling for several seconds before carefully rolling off the bed. I tuck the blanket closer to Ally. I open the door a crack and slip out.

I go down to the den and grab *Russia: From Slavic Tribes to Potential Superpower*. I take it to the office. I flip it open to page 4, word 14: law. Page 6, word 2: enforcement. Page 10, word 23: discovered. Page 70, word 32: Mach. Page 23, word 7: Ten.

Law enforcement discovered Mach ten. He must mean MAC-10. Illegal firearms wouldn't have been the first evidence we would have tried to get rid of, but it would have been on the list. It doesn't directly link us back to the Bratva, but it's enough for them to keep digging. If they figure out we're transferring the weapons through furniture delivery, that could be connected back to us.

I send an encrypted message to Ilya, telling him to cancel all gun deliveries for the next two weeks.

I glance out the window. It's still dark outside. All I want to do is crawl back into bed with Ally, but the police are a molehill and the Colosimos are turning into a mountain. Instead, I open up my laptop. There are sixteen emails in my Mariya's Revenge account and they must all be important because my people know not to contact me unless it's urgent.

I answer them one by one. Ilya calls to tell me Rodion's wife is flipping out, refusing to do anything the Bratva says. Her husband was new to the family. I don't blame her for being distraught, but at the same time, she has to be brought under control. I tell him I'll call her around 7:00.

It's like the world is full of children and I have to save them all from setting themselves on fire.

At 7:00, I call Rodion's wife.

"They could come back to torture and kill me," she says. "I should tell the police everything. Maybe they'll protect me."

"The police aren't going to do shit for you," I say. "You know that. We have people watching your house, but it's unnecessary. They don't want you."

"It's not enough. You should set me up in that new hotel—the five-star one with the gold lion statues. Or I could stay with you. You have a lot of extra rooms, yeah?"

I stifle a sigh, disappointed in Rodion's choice of a wife. Like so many other Bratva women, she's mixed disloyalty with moral bankruptcy, which is a venomous cocktail.

"No. You're going to stay in your house," I say.

There's a soft knock on the door. I walk over to it. Ally is standing on the other side, holding a mug and wearing one of my button-up shirts. It drapes over her thighs and only the button near the center of her chest is fastened. I indicate for her to step in before closing the door again. She sits down on the couch.

"If you're not going to help me, I'll go to the police and tell them everything. I'll tell them about you and—"

"You do that," I say lazily. I watch Ally set her mug down on the end table and rest her head on the armrest of the couch. My cock stirs. I'll never be able to look at another couch without thinking about our session last night. "I'd tell you I'll see you in court, but you know I won't. It's in your best interest that, when the police ask later why I called, you tell them I called to give my condolences. It's up to you whether the condolences are for you or your loved ones."

I hang up, setting the phone down. I walk back over to Ally and crouch down beside her. "Hey."

"Hey," she echoes. "What happens if the police were listening to that phone call?"

I run my hand down her arm, her skin soft and cool. "I don't know what you mean."

"You just threatened that woman."

I smirk. "Did I? I don't recall anything I said that sounded like a threat."

She nearly rolls her eyes. I give her a quick kiss and she smiles.

"I wasn't sure where you went," she mumbles. "I looked around. I thought you'd be in the den."

"Where did you think I'd go?"

Her shoulder barely lifts and drops. "I don't know. We were drunk last night. Nothing you said has to mean anything."

"Everything I say means something," I say. "I said I'm going to keep you and that means I'm going to keep you."

She smiles. I kiss her again.

"How long have you been awake?" I ask.

"Um, maybe forty minutes," she says. "After I looked for you in the den, I went into the kitchen to find something to eat, but your kitchen is nearly empty except for alcohol and the ingredients for the cinnamon chai tea."

"Mmm. Yes, I don't keep much around here. Irina isn't supposed to work today, but I could get her to grab some things if you want to write a grocery list."

"Nah, I don't want to inconvenience her." She sleepily rubs her cheek. "I'll just go back to my apartment while you work."

I take her hand in mine, intertwining her fingers in mine. "What if I don't want you to leave? Do you want to write me a list and I'll go get it?"

She opens one eye. "Could we both go to the store?"

It hadn't occurred to me. But the look in her eyes is hopeful, for some reason. I wonder what this means to her—two normal people doing normal-people things in a normal-people place.

"Yes," I say. "I just need to make a couple of more calls and we'll go."

She smiles again, closing both eyes again. "Thank you."

I raise our clasped hands, kissing her wrist before letting her go. My phone is already vibrating, but I let it go to voice mail. I sit down at my desk, watching her snooze for a few seconds before turning my attention back to work.

∽

In the grocery store, Ally has a slight limp while she walks. After I put some tomato sauce into the cart, I let my hands slide under her shirt, her soft skin tempting me in the worst way. I almost completely lost control last night. I'm not surprised she isn't quite walking straight.

I glance around us a few times, my natural vigilance taking over, but it's easy to forget about Bratva life while I'm with Ally. I could imagine a life where I have some average job, she became my fiancée in a normal way, and we're just an enamored couple. No different from a thousand others strolling through the city right now.

A few times, she peeks at her phone.

"Do you think I should call my parents?" she asks.

"No. They'll come around on their own."

"Maybe," she says. "But the right thing to do would be to reach out first."

"Your father insulted you. Repeatedly."

She takes a can of corn off the shelf and sets it in the cart. "He was angry."

"He was an asshole."

She tries to shove me. I let myself sway before we continue walking down the aisle.

"He's still my father," she says. "He was a good father. He *is* a good father."

"You should never let anyone talk down to you," I say. "It allows them to think they can walk all over you."

She crosses the aisle to check the various cans of green beans. I glance at the canned carrots, but it all just reminds me of living in poverty.

As I turn back toward Ally, a man walking down the aisle stumbles into her. He grabs her shoulder, pulling himself back up. Instinctively, I step toward her, my hand tightening into a fist.

"I'm so sorry," he mumbles, sounding intoxicated, before walking on. I follow his movements until he bumps into somebody's cart.

"Are you okay?" I ask Ally, resting my hand on her shoulder. She nearly jumps.

"Oh yeah, fine," she says. She has a can of green beans in one hand and a piece of paper in the other.

She didn't have a grocery list before.

"What is that?" I ask.

"I don't know," she says. She sets the can down on the shelf. She unfolds the note. It has one word, handwritten, scrawled on it.

L'osservatore.

"What does this mean?" she asks me. She must see something in my face because I see the concern flood her eyes. "Is this Russian?"

I shake my head. "It's Italian."

"Tell me what it means."

I turn, taking several quick steps to the end of the aisle. The man is gone. I glance back at Ally. I could find the man quickly, but with Ally, I'd need to ensure we were both protected, which would make me too slow. I'll have to let him go.

I return to her, putting my arm around her waist. I pull her away from the cart. She tries to reach out toward it, but I stop her.

"Forget the cart," I say. "We need to go."

"Tell me what that word means," she says. She tries to drag her feet, which isn't very successful but is incredibly annoying.

"It means 'the watcher,'" I tell her. I direct her to the end of the corner, check east and west, and proceed around the corner. The doors are within sight.

"And?" she prompts.

"It's an old custom. It means that a target is under surveillance. In the old days, it was an honor tradition—forewarn your enemy, so they have a chance to defend themselves. Over time, especially with the Colosimos, it turned into a threat."

"A threat?" she echoes.

"Marco Colosimo is telling me that he can come after you or me even though I have full knowledge of the fact that he's watching us. He's telling me I can't do anything about it."

"But he didn't just kill me."

"He's playing mind games. I'm certain he came up with that whole scenario. He's telling me that he can get that close to you—close enough to stab you—and there's nothing I can do. Son of a fucking bitch."

I guide her back to the car and put her in the passenger side before checking around me. I know it was likely only a threat—a taunt—but Marco is smarter than I originally thought. And it would be incredibly clever to give me less than five minutes to prepare for an attack.

He knows it would haunt me to have Ally so close and lose her.

Worthless Mafia fuck.

I get into the driver's side, locking the doors. The drive is silent as we return to the mansion.

"So, the Colosimos know about us."

"After the gala, everyone likely knows." I shake my head. "I'm sorry. I didn't consider them a threat when this started. His father is dead. Marco shouldn't have ascended this quickly. The Mafia shouldn't have trusted him enough for him to make all these brash decisions. They must have already been preparing for him to take over."

"And he'll hurt me?" she asks.

I take a deep breath. It would be a huge risk for Marco to go after the chief's daughter, but then again, it was a huge risk for him to go after the Bratva, and yet here he is. Threatening me. Threatening my woman.

Before I can answer, she slides over the center console. She sits on my lap, her legs on either side of my legs. Even in mortal danger, my cock is pleasantly surprised.

"I don't think so," she says to me. She bounces twice on my lap. "I know you. I know you wouldn't let that to happen."

I know she's trying to distract me, for both our sakes. I know there are at least four calls I need to make to ensure the Colosimos don't leave my life in ruins. But as her lips press against mine, all of the sirens in my mind quiet. All I sense is the sound of her shirt buttons hitting against the center console, her breath in my ear, and desperation concealed like a gun.

Ready to fire.

Sex while sober isn't something I do.

It isn't alcoholism, or some vague notion that sex is something I need to suffer through. Alcohol just makes the storm in my head manageable and makes me hate whoever is underneath me a little less.

But Ally on top of me is like taking MDMA and Coke while driving a Mustang down an open road with no speed limit.

Reckless. Wild. Fucking irresistible.

She rests her head against my chest as she wiggles out of her silk underwear. Her pussy bumps against my erection as she squirms above me, and I grip onto her arms to help her lift each of her legs and kick off the underwear.

She fumbles with my belt. As I raise myself up, she pulls my pants and boxer briefs down, rocking herself back and forth as she tries to slide them past her legs and down to my knees.

When she continues to try to get my pants lower, I pull the seat lever. The backrest of the seat jerks backward and she falls onto me. She lifts herself up onto her hands, looking down at me with a smirk. I grab her wrists. With the weight of her upper body in my grasp, I slowly lower her arms above my head. Her body presses up against mine, her lips nearly pressing against my lips.

I close the distance between us. The kisses act like liquor shots, each one getting more reckless. As our kissing becomes more frantic, my hands move to the back of her thighs, right under her ass. I pull her forward, so the tip of my cock is pressing against her entrance.

She reaches down, her small hands guiding my cock into her. Even with how wet she is, there's resistance. I've taken her quickly both times before, but with her on top, she eases her way down with a pace I'd never tolerate with anyone else.

It's slow, painstaking, damn near agonizing.

But when I'm buried in her, she looks at me. There's the softest vulnerability in her face.

I love it—because it's mine.

And I hate it, because—like all things I've ever loved—it will one day break.

Her hands pressed against my shoulders, she slowly lifts herself up and down an inch, acquainting herself with my size. The soft patter of her fingertips keeps moving across my shoulders and the front of my chest. Her lips are slightly curved in an uncertain smile.

In someone else, the nervousness would be a sign of weak character, but with Ally, I'd let her self-consciously lead me through a battlefield if it's what she wanted. I'd let her take me anywhere. No questions asked.

She's the patron saint of bad ideas. She's Pandora's box, which I'd open over and over.

I slip my hand under her shirt, tracing her spine. As she settles over me again, my fingertips dig into the flesh of her hips, keeping her down.

"Lean forward," I tell her. She obeys, our lips close enough that I steal a quick kiss. I rock my hips against her. Her eyes melt, like black rum in her irises. "Sway your hips."

At first, her hips move slowly, rocking against me, but as her breath quickens, she grinds against me with determined enthusiasm. My hands settle on her thighs, feeling her muscles rippling under my palms. I slow my breathing, trying to concentrate on the ceiling of my car and not the hitches in her breath or the delicate moans that sometimes follow.

But, God, it's like trying to pay attention to the candlesticks instead of the ceiling in the Sistine Chapel.

I grab her left hip and her right ass cheek. I slam her up and down my cock, her body bouncing high enough that she has to steady herself with her hands on my chest and her hair still sways like it's caught in a storm.

As I drive back into her, I grab the back of her neck to pull her down to me. When we kiss, her lips frantically crash against mine. She nips at my lower lip, her hips gyrating against my hips, getting her clit to rub against my abdomen.

When I start bouncing her again, she leans forward to meet my movements and her cheeks are flushed. It almost makes me angry again because I know I can never completely own her. She will always belong to other people, because of her devotion to improving the world, whereas I need her to be fully mine.

Her hands grip onto my shirt, her eyes squeeze shut, and she starts bobbing with my movements. Her pussy is pulsating around my cock. As her thighs tighten against my legs, I drive into her harder.

Her climax is unrelenting. Her fingernails dig into my chest as her pussy repeatedly clenches my cock, squeezing me until I can't hold onto the edge anymore. Euphoria blinds my vision as I erupt, my seed surging into her.

She collapses onto my chest.

We're both heaving for breath. I close my eyes, trying to steady my thoughts, waiting for that post-sex regret to sink in, but all I can think about is how much I'd rather be here than anywhere else.

I sink my fingers into her hair, follow the strands down her back, and let my fingers trace her shoulder blades through her shirt. She plants a kiss under my jaw.

"It looks like I did all right," she says. "Not bad for my first time on top."

"Oh, you were flawless," I say. "But if you want more practice, we can arrange daily sessions."

She smirks, rocking her hips against me. I grab her, kissing her hard. She lays her head on the side of the headrest next to me.

"You said I shouldn't be living in fear," she says. "And I don't want to. But you're much better at being in control."

"Don't underestimate yourself," I say, my voice sounding harsher than I mean to be.

"You also …" she starts. She kisses my cheek, nervous again. "You also mentioned that your parents lived in fear of each other."

She doesn't ask anything. The statement joins the steam on the windows, slowly evaporating as the seconds pass by. I could let it go. I don't need to answer anything when she never asked a question.

"Yes," I say. "It's complex. My parents had a good relationship for several years. They were happy. But my father began to rise in power and their relationship became more and more strained. When he became the Bratva boss, something changed. It could partly be that my mother simply didn't like that he had so much power, but it was mostly my father's ego. He became violent. I didn't intervene—he was my father and he was the Bratva boss, so he had power over me in nearly all aspects of my life. I left the house when I was sixteen. Within the Bratva, I heard rumors that my mother had been seen with an FBI agent. I thought my father would beat her and she'd fall back in line."

I take a deep breath. Ally's thumb rubs over one of my shirt buttons as she listens carefully.

"The police report … she was found beaten to death. Everyone knew it was my father, but in the Bratva, what happens in the house has no effect on anything else. It's a man's domain and he gets to decide how punishments are dealt. That's especially true for the Bratva boss. I wish I could say I tried to let it go or that I thought of going to the police, but as soon as I heard, I knew I was going to kill him."

She stops fidgeting with my buttons. Her fingers are slightly curled above my shirt, her wrist still resting on it.

"It was simple enough. I told him to come to his nightclub, Original Menace, because a Colosimo tried to put poison in the vodka. I said I had captured the man. Like the Colosimos, he took pleasure in torture, so I knew he wouldn't give up the chance to torture someone before killing them. He came. And I killed him."

Ally raises her head. Her eyes search mine, looking for guilt or regret.

"The way I act isn't armor or an act to intimidate people, Ally," I say. "I killed my father because I wanted to kill him. My mother's name was Mariya. I named my vodka Mariya's Revenge because I feel no shame over what I did. I can look at those words every day, remember I killed my father, and I wouldn't ever take it back."

Her fingers rest over the button again, but she doesn't fiddle with it.

"You're not angry that she went to the police?" she asks.

A muscle jumps in my jaw. "Angry? No. I understand why she did what she did. I'm certain she thought it was the only way to get out from under his thumb. I can't say that I'm happy about it, though. She had to know it could have screwed me over and she could have told me she was going to do it, but she was a desperate woman in a desperate situation. I don't blame her for her choices."

She looks down at her hand on my chest but doesn't say anything.

"I need you to know that this is who I am. If somebody hits me, I'm going to hit them back twice as hard to prevent them from doing it again. If somebody tries to fuck with something I care about, I'll kill them myself and I won't regret it for a second. I won't feel sorry for their wives and I won't cry for their babies. If you can't handle that, you should leave now."

She grips my shirt like she might drift away from me by accident.

"I believe you," she says slowly. "I believe you should have taken your father to court. Spouses are the first suspect in any murder. But I understand why you did what you did. I don't think this is some evil coming out of you, even when you act like it is. You cared about your mother and that pain caused you to react on instinct. It's not completely excusable, but it's understandable."

Her eyes are soft black silk threatening to suffocate me under their pity. My chest compresses. I need anything but this emotional bullshit.

"If you want more practice, we should start on a new lesson." I cup her cheek, my thumb brushing against the edge of her mouth. "I'd like to see if you were bluffing about your mouth during our phone conversation."

She smiles slowly, the edges of her lips pushing against my thumb.

Fucking priceless.

16

ALLISON

Sitting alone in Lev's dining room with a variety of Thai dishes spread out in front of me should make me feel isolated. Lev left to talk to Mariya's Revenge board members about the advertising for the new orange cream vodka and I should resent him for it. I should be running for my life after what he told me about the man in the grocery store.

But I'm dancing in the afterglow.

It's like I made a deal with the devil for unadulterated happiness and he granted my wish. Twice in the last hour.

As I eat some jasmine rice, my phone starts to vibrate near my bowl.

Dad.

My hand lingers over my phone. Reality is threatening to take down my fantasy life, but I could never abandon my parents for a dream.

There's only one more ring left before it goes to voice mail.

At the last second, I tap on *Answer* and bring the phone up to my ear.

"Hi, Dad," I say. There's a couple of seconds of silence. I don't know if it would be better or worse if he had called me on accident.

"It's both of us," he says finally.

"Oh. Is this an intervention?" I ask, the bitterness cutting into my tone.

"No, no," he says. Several more seconds of silence pass by.

"We just wanted to apologize," my mother interjects. "Especially your father."

"Yes," he says stiffly. "I shouldn't have talked to you like that. I was just shocked. I don't think you're a foolish person or anything like that."

"We still want you to reconsider your engagement," my mother adds.

I imagine them standing over their phone, the silent gestures and looks between them. They are trying to build a bridge back to their daughter. I've caused their stress. I burned that bridge. If I could repair it by telling them I'll end the engagement, I would.

And I can, because Lev is willing to give up the evidence against me.

I grip the phone tighter. "We could talk about it."

"We should have dinner together. Come to our house," my father says, the words jumbling as he rushes to say them. "Without Alekseiev."

If they have me in their house, the three of us, there is no way the discussion will go well. It will either end with them yelling and screaming, or they'll manage to get the truth out of me. Neither option is appealing.

"What if we have dinner at my place?" I ask. "Julia can join us."

I hear static and muffled voices. Someone must have covered the speaker. The static returns as someone lifts their hand off the speaker.

"We'd like that," my mother says. "How about Sunday night? Tonight, your father has to work, and Saturday night, I'm having drinks with your aunt."

"Sounds great," I say.

"Good. Thank you, Ally," she says. "You know we love you. We only want what's best for you."

"I know," I say. "I love you too."

"Have a good night, Ally," my father says.

"Good night."

The line goes silent.

I hang up. The deal with the devil seems less appealing now. Nobody ever tells you that once you sell your soul, the rest of the world starts to shrink until all that's left is you and the devil.

∼

In my dreams, we're at Lev's dining room table. Lev sits at the head of the table; my father and mother sit on either side of him while I'm on the other side of the table. I can hear all of them talking, but they're too far away for me to decipher what they're saying. They keep glancing over at me.

Water starts to seep underneath the walls. I try to warn the three of them, but they're consumed in an argument. As the water starts to reach my knees, my father grabs the front of Lev's shirt. Lev yanks my father out of his seat. My father hits Lev. Lev hits him back, my father's body slamming against the wall as they fight. I try to tell them about the water, but nobody notices.

I turn to the man sitting beside me. "Why won't they listen to me?"

Jeffrey Douglas, his skin peeling off, his eyes glazed over, reeking like pepper spray, shrugs. "The only people who listen to defendants are fucking morons, because defendants have every reason to lie. You're the defendant."

The smell of pepper spray starts to get into my throat and coat my nostrils. I put my hand on my throat, feeling it swell shut. Jeffrey reaches forward to touch me. I jerk away. He reaches forward again.

The smell of pepper spray starts to fade. A smoky, piquant scent wafts in. Lev is still fighting with my father on the other end of the table as the water reaches our waists, but I'd know that scent anywhere. It's his.

∽

I recognize Lev's hand on my shoulder first. Then, the weight of his comforter. I open my eyes and see him crouched down beside me. He raises an eyebrow.

"You were kicking in your sleep," he says. "I didn't picture you as a violent sleeper."

"I'm not," I mumble, sitting up. "You're done working? What time is it?"

"A little after midnight," he says. "Yes. I'm done working. I wouldn't have woken you up, but it didn't look like you were having a happy dream."

"It was just—" I shake my head. "It was dumb."

He brushes a couple of strands of hair away from my face. "You still look unhappy."

"I'm fine."

He gives me a quick kiss. As he stands up, I grab his arm and pull him back toward me. His arms cradle me as we kiss. I imagine each kiss conveys something we're not telling each other. My lips tell him about my parents' call, my concerns, the fact that I know leaving him is my best option, but I can't seem to let him go. I imagine his lips are telling me that he'll take care of me forever and that when the novelty of our relationship wears off, he won't find some model to fuck. Harsh truths, one after another, conveyed but not spoken. They taste bitter and sweet at the same time.

I put my hand on his chest, pushing him a little bit. He resists our separation, kissing me once more before I put both my hands on his chest and put some distance between us.

"I just want to get some wine first," I say. "Stay right here. I'll be right back."

I whip the blanket off and slip past him. I walk quickly, running my fingers through my hair like I'm expecting to find Jeffrey Douglas' decaying skin in the strands. I nearly trip as I go down the stairs. I grab a bottle of wine from his home bar and take a breath.

I touch my lips. I'll have to tell my parents that I'm not going to leave Lev. I just can't see any way that I'd return to my previous life. Looking back now, it seems so empty.

When I return to his bedroom, he's pulling off his shirt. When he turns, everything about him lures me closer. His body reminds me of the depictions of barbarians, nearly every muscle a reminder that he doesn't need a gun to overpower anyone. Even where his waist narrows and the muscles ripple across his abdomen, he makes every other man I've ever seen appear trivial.

My hands are on him before I realize I've walked straight up to him. We kiss once, twice, three times as my heart beats wildly in my chest. His hands move to my waist, slipping under the band of my underwear, squeezing my ass.

He kisses beside my ear before pulling away for a second. "Your phone was ringing."

I pull off my shirt. "It can wait."

His gaze focuses on my breasts, pulling me tight against him. The heat between his legs presses against me and it still makes me shiver.

My phone starts ringing.

Lev kisses the top of my head. "You should answer it. I can jump back in at any time."

"No, no, I can call them back," I say, but I'm already grabbing my phone.

Nobody should be calling me after midnight. It's Julia.

I answer the call. "Julia? What's going on?"

"That's what I was going to ask you," she says. I glance at Lev. She knows about the engagement.

"Maybe we should talk about this later," I say. "I meant to text you. We're going to have dinner with my parents on Sunday."

"Uh, okay," she says. "But, Ally, is your dad okay?"

I stop. "What? Why wouldn't he be okay? Did he call you? He shouldn't have called you. If he has a problem, he should have the conversation with me."

There's a long pause.

"Julia?" I ask.

"Ally, I thought—" she stops. "I thought someone would have called you to assure you everything was okay. Nobody has called you?"

"Julia, what the hell are you talking about?"

"I'm sorry, Ally." There's a rustle of noise on the other end of the line. "There was a shooting outside of the police station. All I know is that some policemen were shot. I heard about it from some of the other EMTs. I wish I had been closer to my phone when the call came in. It happened nearly an hour ago. You haven't gotten a call from your mom or dad yet?"

I can barely breathe. "No. No, I haven't."

"I'm sorry, Ally. I'll try to get more information. I've heard that four policemen were brought into the hospital, but everything was such a mess. I'll call some people, okay? We'll find out what's going on. Hang on, all right?"

"All right," I echo.

"I love you, Ally. It's going to be okay."

She hangs up. Lev has moved beside me, his hands on my arms.

"What's going on?" he asks. "What happened?"

I shake my head. "I have to call my parents."

I turn away from him and dial my father's number. It rings. And rings. And rings.

"This is Chief Harrington," his voice mail answers. I hang up and immediately dial my parents' landline. It rings. And rings. And rings. I hang up before the answering machine picks up.

"Something happened with your dad," Lev guesses. "Do you want me to drive you to their house? The hospital?"

"I want somebody to answer their fucking phone," I snarl. "What is the point of owning fucking cell phones if you're not going to answer them?"

I dial my mother's cell phone. It rings three times. I hang up and toss the phone on Lev's bed. I cover my face with my hands, settling on the bed as I try to think. It's past midnight. They're sleeping. It makes perfect sense that they wouldn't answer their phone.

I stand up. The world is unsteady as I start walking toward the door. Lev's hand grips my elbow as he steadies me.

"Where do you want to go?" he asks.

"Home," I say. I use the heel of my hands to hide any evidence of tears. "My parents' house."

He nods.

～

The lights in my parents' house are on. It should be reassuring, but I know if my mother was in a rush to leave the house, she wouldn't be worrying about the electric bill. Lev is still pulling into the driveway when I open the passenger door and bound out. I hear his voice, concerned and nearly angry, but I ignore it as I pound on my parents' door.

After nearly five seconds pass by, I try the doorknob. It's locked. I slam my fist against the door three more times.

Lev runs up beside me.

"Ally, two cars are in the garage—" he starts. The door swings open. My mother looks at the two of us, her eyes wide and confused.

"Mom." I grab her, hugging her tightly before pulling away. "Where's Dad? Is he okay?"

I'm nearly choking on my own voice. Lev's hand settles on my back, his other hand on my hip.

My mother's face softens. "Oh, Ally, I'm sorry, he's fine. We should have called. I'm sorry. He's not here. One of the officers picked him up and took him to the hospital to check on the policemen, but he's fine. Come in. Please, come in. I'm so sorry to make you worry. Come in."

My parents' house is a tribute to law enforcement, the Marines, and houseplants. The walls are covered in newspaper clippings and photos of my father and grandfather's service. The floors are covered with houseplants that prickle my legs every time I pass them.

My mother gestures for us to sit in the living room. "I've got some coffee started. I'll get some tea for you, Ally. Is coffee good for you, Lev?"

"I'd be grateful for that, Mrs. Harrington," he says.

I sit down on our couch—the same couch I filled out college applications on while my father helped me with the essays. Lev sits down beside me. His hand squeezes my knee before he leans forward to kiss my temple.

"Everything is good," he says. "Just breathe. Your father is fine."

I don't say anything. My hands are shaking. He folds his hands over mine like he's keeping them warm. I should be reassured—none of my worst fears came true. My father wasn't even hurt. But all I can think is: not *this* time. He wasn't hurt *this* time. If he'd died tonight, I'd know that he was angry at me over a lie and that I ruined a man who gave me everything I could ever need.

The second thought creeps in slowly, but I push it away before it has time to make itself at home.

My mother returns with two cups of coffee in one hand and a cup of tea in the other. I take the tea from her and Lev takes the coffee.

"Thank you so much, Miss Harrington. I'm so sorry if we scared you," Lev says.

"Oh no, it's—it was my mistake. I should have called Ally."

Lev is like the serpent in Eden, lulling her into a sense of faith in his words. I'd never noticed it before, but he did the same thing to me when he convinced me to marry him in exchange for keeping Douglas' murder a secret. He must do it with every model he meets. He must do it with the board members in Mariya's Revenge, assuring every one of them that the Bratva rumors won't hurt their bottom line. He must do it with all of the Bratva members, allowing him to stay in power while they all kneel to him.

I thought his power over me was because we were compatible—not quite soul mates, but like the statues of Lady Justice, where I was the set of scales, weighing evidence, and he was the sword, carrying out justice.

Lev and my mother continue to talk, the conversation branching from Mariya's Revenge to my mother's green thumb. He tells her that his mother was killed and his father was a 'deadbeat' that disappeared. He lies so seamlessly, it's embarrassing that I ever believed anything he ever told me.

The second thought sneaks back in: how certain am I that he was at a Mariya's Revenge board meeting earlier tonight?

He told me quickly about it before leaving, saying he was discussing advertising for their new flavor of vodka. But he came home late and I never asked him about the meeting.

The way my mother is acting toward Lev, my father must not have told her the full story. On one hand, it seems insane to me that he wouldn't forewarn his wife. On the other, I didn't warn either of them.

"Ally used to think that snakes lived in our snake plants," my mother says. "She thought the eggs grew in the leaves and they'd come slithering out someday. She wouldn't go anywhere near them. Do you remember that, Ally?"

"Sure," I say, setting my tea down on the end table and standing up. "Lev, could I talk to you outside for a moment?"

If he's surprised, I don't see it on his face, but my mother raises both her eyebrows.

"Of course," he says, standing up. "We'll be right back, Mrs. Harrington."

He follows me out of the house. I walk out toward the mailbox, so I know we're too far away for my mother to eavesdrop. He keeps his hands in his pockets. In our rush to leave, the last two buttons of his shirt were left undone.

"I need to ask you something and I need you to be completely honest," I tell him.

"Okay."

"I mean it," I say. "Do not lie to me, Lev."

"I get it, Ally."

"You had no problem lying to my mother," I snap. "Let's not act like lying is a moral line you won't cross."

"You'll notice that I lied to her, but I didn't lie to you. If I don't want you to know the truth, I just don't tell you anything," he says. "That's how it was and that's how it's going to be."

I take a deep breath. It doesn't feel like I get enough air in, so I take another one. He reaches out toward me, but I take a step back from him. I look straight at him. Even in the dim lighting, he is intimidating and stunning.

"Do you—" I stop. "What do you know about the shooting tonight?"

He takes a step back, his head tilting. It's the first time I've seen him seem confused.

"What do you mean?" he asks. "I know what you told me."

"Come on, Lev," I say. "I know about your business. I know who you are. You're well-connected in the criminal world. Most criminals won't move if they think it would upset the Bratva."

"Ally, this could have been anyone," he says, his hands swinging out in front of him like he's presenting evidence but there's nothing there. "You must know that the police piss off a lot of people. It's part of their job. Criminals don't go to people asking for permission to do things. Yes, many of them are careful to not piss off the Bratva, but they wouldn't think I'd be upset about them shooting up a police station."

"You should be," I say. "That could have been my father who died. Those four policemen who were shot didn't deserve to be attacked like that."

"I didn't say I wasn't upset. I said they wouldn't think I was."

"Are you?" I retort. He stares at me for several seconds, his green eyes striking through me like the reverberations of a bass drum.

"The truth?" he asks.

"Yes."

"I don't care about those policemen," he says. "The police have had it in for me for a long time and—"

"Because you're a criminal who hasn't served your time," I interject.

He takes a deep breath, his fingers flexing. "But I care that you care," he continues. "I care that you're upset. I care that this hurt you. I'm sorry if that's not enough for you, but I warned you about this. I told you I wasn't crying over people's deaths."

I fold my hands over my chest. He looks away from me. His lip is slightly curled up in a partial snarl. I can feel the distrust breeding between us. It hurts, but it almost feels necessary. It feels safer to distrust him.

I can't be certain if he's involved or not. And that will always be my problem. It will be worse once I try to climb that ladder into becoming the district attorney. I'll always wonder if the case I'm prosecuting is one he knew about beforehand. I'll see the photographs of the victims and wonder if my husband ordered the murders. And if I saw something so heinous that I felt morally obligated to turn him in, my ties to a Bratva boss would cast such a long shadow over me that I'd never be free from it. I'd always be the Bratva boss' fiancée, his wife, his woman.

"I want to go back to my apartment," I tell him. He nods. When he looks at me, there's nothing in his eyes. They're cold like when we first met.

"That's for the best."

17

LEV

I've chosen a life of impassivity because rage is not an option. I've seen rage in my father's fists like a bull trapped in a pen, and it only led to an FBI investigation and his death. I cut out those malignant emotions. It's saved me from making the kind of reckless decisions that lead less capable men to end up on the wrong side of a gun barrel.

But as I'm driving Ally to her apartment, the anger comes after me like a rabid dog. I focus on the rational aspects.

It's understandable that she'd see me as the source of all criminal activity in the city.

It's understandable that she wouldn't trust me completely.

It's understandable that after her scare, she'd lash out.

But the anger screams in my ear, telling me that no matter what I do for her or how much of myself I give, she will never trust me. I was willing to give her my leverage and she still believes I'd endanger her father. It doesn't even make rational sense for me to go through all of this effort to get her father on my side, only to attack the police station, but she still believes I would.

One hand on the wheel, I toss my phone into her lap. "Text Ilya. Tell him to send people to watch over your apartment."

"I don't need anyone—"

"It's not up for negotiation," I cut her off. "Either people are going to watch the apartment or you're going back to my house."

"I can't believe ..." She shakes her head. "Never mind. Fine."

She texts out the message and tosses the phone into my back seat. She turns away from me, staring out the side window.

I park a couple of feet away from her apartment building. Ally opens her door and gets out. She turns like she's going to say something to me, but a second passes, and she shuts the door.

I watch her step into the building before I stomp on the gas and drive away.

At a stoplight, I grab my cell phone. There's no text to Ilya. I growl through clenched teeth and quickly text him before driving again.

The cars and buildings start to blur together as I pass through the city. I imagine letting my hand slip on the wheel, speeding into another lane, and letting another car crash straight into me. It's not some pathetic death wish. I just need a little more adrenaline, a little more stimulation, a little more physical pain to distract me from my thoughts.

I need a way out of this.

I start driving east. The skyscrapers slowly die out, replaced by brick stores, their American flags snapping in the wind. I keep driving until I see the whitewashed store with a pinwheel instead of a flag.

I park in front of the store. The decal on the window says *Soft Horizon Salon*. When I step inside, every instinct in my body tells me it's not safe to be there, but I ignore it. I walk up to the owner, who's standing behind a podium, jotting into a datebook.

"Hello, Sarah," I say. The chemical smells of a salon sting my nose. "How's business?"

Sarah Lyle, her bleached blonde hair curled around her shoulders, glances up at me. She tucks her arm closer to her body, but doesn't show any more signs of fear. She's wearing a tank top that's tight enough that the outline of her bra is visible and her long pink nails click against the datebook as she sets her pen down.

"Mr. Alekseiev. You don't have an appointment," she says.

"No. I don't," I say.

"I'm surprised you're here," she says. "I was under the impression that you thought my business was too risky to be seen around."

A man getting his neck shaved peers over in our direction. There's also a woman getting her hair dyed. The woman is married to a gangbanger. I don't recognize the man, but that doesn't mean he won't become an issue.

"I need information," I say.

She rolls her eyes. "Of course you do."

I slam my hand down onto her hand. She yelps and tries to wrench it free, but I don't let go.

"Don't try me today, Sarah," I say. "I wouldn't even need to touch a hair on your head to ruin you. If I tell the police that you allow criminals to conduct their business in your shop and launder money for the Colosimos, they will tear this place apart. Even if they don't find anything, the police presence alone will kill your business. And once they think you've fucked up, one of your criminal friends will kill you."

I loosen my grip and she tugs her hand out of my grasp. She keeps her voice low. "What do you want to know?"

"Tell me about the police shooting," I say. "Who was behind it?"

She shrugs. "Nobody here."

"Sarah," I growl.

"It was a random act," she says, tucking her hands in her back pockets. "One man who lost his mind. I'm sorry that's not the answer you want to hear but it's the truth. A gang member was leaving when the shooter was brought in—he heard about it. He's not affiliated with anybody."

"Fuck." I hit my fist against her podium. She jerks back. As I rub my forehead, she leans on the podium, her breasts nearly spilling out of her tank top.

"Did you want somebody to get into a lot of trouble?" she asks. "Possibly the Colosimos? I've heard you two aren't getting along."

I shake my head, rubbing my knuckles against my temple. "No. I just wanted to retaliate against someone."

"For hurting the police?"

"For hurting someone I care about."

"Hmm." She picks up her pen and taps it against her lips. "You look exhausted, Mr. Alekseiev. I don't have another appointment for another twenty minutes. Maybe I could help you sleep."

"Fuck off," I say. I turn around, wrenching the door open.

As I walk out, the anger bites at my ankles again. There has to be a way to get rid of this rage. There has to be a way to kill it.

∽

Mariya's Revenge headquarters is a five-story building predominantly constructed of glass. As I stride to my office, people avoid me, keeping their heads bowed to appear busy.

I stop at my secretary's desk. Letitia is a twenty-six-year-old former model. I know there's a lot of snark around her, accusations of her getting the job because of her looks, which is true, but she's also the most efficient woman I've ever met.

She hands me a red folder. "Hammond wants your opinion on a new advertising agency, Quality Boulevard. Cooper is adamant about making a Mariya's Revenge app. Gardner heard that you were dating the police chief's daughter and he said—I'm quoting here—that you better fucking know what you're doing. And a man claiming to be the police chief's son is here."

I stop mid-turn. "The police chief doesn't have a son."

"Yes," she says. "That's why I said he was claiming to be the police chief's son. I looked into it after he left to get some coffee. He's an Italian man, no facial hair, well-dressed, about five ten or five eleven, a hundred seventy to a hundred and eighty pounds. Late twenties or early thirties. Kind of slimy."

I tap the folder against her desk. "Thank you, Letitia. You are irreplaceable."

"I know."

"Send him in when he returns."

"Absolutely," she says, turning back to her computer. I enter my office, setting the folder on my desk before sitting down.

Marco Colosimo, coming straight to the throne to test me. Any other day, it would be a mild irritation, but this morning, if he wants to try to hurt me, it will make my day to ruin him.

Letitia would have told me if Marco had come in with anybody else, but it still gnaws at me to see he's alone. He's taunting me. Showing me that he doesn't need any guards, even when he's in the center of my kingdom.

I watch him through the glass wall as Letitia opens the door.

"I'm sorry to interrupt, Mr. Alekseiev, but Mr. Harrington is here," she says. She gestures for him to step in. He likely only took on the identity of Ally's nonexistent brother because he believed Letitia would let him in on his word, but his use of her last name still adds to my anger.

"Lev." Marco walks straight over to me as Letitia leaves, closing the door behind her. I stare at him, but I don't take his hand when he raises it.

"You could have told Letitia who you are," I say. He drops his hand. "It wouldn't have changed the outcome. She wouldn't have let you in without my permission even if you said you were Hitler or Jesus."

"Yes, but we all like to play pretend here, don't we?" he asks. He takes the chair in front of my desk without asking. "Or is it true love for you and Miss Harrington?"

A bait and switch—I can either agree with him, proving to him that he's figured out my con, or admit that Ally and I have more going on than that.

"You know how true love is," I say. "An eternal vow until the next woman opens her legs."

He smirks. "Wow. It hurt you to even say that, didn't it? She is a beautiful woman. I don't blame you. Good connections, too. It's almost in her blood."

"It's a fraud, Marco. You should be smart enough to figure out why I'm doing it."

"I considered that," he says. "Which is why I chose to leave my note in a public place. I heard that you were very protective when the two of you left the grocery store. It may be a fraud, but you wouldn't be the first man to fall for a prostitute."

I lurch forward, my hand on his throat before I can stop myself. My thumb presses against the soft flesh as his hand clenches around my wrist, fear flickering in his eyes like hazard lights.

Through the glass, I see Letitia turning away. I let my hand relax and let my arm fall back to my side.

Marco rubs his throat. "So. Not just a hooker to you."

"Watch yourself, Marco," I say. "I pay Letitia well enough that she will have no problem claiming that you attacked me and I killed you in self-defense."

"Sure," he says. "She could claim that. But how do you think the police investigation will go? Only an Alekseiev would be ignorant enough to think that fucking the chief's daughter wouldn't lead to the chief despising him. You Bratva fools will never understand family loyalty. You're too far up your own asses."

"Did you come here to just toss around schoolyard insults?" I ask. "Because while you scrounge around for cash, I make more money in an hour than you'll see in a week."

His lip curls up in a sneer. "Yes, well, all that difference in income and we're still both in this office, aren't we? I just wanted to remind you that dating the chief of police will only give you minor protection from the boys in blue. It won't protect you from my men."

"I have my own soldiers for that." I lean against my desk. "But when I stuck your father and Vozzella like the pigs they are, I barely broke a sweat. So if your men want to die, send them right over."

Marco thrusts out of the chair, his fists clenched. He's nearly shaking with anger. My jaw is clenched, but I keep my expression as neutral as possible.

"I suggest you leave," I say. "I'll tell Letitia to give you a parking voucher."

"Don't bother."

He storms out, fury following each of his steps like a trail of blood. I sit down at my desk, snapping open my laptop. I open the folder Letitia gave me, scanning over her notes.

I call Hammond. I tell him to hire Quality Boulevard to see what they'll come up with.

I call Cooper. I tell him we're not going to make an app.

I call Gardner. I tell him to mind his own fucking business.

I call Ilya. He tells me that the soldiers report that nothing has occurred at Ally's apartment.

I pace in my office. There are so many broken pieces that I'm holding, something is bound to cut me. I don't know what I'm willing to lose. I've never been forced into a position where I might have to give up something—at least not since the day I left my house, leaving my mother to fend for herself.

I sit back down in my chair. My phone beeps.

Ilya: 5*4 31 6

I don't need *Russia: From Slavic Tribes to Potential Superpower* to translate the text. 5*4 means 54, the code for one of our weapons storehouses. Ilya would only be alerting me if it had been ransacked. There aren't enough words in the message for him to be reporting any fatalities, which should be good news, but it also likely means no one was there to stop the thieves from taking everything.

I grab my phone and jacket and leave my office, telling Letitia to tell anyone who calls that I had a personal emergency.

As I get into my car, adrenaline is ripping through my brain like bullets. This is Marco letting his emotions get the best of him. He must have paid someone a lot of money to find out where one of our warehouses was. He can't afford to make those types of payments, but he's willing to implode his own syndicate to go after mine.

Emotions will lay waste to even the richest of empires.

I try to keep my cool while I drive, but even passing by police cars, it's difficult to not slam on the gas. As I pass the police station—the flag hanging at half-staff—my phone rings. I glance at it.

Petrov.

He's a promising soldier, willing to die to prove his worth. But there's no reason he would be contacting me instead of Ilya unless it was an emergency.

"What?" I answer.

"Boss, a Colosimo tried to get into Miss Harrington's apartment. He's dead, but Mr. Sevostyanov wanted us to call you."

"Stay there," I order. "Deal with anybody who looks suspicious. Send someone to do a sweep."

"Yes, sir."

I hang up. Marco's attack may have been a reaction driven by emotion, but he's smart enough to attack me from more than one side and on opposite sides of the city.

The warehouse or Ally's apartment. My business or Ally, who could never understand how much danger she's in. The kingdom I've poured sweat and other people's blood into for the last five years or a woman who will never give me the benefit of the doubt.

I yank on the steering wheel, letting the back of the car fishtail.

I text Ilya to go to the warehouse as I step up to Ally's door. I knock. As I'm about to knock again, she opens the door.

Her eyes, slightly red-rimmed, regard me warily. Drops of water cling to her temples like she just splashed water on her face.

"I'm coming in," I tell her. I slide in past her, our arms bumping against each other. I walk around the apartment, checking for Julia, but she's not inside.

"Lev, you can't just barge in," she says. She sounds tired and even as she gestures around the apartment, her movements are lethargic.

I ignore her, walking toward the window that faces the parking lot. I drove around, checking for anyone suspicious, and checked in with Petrov, but anxiety drills into my chest. I've tried to shake the fear, but if Ally was hurt because of the Bratva's actions, it would be another burden I can't fathom carrying.

I turn toward her. She's watching me, her arms crossed over her abdomen, and she seems lost in thought.

"You need to come back to the mansion," I say. "It's for your safety."

"I can't right now," she says, looking away from me.

"I know you're upset because you think your father almost died, but he didn't. You need to prioritize your own safety now and not focus on some worst-case scenario that didn't happen."

She whips around, fire suddenly in her dark eyes. "God, you are the champion of assholes. It must be difficult to be that self-absorbed. I'm not prioritizing my father right now. I'm prioritizing—I'm figuring something out and I can't do that when you're around, messing with my emotions."

"Your emotions aren't a priority right now either," I say. "Your safety is the priority. You need to get over what you're feeling and just come with me. I'm not fucking around."

Her arms tighten around her abdomen. "I'm usually very responsible. I do everything by the book. I never forget things. But you came into my life and everything turned into a mess."

"Yes, I get it. I'm terrible. I'm the worst person on earth. Let's go." I grab her arm. She looks down at my hand, then back at my face.

"I was going to take my birth control pills last night," she says. "I realized I was two days behind. I missed the night of the gala and the night before."

The images clash in my mind. The pills. Sex in the den the night of the gala. The lack of a condom.

"You should have told me," I say.

"I didn't realize it," she says. "I didn't know."

Pregnant. I reel with the realization, trying to absorb it and failing completely. Later on, I'll have to cope with the fact that Allison is pregnant with my child. Her child. Our child. My heir. But right now, I have to focus on the present circumstances. And those circumstances are that Ally is now more in danger than ever, as am I.

Karma is a mean bitch and she's coming back to bite me. Since I took Marco's father, it only makes sense that Marco is going to try to hurt me in the same way—except I killed my father, so Marco can't do that. The closest Marco could get is killing my fiancée or my child and it's looking like, while he's at his most wrathful, he can kill them both in one shot.

It's some Old Testament bullshit. I've worked too hard to build myself up to be taken down so easily. I've taken the ashes that my father left behind, turned them into gold, and a single woman is going to destroy everything because I was foolish enough to allow her into my life outside of the bedroom.

"How could you forget to take your pills?" I ask. "If I thought you were going to be that irresponsible, I would have done something about it."

"I forgot. I'm usually responsible but after we met—"

"Don't blame this on me," I snarl. "You did this on purpose. You wanted to trap me."

Her cheeks flush. Tears threaten to fall from her eyes. It almost makes me regret my words. Almost.

"You're the one who wanted to marry me," she retorts. "You're the one who trapped me. I didn't need to do anything."

I turn away from her as I slam my fist into her kitchen counter. I hear something crack underneath my knuckles, but I don't check it. I know this is my fear manifesting as rage, but it doesn't change the racing thoughts and the evolving anger.

It looks like I have become my father after all. Much as I want to force her to come with me to the mansion, I can't bring myself to do it. That alone tells me I'm in too deep—the fact that I'm thinking twice about exerting control.

"Stay away from the windows," I order. "I'll keep some men on the building."

I leave the apartment, an ache in my hand and a river of fear in my chest. I swallow to keep it down. I know it's too massive to ignore, but I'll keep forcing that fear down.

I have to tame it ...

Before it can drown me.

18

ALLISON

Shortly after I realized I'd missed two of my birth control pills, Elizabeth called, offering to let me sit in on another criminal case. I agreed, my mind too numb to consider saying no. Now that I'm sitting behind her again, everything reminds me of pregnancy, of Lev's accusations, of Jeffrey Douglas.

"Mr. Carlson," the defense lawyer, Matthew Davis, says as he strides to the witness box. "Your PTSD diagnosis makes it difficult for you to differentiate a threat from something innocuous, correct?"

You wanted to trap me, Lev's voice echoes through my thoughts.

"Yes," Timothy Carlson nods furiously. "My three children, my babies—they know not to jump or scare me. And I did this all for them. I wouldn't have taken anything if it weren't for them. I wouldn't risk prison unless I thought I needed to do it."

I wouldn't have risked prison if my life hadn't been in danger. I wouldn't have done any of this if it weren't for my father's career being on the line. Now, I'm probably having a baby, complicating all of my choices.

"Thank you," the defense attorney says, sitting back down.

Elizabeth shoots out of her seat. She strolls around the table.

"Mr. Carlson, you claim that you wouldn't have taken anything if it weren't for your children. Would you have also not killed your neighbor if it weren't for your children?"

"What? I mean, I guess. They were why I was in his house—"

"You blame your children for why you murdered a man?"

"It wasn't murder. It was self-defense. I needed money. I needed to feed my family."

It was self-defense. I didn't mean to kill Jeffrey Douglas. I needed to hide his murder to protect my family.

"But this isn't even your first crime. You have a long criminal record. You've been caught breaking and entering three times. There are plenty of veteran organizations that will help you get a job. Have you tried to get ahold of any of them?"

After Douglas' death, I watched Lev kill a man. I didn't report it. I didn't do anything. I learned he was the leader of the Bratva and it didn't even occur to me to turn him in.

"I've—I've considered it," Mr. Carlson says. "You don't understand. The tension in my head. It's like a rubber band. I can't handle it."

"There must have been plenty of tension while you were breaking into Mr. Cruz's house and you managed it just fine," Elizabeth retorts.

"It's different." Mr. Carlson shakes his head. "It's all different. It's not my fault. I had to—my kids. I had to do it for my kids."

I can't turn into this kind of person. I can't go on justifying crimes, hiding behind excuses, blaming other people. I put myself into this mess. I didn't trap Lev, but I allowed him to sway my moral compass. That's my responsibility.

And if I'm not going to be justifying crimes, I can't marry Lev.

Elizabeth winks at me before she sits back down. She asked to have lunch with me again after court was dismissed. After everything that's happened since the last lunch, it feels strange to return to how it used to be.

It feels like it's my court trial, and I don't see a jury ever returning with a verdict that exonerates me.

∽

Last time, Welkin's was alluring, reminding me of what my future could look like. I saw the grayish-blue walls and thought it was the color of the sky before dawn. Now it reminds me of a guillotine's blade.

"You seem worried," Elizabeth says after our waitress serves us wine. "Don't be. We've got the stronger jury members on our side and they'll sway the weaker ones."

"I'm not worried about that." I fiddle with my napkin. "I'm not worried about anything."

"Good," she says. "Because I want you to have a clear head when I ask you something."

I unravel my napkin, letting the silverware fall out. "Shoot."

"Do you want to take an internship in the district attorney's office?"

"What?" I ask, sitting up. She smiles at me, knowing the gift she's just offered me.

"You'd be able to continue to attend trials, assist in investigations, prepare documents, and do legal research," she says. "It'd also look great on a JD program application. Any law school would put you at the top of its list."

I cover my mouth with my hand, trying to hide my smile. This is more than I could have dreamed. Just the chance to work side-by-side with the DA employees is too good to believe.

"Allison?" she asks.

"I'd love to do that," I blurt out. "Do I need to sign something?"

"You will, yes," she says. "But there is one stipulation."

"Of course," I say. "Whatever you want."

"You have to break it off with Lev Alekseiev."

I open my mouth, waiting for the right words to come. I expected her to say I needed to put off going to law school for another year. I expected her to say that I need to not talk about my work with anyone else. I didn't expect this.

"How ... how do you even know about that?" I ask.

"I know a lot of people in law enforcement," she says. "We work closely with the police, Allison. I work closely enough with them that they told me that you two were at the gala together and it's a well-known fact in the police department that Lev Alekseiev's father was a leader of the Bratva. It's believed that Lev is still connected to them. I can't have anyone in my office connected to the Bratva in any form. I know it must seem cruel for me to give you this ultimatum but it's an issue of ethics. If we get any case where there's even a slight potential of the Bratva being involved, there will be accusations that we didn't pursue the case hard enough because one of our own was dating a man that profits from them."

I nod and swallow hard. "That makes sense."

Elizabeth takes a sip of her wine. This should be easy. I never got rid of the evidence that Lev offered me, but I can't imagine him using it against me now. I could see him doing many terrible, violent things, but I can't picture him throwing me to the wolves.

Though I've been wrong about a lot of things already.

"It's fine that you're conflicted," Elizabeth says. "I can give you a week to decide, but after that, I'll need to give the internship to my assistant district attorney's son."

I nod again. "Thank you."

"I have to say I'm surprised, Allison. I didn't think you'd be the type to get in bed with someone like Alekseiev."

"Oh well …" I shrug. "I didn't know he was rumored to be associated with the Bratva."

Elizabeth tilts her head. "Interesting. Your father told me that he told you about Alekseiev's Bratva connections."

My cheeks burn hot. I grab my wine, taking a long swig of it. Right after the district attorney offered me a dream internship, she caught me in a stupid lie about the Bratva. Even with her stone-cold poker face, I'm certain she's second-guessing the offer. If I lied about this, I could easily lie about anything that comes into the DA office.

I'm falling apart from the inside out. I've got a sickness, and I breathed it in when Lev and I kissed.

19

LEV

A week later

When Ilya calls to tell me there's been an issue reported at the hardware store, I'm halfway grateful for the distraction. Being alone in my office, thinking of Ally, who I haven't seen in a week after our big fight, is driving me insane. Then there's the probable baby now in the equation who keeps popping up in my thoughts. Me. A father. I can't begin to get my head wrapped around that, so I mostly ignore it for the time being.

Entering the hardware store, three customers are milling around. I signal to Ilya and Petrov to tell them to leave. Daniil and another one of my lieutenants, Novikov, move up closer behind me as I walk up to the register.

I see the movement—the cashier's hand dips down too fast to be subtle. I grab Novikov's shirt, yanking him back against the shelves with me as I rip my Glock out of its holster.

Novikov and I back up as a shot goes off. I whip around in its wake and pull my trigger twice in quick succession. The cashier's body jerks back as Novikov and I manage to get behind the shelf.

I check Daniil. It looks like his shoulder is bleeding, but he's managed to get behind one of the other shelves. I check behind me. I can't see Ilya or Petrov, but that likely means they're both safe.

Another gunshot goes off.

I peer around the corner. The cashier is definitely dead or mortally wounded. Someone else is shooting.

Tracking stolen guns isn't practical, but with a gun in Sarah Lyle's face, she told me this was where the Colosimos were storing the weapons they took from us. I hope—for her sake—that she did not forewarn them that we were coming.

As Daniil tries to look around the shelf he's hidden behind, nearly letting his whole head protrude out, and several shots go off. His head slams back. He screams, high-pitched enough that Novikov flinches.

It's as good of a distraction as any.

I tilt to the side, seeing the movement of two men. I shoot the taller one as he turns toward me. His body stumbles back. I shoot the second man as he aims at me.

There's another shot. A hot, stinging sensation runs down my arm. I lurch backward and check my arm, finding a line of blood. It looks like the bullet only skimmed me. As I'm examining my wound, the oddest thought occurs to me. Not only do I not want to die here—nor do I plan to—but I realize that I can't die. Allison and the baby need me alive to protect them, whether or not she ever wants to see me again.

Several shots echo in the store, drawing my focus back to the situation at hand. It's a storm of noise, occasionally punctuated by screams and yells. I turn to check the register. There are three more men, but they're barely focused on us as bullets assault them from the west, destroying the cash register, the counter, and the wall behind it.

I signal to Novikov before I charge out, and he covers me. One of the men is down or hiding, but I take out the man hiding behind a stack of cardboard boxes. There's a shot behind me as Novikov takes out the Colosimo half hidden in the stockroom.

I keep my gun raised as I peer behind the counter. Six men. It seems safe to assume they're not all here earning minimum wage.

I spin around as I hear movement behind me. Ilya raises his hands with a nervous smile. Petrov is behind him, looking immeasurably more serious.

"You shouldn't have wasted so many bullets," I tell Ilya. "You turn into a maniac during a firefight."

"Just backing you up." He nods to Petrov and Novikov. "Do a sweep in the back."

They both nod, jumping over the counter. As they disappear, Daniil groans down the aisle.

"Shit," I mutter. I turn back down the aisle, finding him. Blood is gushing from his head, but he's alert. I crouch down, grabbing his hand away from his face.

His ear was shot off.

Not a great scenario, but not the worst either.

"Get him to our guy," I say. Ilya nods, getting his phone out. He sends a text out as I find some industrial wipes. I hand them to Daniil. It looks like he was shot in the shoulder as well. Ally would have been more sympathetic, but someone else's idiocy isn't my problem.

Petrov and Novikov return.

"The guns are back there," Petrov reports. "Nobody else is here."

"Get them to the 73 warehouse," I tell them. They both nod once before returning to the stockroom.

"Your arm is bleeding," Ilya says.

"It's fine." I run my hand over it, the sting twisting all of the way down.

"You weren't as sharp as usual," he says. "Sloppy work from one of the best shooters I've ever met. What happened?"

"There's a time for you to speak your mind, Ilya," I growl. "Now is not that time."

He nods. Daniil curls into the fetal position below us, the industrial wipes turning bright red over his ear.

～

I wash the blood off in the shower. The wound on my arm stings, but after a while, I don't feel it at all.

I look up into the showerhead, letting the water blind me. I imagine Ally in front of me, the water flowing down her curves and her ass pressed up against my groin.

I run my hand over my cock, imagining her soft hands. I imagine her mouth, her lips tight around the head. I press my hand against the wall of the shower. My fist glides up and down my cock. I close my eyes. Ally on her knees. Her eyes, gazing up at me. The look of need. Her hand raising, cupping my balls.

As I get closer to my limit, I imagine jerking her around, pressing her up against the wall. I'd bury myself in her, feeling her breathing quicken with my chest against her back. I'd fuck her as her hands tried to grip onto the wall. Her supple ass pushing up against me as she struggled to keep her balance.

When I come, there's a flood of pleasure. I lean against the wall. As the seconds pass by, the pleasure is replaced by a hollow solitude.

I step out of the shower, but Ally's mirage follows me out. She dances naked in the center of the bathroom. When I get dressed, I see her in the closet from when we picked out her clothes after our first run. When I go down the stairs, I recall her standing in the doorway, prepared to run away from the deal I was giving her. Even her words and her laugh reverberate in the house like ghosts.

I make myself a drink, hoping to drown the memories out. I check my phone.

Ilya: I'm coming over with the report. Don't shoot me.

He's worried. It's annoying as fuck, but as my right-hand man, he's equally concerned about me as he is about the Bratva. He's right about how shoddy my marksmanship was today. My father gave me a gun for the first time when I was five and I practiced obsessively when I was a teenager. I should have been able to take out all of those men easily. But my mind was preoccupied.

The doorbell rings. I finish my drink and get the door.

∼

Ilya sets his old-fashioned down beside my whiskey on the coffee table. I still smell smoke wafting from the fireplace. I cleaned it out thoroughly enough that nobody would ever know that Ally turned it into our burned bridge.

"The only choice left is to kill him," I say.

Ilya shakes his head. "Killing the don is what led to this. It would also lead to too much attention from the police. I'm certain they assume that Duilio Colosimo's disappearance means that the Bratva took him out, but they can't be certain. For all they know, he skipped town or one of his own members killed him. But if his son is killed as well, they will go after the Bratva without reservations."

"If we don't kill him, he will become a much larger problem than the police."

"We could offer a deal," Ilya suggests. "There's no way he would pass up a decent deal for peace. We overpower him in every way. He knows, at best, this ends with us suffering some casualties while the Colosimos are annihilated."

"He's willing to burn generations of his family's work to get back at me for killing his father. He's not going to fold because we offer him an increase in his profit. Even if he was, I'd rather be skinned than negotiate with him."

"Lev—"

"No," I cut him off. "He threatened Ally. He came into the office. He took my goddamn guns. If he disrespects me one more time, I'll have no problem cutting off his goddamn balls in the middle of the police station. *Ponimayesh?*"

Do you understand?

"*Da*," he says. *Yes.*

I pick up my drink, finishing it off. He picks up his old-fashioned, taking a gulp. There's an uneasiness in the room and it's not just coming from Ilya. I can almost sense Ally sitting on the couch's armrest, where we had sex without protection. For a brief moment, I think of the baby, then banish that thought. But I can't banish Ally from my mind. Her voice infiltrates my thoughts, soothing but disapproving.

You should take him to court.

There has to be another way.

You're pathetic. You're just a common thug.

"You should get back to Sophie," I say. Ilya nods, downing the last of his drink. He stands up, placing the glass on the bar.

"You know," he says as he moves toward the doorway. "I would have cracked a long time ago if it weren't for Sophie."

"I know," I say. "She's been good for you."

"I don't know what happened between you and Allison—"

I scowl at him. He pauses.

"I don't know what happened," he repeats. "But letting her go is a mistake. Sometimes you need someone else to keep you from going over the edge."

"That's why you're here," I say. "And you're better with a gun."

"Thank you," he says. "But Allison is who you need. Sophie agrees. Before Allison, you were relentless and created a legacy—but you were just like Marco. You were willing to give up everything. The only difference is that he's doing it for revenge and you were doing it for power. Allison gave you something that you wanted to hold onto."

"Ilya," I say. "I'm closer to you than anybody else in the world. But if you compare me to Marco Colosimo again, I will cut your bowels open, dump you in the sewer, and let you be eaten alive by rats."

He nods once. "Understood."

He leaves quickly, the entrance door softly closing behind him. I pour myself another drink. Ally's voice continues to cling to my thoughts.

I don't regret it.

I imagine she does now. I'm not certain I can say the same.

As I drink, I play through the memories. Her words become a symphony, accompanied by her breathing, the sweet sounds she made while we moved together, and the softness of her voice afterward. I imagine her body over mine, soothing me in her warmth and her reassuring hands. The creak of her movements in my bed. The quick patter of her heart. Just as quickly, I imagine a child cradled in her arms—

Creak.

I open my eyes. My bed doesn't creak.

I sit up. I don't recall lying down on the couch. I stare into the dim light from the den's lamp, listening.

The faintest tap. Someone is inside the house. Ilya left and Irina shouldn't be here today.

I quietly move to my home bar. I lift it up less than an inch and shift it forward. I reach behind it, finding the holster where my Ruger is kept.

Gun in one hand, I take the cocktail shaker in the other. I reach it into the doorway, using the reflection to check for anyone in the hallway. When there's no one, I set the shaker down and step out into the hallway.

I listen again. Nothing.

I search the halls and the rooms on the first floor. Empty. I keep my gun raised. As I move toward the entrance, mind racing, I notice a small dark shadow underneath the door.

Not a shadow. *Blood.*

I jerk the door open, fear gripping me as I picture Ilya, dead on my doorstep. More than my second-in-command, the man is also my closest friend—something I rarely acknowledge. But if he's been killed …

I take several steps out, my finger over the trigger. Another dead body lies farther out in the yard, but no moving targets.

I check the body at the front door. It's not Ilya. Relief washes over me, along with regret as I see that it's Bogdanov—a low-ranking soldier. Even so, he was one of my men, and I treat all their deaths the same —with the aim to avenge the loyal fallen. His throat has been slit, blood painting his lower neck and most of his chest. Tension ricochets in my body as I go farther out to check the other body. Semyonov. Another soldier, who had three kids. A knife wound to his eye, one to his throat, and three to his chest. Ilya must have assigned them to the house.

Fuck.

I pull out my cell phone, then hear a sudden sound, deafening, followed by indescribable pain.

For a split second, I feel my body crash into the cement and the blood-drenched grass before everything is gone.

20

ALLISON

"Could you pour us some wine?" Julia asks as she sets the pot roast back into the oven. "It should be ready soon after your parents get here."

I take two glasses out of our cabinet. After I pour one glass, I stop before I pour into the other one.

What is the likelihood that I'm pregnant? I try to recall the statistics—it's either fifteen percent or twenty-five percent and both seem like a high risk.

I set the wine bottle down and fill my glass with water from the faucet instead. When I hand Julia her glass, she glances between the glass of water and my face.

"Are you driving somewhere tonight?" she asks.

"No," I say. Avoiding her maternal gaze, I look over at our dining room table. I can almost see Lev sitting there, refusing to drink more because he knew how I felt about driving under the influence.

Her eyes narrow. "This dinner isn't to tell your parents that you're pregnant, is it?"

I nearly spit out my water. She rubs my back as I cough into the sink. It only makes me feel worse.

"Um," I manage to get out. "No. The dinner is because my parents wanted to talk about my relationship with Lev."

Her hand on my back feels too small. Lev's arms, steady and toned, gave me security without feeling restrictive. When he held me after I told him about the car crash, he turned all my panic into the heartbeat of something new.

"I could see why your father wouldn't like him." Julia sips from her wine. "Why isn't Lev here then?"

"Well ... we broke up."

She rubs the back of her neck. "I think you might have spiked my drink because I'm already confused. Why are your parents coming over if the two of you broke up?"

I shoot her an apologetic look. "We were kinda engaged."

"Are you shitting me?" She sets her glass down. "What the hell, Ally? Take a few steps back. So, at one point, you got engaged. And at some point, this became past tense. Have I been downgraded to your next-door neighbor or something? Why didn't you tell me?"

"It was chaotic. Everything was overwhelming," I say. "But it's over now. So, my parents should be happy."

"Are you happy?"

"Yeah," I lie.

She eyes me suspiciously. "And this engagement had nothing to do with a pregnancy?"

"No," I say. "That ... is something else entirely."

"Excuse me?"

"I missed two of my birth control pills. So ... I might be."

Julia throws her hands up in the air. "Holy shit, Ally."

"Can we please change the subject?" I ask.

"Not yet. What does Lev think about all of this?"

"He doesn't want it. I doubt there's any pregnancy anyway," I say. She frowns.

"Well, I guess that works out," she says. "It's still not great. I'm sorry."

"Let's just forget about it. Tell me about your day."

She sighs, taking another sip of her wine. "Fine. In comparison, my day has been boring, which is saying something. So, the first call I get, it turns out to be a guy with a huge swastika on his neck. His friends have similar tattoos. This guy has overdosed, I'm trying to save his life and get him into the ambulance while his friends are trying to prevent me from helping him because Faiza is with me and I guess they didn't like the look of him or something. The police end up coming to help us. On my second call, a man was beating his kid and the kid had locked himself in the bathroom. That's all we were told, but once we got there, we found out that before the kid locked himself in the bathroom, he'd stabbed his father in the abdomen four times with a pair of scissors. We ended up needing the police to help restrain the man as we tried to help him and the man still tried to attack us."

"Don't you ever want to just walk away?" I ask.

She shrugs. "I used to. But, after you've done this for enough years, you stop reflecting on who's worth saving or whether or not they did something terrible. It's not like the courtroom. We're not placing judgments. I just know that I want to do a good thing and I don't need society's approval for that."

"That almost sounds critical of the legal system."

"The courtroom is your thing and I love you," she says, squeezing my arm. "But I don't want to regret anything. I didn't want to put less effort into saving that father and finding out later that he'd been an immensely loving father that accidentally ingested some drugs. Morality is subjective. For one man, an eye for an eye is good. For another man, killing to protect his loved ones is good. For a wonderful, amazing roommate, the legal system is good. It is what it is."

Lev killed to protect me. And I hated him for it.

Julia sips from her wine. "So, now that you're breaking up with Lev, is it because he was bad in bed?"

"What? No."

"Which means that he was great at it," she teases. "That guy was an arrogant ass, but with that much confidence, his cock must have been massive. It'd have to be with the size of his balls. The man called me out without flinching."

"You deserved it."

She laughs. "I absolutely did. I'm glad I didn't waste too much time trying to like him, but I have to give him some credit. He would've defended you against a prison full of angry felons if they'd insulted you."

"He did defend me in front of my father."

Both of Julia's eyebrows shoot up. "Wow. Going up against his fiancée's father. That must have been rough."

It's not something I'd considered before, but she's right. This whole con was based on the idea of getting my father to trust and like Lev, but Lev went after him the moment Dad called me reckless and foolish. He ruined his chances from the start. All because he defended me.

I drink my water, wishing it was wine and that I could have one more night with Lev before everything went to shit.

When my parents knock on the door, I've replaced my water with a glass of grape juice. I take their coats, our greetings to each other jumbling together, and hand them each a glass of wine as Julia serves the pot roast onto four plates.

By the time we're sitting down, it should be easy to pretend everything is exactly the way it used to be before I met Lev. But it's hard to ignore how much I crave his hand on my hip or his breath hot against my ear as he whispers something to me.

It's also hard to ignore the way my father keeps looking at me, clearly waiting for a chance to give a speech about how I'm ruining my life.

I turn to him after everyone's second bite. "Lev and I broke up."

Dad's face lights up before his whole body relaxes, a small laugh eclipsing the story Julia was telling my mother.

"Oh thank God," he says. "I knew you'd figure it out, Ally. I'm so glad. This is great."

"They broke up?" my mother asks. She playfully smacks my father on the arm. "See, Peter. You didn't need to worry about anything."

My father takes my hand, squeezing it over the table. "This is great. Everything is still going to work out for you. Did Elizabeth offer the internship to you?"

I nod.

"Wonderful. Your future is set." He beams. "This is phenomenal. Everything is falling into place for you."

"We're very happy for you," my mother adds. "Elizabeth seems to think you'll be able to do anything you want after the internship. It's such a great opportunity."

I nibble on my food. The conversation drifts to Julia's day, then my father's day. I know why my father is so happy about this news—his daughter is no longer dating a dangerous criminal. But it's jarring to hear that they care more about my future than my current happiness. I'd hope that if Lev were anyone else, they'd at least ask how I was dealing with the breakup.

"Officer Wilcox was ready to fight the nurses to get out of the hospital," my father laughs. "But Morris is nearly ready to order room service there. Yesterday, he tried to get a nurse to give—"

He stops as his phone beeps. He pulls out his cell phone.

"Peter," my mother warns.

"It's the station. I have to answer it," my father says. He taps on the screen before putting it up to his ear. "Chief Harrington."

His eyes shift back and forth for half a second before he looks directly at me. His forehead furrows.

"Yes, I do," he says. "She's right here in front of me."

I sit up straight, setting my fork and knife down. The confusion clouding his face slowly changes. His eyes widen and his body stiffens. He looks away from me, slowly standing up.

"Good," he says. "I'll be there soon. Keep the media as far away from it as possible. Call in our best people. If this is a Mafia war, we need to cut it off at the knees. Even if it's random, it could lead to trouble. Good. Go."

He hangs up.

"What's going on?" I ask, standing up as he grabs his jacket.

"Nothing," he says. "Stay here."

He turns to my mother, giving her a quick kiss. He mutters something to her and she nods.

"Dad," I say. He touches my shoulder in a half-hearted attempt at reassurance before nearly sprinting out the door. I turn to my mother. "What did he say to you?"

"He just told me he loved me," she says, avoiding my eyes. "Let's finish dinner."

"He mentioned the Mafia," I say.

"We could turn on the TV," Julia suggests. "If it's something big enough for the chief to be there, it could be breaking news."

"No," my mother says. "Let's just eat. Julia, tell me more about this evil man who hit his son."

Julia glances between us before describing the situation with the abusive father who'd been stabbed four times.

I stand up. "I'm going to pee."

Before anyone can question me, I rush into the bathroom. As soon as the door is closed, I pull my phone out of my pocket and check the local news.

On the first website, there's nothing notable.

On the second one, there's the same news.

On the third one, there's a breaking news alert.

Reports of Explosion at House of Mariya's Revenge Owner

My heart stops beating, but I barely notice as I reread the alert over and over.

Several social media accounts have reported hearing an explosion and seeing a fire at the residence of Lev Alekseiev, owner of Mariya's Revenge and several nightclubs.

I scroll, waiting for more words to appear, but that's all that's written.

I shove my phone back into my pocket. I hear my mother's concerned voice at my prolonged absence, followed by Julia trying to reassure her. I lock the door, yank open the bathroom window, and climb out onto the fire escape. I hear the bathroom doorknob rattle, but I don't think twice about it.

I climb down the fire escape and then hesitate as I measure the distance between the ground and the ladder, thinking of the baby I might be carrying. But Lev is that child's father and I have to get to him. Trying to be careful, I jump down the last couple of feet. When I land, I take off running to my car.

∽

The drive to Lev feels like it takes years. When I get there, the front of his mansion is on fire, the flames illuminating everyone standing behind the police tape. Four firetrucks have pulled onto the lawn. Even as jets of water pour onto the blaze, waves of heat billow across my face.

Groups of firemen watch the house burn. It could be some kind of ineffective tactic or maybe they don't care because he's associated with the Bratva.

I duck under the police tape. A policeman tries to stop me but lets his hand drop when he sees my face. I don't know if it's because of my desperation or if he recognizes me as the chief's daughter.

I grab the arm of one of the firemen. His helmet is under his arm, but his face shines with sweat.

"What's going on?" I ask.

The fireman points behind me. "You should be behind the tape," he says.

"I'm the police chief's daughter," I say. "Tell me what's going on."

He looks me over for several seconds, the light of the fire making one half of his face glow while the other half is in shadow. "There were multiple explosive devices in the house. We haven't located any survivors, but we can't get that far into the house without risking our men because the explosions increased the risk of structural failure. All we can do is prevent the fire from spreading."

They haven't found Lev.

As the firefighter turns to look back at the fire, I run. I'm within ten feet of the house by the time the firefighters start yelling. The entrance door is gone—removed or reduced to rubble—so I run straight in.

It's like stepping into hell. I check my arms and legs to see if I'm burning as the heat cuts into me like a knife. I should be thinking about the baby, something says in the back of my mind, but Lev is uppermost right now. I have to find him. He needs me. And I need him.

Lev favored three places in his house: his office, his gym, and his den. His office and his gym are both on the second floor, so I head to the den first.

The ceiling is splintering. I can't recall what room is above this one, but it's ready to come crashing through. I glance around the room from the archway.

He's not here.

I backtrack, checking the stairs. I try to step on the first two steps, but they both collapse under my weight. I grab onto the railing, but the metal sears my skin. As I jerk backward, I bump into a solid body.

I spin around, a merry-go-round of elation. It's not Lev. It's a firefighter. He grabs me, throwing me over his shoulder. I start to struggle, but it does no good as he jogs me out of the house.

I'm too embarrassed to even raise my head as he takes me to the firetruck farthest away from the mansion and lowers me to a seat on the metal ledge on the back.

I cover my face with my hands, trying not to scream in frustration.

The grief takes hold faster than I can control it. The tears sneak down my face, clinging to my cheeks before dropping into my lap.

The firefighter holds out an oxygen mask. I take it. I doubt I need it, but I've heard the horror stories of people killed by smoke inhalation.

The scent in the mask is oddly sweet.

Something isn't right.

As my head starts to wilt and my eyelids become heavy, I try to peer up at the firefighter. He looks all fuzzy but I'm certain he's not familiar.

I take one more breath before my body lets go of consciousness.

21

LEV

My head is a coal mine, explosions with echoes of pain, clouds of dust turning my vision into blurs and darkness, and gases churning all my thoughts into disoriented fragments.

I force my eyes open.

The blurry room slowly comes into focus. I try to move my arms. Steel on my wrists. I push my hands together, finding the chain of the handcuffs. I move my hands backward, touching what's between my hands and my back. Large circular wood. Too smooth to be a tree. Support beam.

Round support beams. Hickory floor. Two doorways come into focus. I used to slam one of them shut, an angry teenager who only wanted to fuck and kill.

I grew up here.

This is Marco's bullshit. In order to inflict mental torture, he thinks my childhood home is the optimal environment. It must be exhausting to keep coming up with torture methods instead of simply shooting someone in the head.

I run my fingers over the cuffs. They aren't cheap, kinky ones or shoddy antiques. If the support beam was built out of brick, I might have a chance of smashing it apart, but otherwise, they're too sturdy to break.

I slam the side of the handcuffs against the support beam, attempting to hit the part with the rivet. It may be impossible, but I'm not going to wait around to be tortured.

The house vibrates as I jab the metal against the beam. It shouldn't surprise me when somebody comes through the front door, but it pisses me off that it's Marco.

He walks up to me but keeps four feet between us.

"I bet with all of your careful plotting and bravado, you didn't see yourself ending up here," he says. His voice is casual, but his arms are stiff and all of his weight is on his right leg like he's prepared to bolt. He takes a few strides to his right and points downward. "The wood is still stained with your mother's blood here. And since that's the smaller bedroom, I assume that was where you used to sleep."

We stare at each other. I force a smile.

"If you thought bringing me back here would cause me to break down, you haven't figured me out," I say. "I'm more likely to get upset over a bad steak."

"I also heard rumors that you killed your father," he continues. "Which could explain why you had no qualms about killing mine."

"I had no qualms about killing your father because he was insignificant."

His nostrils flare. "You're not going to deny killing your own father?"

"I killed a man who no longer had control over his emotions and was a liability to the Bratva," I say.

He's seconds away from snapping. If I can get him close enough, I can eliminate him completely.

"I understand why it might be shocking to you, but I wasn't dependent on my father. Maybe I should have waited a couple of years, so you could grow a spine and kill the son of a bitch yourself."

Marco charges forward. His fist slams into my jaw. The pain hits like a firework—condensed, then rapidly spreading throughout my face. The taste of blood slips over my tongue.

He takes several steps back as I swivel my jaw.

"How's that for spine?" he challenges.

I swallow some of the blood. "I've had girls do worse damage while blowing me. If you think it shows spine to hit a prisoner while both of his hands are behind his back, your daddy didn't teach you shit about being a man."

"If I wanted to be a man, I'd be in the other room with Allison rather than here with you," he says.

I sneer at him. "Your bullshit isn't going to work on me. Allison is having dinner with her parents tonight. I've had people checking up on her."

"Yes," he says. "I know. I also knew that she'd come running if she heard there were explosions at your house. And she did. It's quite admirable how willing she was to run straight into your burning house."

I scrutinize his face. "You're lying."

"But you don't need to worry. I had one of my men pull her out. Dressed as a firefighter, of course. You'd be amazed at who people are willing to trust as long as they're in uniform."

He's not lying. I see it in his eyes.

He's not fucking lying.

I lurch up onto my feet. "I'm going to kill you."

"You talk about spine and cowardice, but all that courage didn't do shit for you or your girlfriend." He turns away from me, walking away. I lunge forward, the house trembling as the handcuffs jab against the support beam. "Thank you, though, for the idea about the jaw-breaking blowjobs. I'll enjoy that."

I hurl myself forward over and over again, even after he's left. My shoulders feel like they're ready to dislocate, but I keep going.

I'll take this whole house down to get to Ally before he does.

~

My shoulders are burning. My arms are burning. My wrists are burning. My body is a wildfire, but I keep hurling myself forward. If there were a sharp object within reach of my hands, I'd start cutting off fingers to get my hand through the handcuff.

And it's not for my sake, which is a change of pace.

Mariya's Revenge is a testament to my work ethic that I can keep out in the open. The Bratva is a private monument to what I can do unfettered. I keep my enemies at heel and the police at bay, a whole city staring up at me like a frightened animal, unable to stop me from doing what I want. I care about my employees and my men, but in the end, it's always been about me.

And I'd let it all collapse into dust and rubble to get Ally out of this.

I'd give up my freedom if it would ensure that she was happy. She's given me more happiness and more purpose than I've ever had with anything else. She doesn't deserve any of this violence.

We all have to die one day. I'd rather give it up for her than anything else. For her and our child.

I pause, hearing a rumble. I've tried to call out to Ally, but she's either unconscious or Marco has her somewhere out of hearing.

A car door slams shut.

I press my back against the support beam. The door swings open. When Marco walks back in, his expression is composed. If I'm going to goad him into a fight, I'll have to get far enough under his skin that he ends up cutting open his own flesh.

"You know, I respected your father," I say. "He was indomitable. You're immeasurably less impressive."

"Oh, you got me, Lev," A sneer on his face, he puts his fist over his heart. "That's exactly how to break my heart. Keep talking about my father. I'd love to hear your psychoanalysis."

"You're far more interesting. Any shrink would wonder how a man as impressive as Duilio could raise someone as weak-minded as you," I say. "It's just sad that after so many generations, the Colosimos will wither and die this way. You were worthwhile enemies—for a time. But you will never live up to what your father did because your father wasn't overwhelmed by emotions. Your father would never throw away the Mafia's legacy—not even to avenge you if you'd been killed."

"You're projecting," Marco interjects, taking a step forward. "Everyone knows your father couldn't give two shits about his family. You think when he was beating your mama, she wondered where you were? You think she thought you knew about it and never came to save her?"

I shrug. "They're both rotting in the ground. You're the one concerned about the dead. On the subject of rotting corpses, I'm most shocked that you took over for your father. We both know he didn't want you to be the don."

His jaw clenches. He tries to laugh, but it sounds more like a cough. "My father had full faith in me. There was nothing he wanted more than for me to take over for him."

"He didn't think you had what it took to become the don," I say. "He thought you lacked self-discipline."

"You're full of shit," Marco says, a slight edge slipping out in his last word.

"You think I'm pulling some mind game, but I know this because your father sold you out to convince me that we were close allies." I smile at him. "He told me that he knew you lacked self-discipline because you pissed the bed until you were ten."

Marco's face turns bright red. He charges up to me, our faces less than two inches apart.

"My father terrorized me," he says, spittle hitting my face. "That's the only reason I had any problems. He—"

I slam my head into Marco's. Marco lurches back, clinging the bridge of his nose. Blood trickles down, skipping past his chin to his shirt.

"Motherfucker!" he shouts. "Fucking motherfucker."

He rushes at me. His fist swings. The pain erupts. My legs buckle.

Before I fall, his other fist swings up. It collides with my jaw, my teeth slamming together. Adrenaline floods my system, blunting the pain. His fist comes at me again. I shift my head enough that it brushes against my jaw before hitting against the support beam. He makes a primal noise, taking two steps back.

When he kicks me, I know it's coming, but he keeps kicking, gripping the support beam for stability. His foot jabs against my chest. I let my body slide forward the slightest bit. He hits my ribs. I move my leg down until it's between his legs, letting him think the pain is crippling me.

It would be, but I focus on the memory of Ally's face.

He hits my ribs again. As he raises his other foot again, I yank my leg back and stomp at his ankle. He stumbles, catching himself on the beam and pushing back, limping slightly.

He stares at me, his chest heaving. He's a rabid animal. There's nothing in his eyes but violence.

"We're going to settle this," he spits out. "And by the end of it, you're going to regret every word that came out of your fucking mouth."

He moves behind me. If he breaks one of my arms, I'm fucked.

Something small is pressed into the palm of my hand.

"Unlock the cuffs," he says. I maneuver the key, getting it into the keyhole. The cuffs pop open. I bring my hands in front of me. My wrists have cuts in them from trying to break the cuffs.

Marco raises his fists, squaring off. I stand up slowly, testing the damage to my body. I drop the key on the floor.

I raise my fists, too.

∽

My father used to tell me that pain was negotiable. He meant that anyone could handle pain if they weren't soft, toughened by perseverance through previous pain, but I'm willing to negotiate now. I tell the pain to keep at bay now and I'll let it conquer me after Ally is safe. I tell it that I'll let it rip me to pieces—tomorrow. I'll let it kill me—but later. Not now. Not yet.

Marco circles closer toward me. He wants me to move, to see where my weaknesses are. Just from his small stature, I know he's going to be faster than me. There's no point in trying to get around that, so there's little point in moving first.

I lower my hands. He charges forward, swinging his fist. I block it with my forearm, grabbing onto the arm with my other hand. I yank him forward, jabbing him in the throat. When he bends over to gasp for breath, I thrust my knee into his face. His head snaps back with a guttural yell. I grab him by his hair, yanking his head down. I slam my fist down into the side of his head. He collapses onto the floor, his face stained red.

"Tell me where Ally is," I say. He spits blood out. As he starts to stand back up, I stomp down between his shoulder blades. He falls onto his chest, his chin hitting against the floor. I grit my teeth together, rubbing my ribs where he kicked me, trying to ignore the pain that is demanding my attention in spite of my bargaining.

"Fuck you," he snarls.

I slam my foot down again. He rolls out of the way and twists back around to grab my leg, becoming an anchor. I strike the side of his head as he tries to get up, but it only gives him an opening. He hits me in the ribs, the same place he kicked me twice. It sends shock waves of pain through me. I take several steps back, gripping my side, as he retreats as well.

My arms are heavy from trying to get free and he's already faster than me. I need to end this now.

I lunge forward. As he ducks, trying to get under me to avoid my fists, I thrust my knee up into his head. He recoils. I grab him by the throat, thrusting him against the beam. My fingertips dig into his throat.

"Tell me where Ally is," I hiss. "Or I'll tear your throat out."

I apply more pressure, feeling the muscles tighten in his neck. I loosen my grip when his lips try to form words.

"I'll tell you," he chokes out. His eyes flicker behind me. I start to turn, but an arm hooks around my neck, pulling tight like a noose. The other hand is close to my ear, fingers pressing against the back of my skull, telling me it's a rear-naked choke, which is far from ideal. I back up quickly, slamming the other man's back against the wall, but it barely loosens his grip. I try to ram him into the wall again, but he's prepared this time.

As his grip tightens, Marco hurls forward, hitting me so hard against the head that the rear-naked choke loosens from my momentum. I jerk forward, grabbing onto Marco, but before I can hit him, the other man punches me in the back of my head. I fall to my hands and knees. Marco kicks my ribs over and over, lightning strikes of pain coursing through me. The other man stomps down, putting his weight into the attack, but it can't compare to Marco's rage.

Time sneaks in and out of my perception. At times, I hear my mother screaming. In others, I see Ally breaking down in Renovate boutique.

All the people I let down. All the people I couldn't save.

"Cuff him again," Marco's voice floats through the disorientation. Hands grab me, dragging me until I feel the support beam behind me. The cuffs snap back onto my wrists, a final victory.

A hand wraps around my throat.

"Before you die, I don't want you to think you won," Marco hisses. "I didn't want to kill you yet because I have other plans for that."

He releases my neck. I hear his footsteps, moving away from me.

"Prepare the disposal site," he tells the other man.

Footsteps.

Door opening and closing.

Silence.

I let the pain rip through me. I let it take over until my body can't take it anymore.

22

ALLISON

Funny the things you remember when you're tied up. Literally.

18 U.S. Code 1201 floats through my mind—the federal statute pertaining to kidnapping. It can lead to life imprisonment and, if the victim dies, it can lead to the death penalty in certain states.

This is not reassuring to most victims, especially when the victim wakes up in a bedroom next to two dead bodies and is informed by a large kidnapper that they were the house's owners.

The cloth gag is damp against my tongue, but the dry sections still cut into the corners of my mouth. The cable ties press my wrists so tightly together, I can feel a patch of sweat between them behind my back. They're tied to more cable ties, tethering me to the leg of a bed.

I glance over at the two dead bodies, my only companions now. After hearing thumping noises over and over, the kidnapper ran out of the room. I thought I heard Lev earlier, but I haven't heard him again, which could mean that whatever gas they gave me caused me to hallucinate or he's dead.

I look away from the dead bodies. Imagining Lev, his skin turning gray and his heart beating one last time, a panic is set loose in my chest. He's chaos and brutality, but I need him—for those things, but also for his control and his compassion.

For his love.

I try to slide my wrists out of the cable ties for the hundredth time. They only cut into the heel of my hand more. I try to pull the bed forward, using my weight, but it doesn't budge.

My eyes flick up as the doorknob turns. I wait.

It's not the kidnapper. This man is younger, smaller, with a swollen nose, a black eye, and contusions splattered across his face.

He walks behind me, crouching down. There's a faint snapping noise and the cable ties are gone. He grabs under my arm and jerks me up onto my feet.

"It's time for you to play your part," he mutters. "And you better not fuck it up."

He shoves me toward the door. I stumble and let myself fall. He sighs, leaning down to grab me again. I lunge my elbow back, but I can't move far with my restraints. It barely grazes him. He grabs the front of my shirt, pulling me as close to his face as possible. I stomp at his feet, but he only pulls me up further, so my toes barely touch the ground.

He hurls me against the doorway. The corner of it jabs into my back. I fall back onto the floor.

"Get up," he snaps. "If you try something like that again, I'll kill you and your boyfriend."

Hope surges within me. Lev is still alive.

I get onto my knees, then my feet. The man points me forward, directing me down a pair of stairs. I walk sideways to avoid falling down. My eyes watch my feet, so when I reach the bottom of the stairs, the first thing I notice is the blood spatter all over the floor.

When I raise my head, I see Lev.

I only have this man's assurance that Lev is alive, but it's hard to imagine considering how messed up his face is. His whole face is one mottled bruise. His eyes are closed, his head lolled on his shoulder. Blood ripples across the front of his shirt like a macabre necklace.

I start walking more quickly, knocking down a chair as I sprint toward him. I land on my knees in front of him. I lean forward to press my lips against his cheek. His eyes open—the smallest blessing. His lips curl up the slightest bit, followed by a grimace. He mouths my name. I cover his mouth with mine, tasting blood.

Hands grab my arms, yanking me away. I scream, the gag barely dulling the sound now. The man forces me to sit on the chair I knocked down. When he tries to put cable ties around my wrists again, I stomp at his feet before standing up again.

He pulls a gun out of his waistband, pointing it at me. "Sit the fuck down and don't move or I'm going to shoot you in the fucking head."

I sit down. He straps my left to the armrest, leaving my right hand free. He moves behind me, one of his hands on my shoulder, and puts his gun in my right hand. His gun directed at Lev prevents me from shooting him outright. I don't know that he won't pull the trigger the second I try to pull mine.

"Good, Miss Harrington," he says. "Now, shoot Mr. Alekseiev."

I shake my head.

"Miss Harrington, your father is the chief of police. I'm sure he's killed criminals. This shouldn't be a problem for you. Mr. Alekseiev killed my father—a man he barely knows—and he killed his own father, a man he trusted. Now it's his turn to be killed by someone he barely knows and someone he trusts. You."

I shake my head again.

"You shoot him or I will slowly kill you both," he threatens, his grip on my shoulder getting tighter.

I shake my head for the third time. He snatches the gun from my hand, aims it, and shoots Lev in the leg. Lev screams. It barely lasts two seconds, but the sound pierces through me like a thousand bullets.

The man puts the gun back in my hand, carefully wrapping my fingers around the grip.

"Shoot him or I shoot the other leg, then each of his arms, and we can both thoroughly enjoy the view of him bleeding out. Then, it will be your turn."

"Do it, Ally," Lev growls, barely audible, his teeth gritted. "For me. I'd rather have you … I'd rather have you kill me than anyone else."

I wait for some indication that he has some trick up his sleeve, but he only grips his thigh, blood seeping through his fingers.

I can't breathe.

"Shoot him," the man repeats. I take a deep breath and look straight at Lev. What a way for both of us to go out.

Then I open my hand, letting the gun fall between my feet. The man curses, quickly bending over to grab it. I stomp at him as hard as I can. He jerks backward and the rage in his eyes could burn whole cities down. The back of his hand hits me like a baseball bat. The chair topples over, the force of the fall breaking one of the armrests and one of the legs. Briefly, my thoughts turn to the baby that could be within me, and how badly hurt it could be. But it will be hurt even worse if I don't get out of this. If Lev doesn't.

With one arm free, I dive for the gun as best I can, given that my left arm is still strapped to the busted chair. The man lurches forward too, grabbing it before I can. I lunge at his legs. We fall to the floor. I crawl forward, the gun straight in front of me.

I don't see the man grab the chair's leg, but it jabs into my arm. I yank my arm back, cradling it to my chest, as the man swipes the gun.

"Marco!" Lev growls. "Don't."

The man aims the gun at me.

"Get up," he orders. "This was about revenge against your boyfriend. I didn't have anything against you. But now, you're going to regret not shooting him for the rest of your life. Do you know how much I can sell you for as a sex slave to the Mexican cartel? Truthfully, not much. But I'm not going to do it for the profit."

Lev writhes in his chair, but the bonds hold fast. His right leg is drenched with blood.

"Marco, don't be an idiot," Lev's voice comes out soft, but the warning is clear in it. "Her father finds out that you did that, there's nowhere you can hide."

"I'll be so far out of her father's jurisdiction, he won't be able to do a goddamn thing," Marco says.

"And what about me? You know I'll track you down, no matter where you go. Let's just settle this like men. One-on-one this time."

"Oh no, see, that's the beauty of my new plan," he says. "I won't have to worry about you or her father because her father is going to be focused on you."

Marco pulls out his phone. He taps on the screen three times before raising the phone to his ear. His other hand keeps the gun raised to my head.

"Oh God," he says into the phone, his voice drenched in fear. "Oh God, I just came to visit my friends in the old house on Prairie Street —the big white one—and this guy, this violent Russian, he killed my friends. And he was bragging about killing the chief's daughter. Oh God. Please send help. Please."

He hangs up. I stare at him, feeling equally numb and broken.

"Goodbye, Lev," he says. The man slices the remaining cable tie free and grabs my arm, dragging me to the entrance door. He gestures for me to open it. I could hit him with the door, I could fight back, but I know he'll be more prepared for me this time and I need to get him away from Lev.

After I open the door, I try to look back at Lev, but Marco pushes me forward. In the front yard, a car pulls up. The kidnapper gets out.

"What's happening, boss?" the man asks. "I thought you were taking care of both of them."

"There's a change of plans," Marco says. "You need to release Lev in five minutes."

I can't say there isn't a flicker of pride in my chest when I see the kidnapper eye the house warily.

"What if he attacks me? It took two of us last time," the kidnapper says.

"That was before I beat him, before I shot him in the leg, and before he started bleeding out," Marco says. "You'll be fine."

Marco yanks my arm, dragging me toward the car. I catch one more glimpse of the house as the kidnapper walks toward it.

For the first time in my life, I hope for a man's death.

23

LEV

Marco's accomplice approaches me slowly. He's a large man, his arms hanging down like dead tree branches. I lean my head back. He's not going to kill me. It wouldn't fit into Marco's plan.

He circles around me. Blood has drenched my right pant leg. With every breath I take, my ribs vibrate with pain. But it's all trivial when I need to get to Ally.

Behind me, the goon's hands yank my wrists up by the handcuffs. He unlocks the cuffs. My arm falls to the ground. The other cuff falls off.

I lunge forward, snatching the broken chair leg, and he knows immediately that he fucked up—badly. He runs at me, trying to grab my arm. I swing the leg, catching the side of his face.

He recoils, touching the line of blood on his cheek. As I swing at him again, he stoops down to avoid it. The leg swings over his head and I grab him by his hair with my other hand. I yank his head back, so he's staring up at the ceiling. I lift the leg up and drive it through his eye. The sounds of him dying are sickening.

When he stops moving, I know he's dead.

I let him drop to the floor and wipe some blood off my chin. Adrenaline swells in my veins, anesthetizing some of the pain, but it still ensnares me. I push it away; I need to focus on coming up with a plan to get Ally.

Steal a car. Speed down the road. Catch up to Marco and kill him.

I open the house's front door. I've barely taken a step out when I hear the police sirens.

This is what Marcus wanted.

He knew I'd kill off his accomplice as soon as I was free. It eliminated one of the people who could testify against him and his accomplice was the only other living person in the house. Three dead people, a missing chief's daughter, and me.

I'm fucked.

Two police cars speed into the driveway. I raise my hands in surrender, the pain in my ribs acting as another reminder that what remains of Ally's life is going to be torture because of me. I can't bear to think of what will happen to our child. To even consider it will cause me to lose what's left of my mind.

Three policemen pour out of the first cars, their guns raised. They start shouting.

"Get on the ground!"

"Lie facedown on the ground!"

I get onto my knees, keeping my hands up. "I didn't do this."

"Shut the fuck up and get on the ground!"

I lie facedown on the floor, my legs lying over the threshold of the house. One of the policemen runs up. Her hands hesitate over my wrists. She must see the marks. Nevertheless, she snaps on the handcuffs. The two other officers run into the house.

"You need to listen to me," I say to the woman. "This wasn't me. The police chief's daughter has been kidnapped. They left five minutes ago. It's the Colosimos."

"You have the right to remain silent," she starts.

"No," I cut her off. "You have to find Allison Harrington. They just left. You need to find them."

"Anything you say can and will be used against you in a court of law. You have the right to an attorney. If you cannot afford an attorney, one will be provided for you. Do you understand the rights I have just read to you?"

The bullet wound in my leg gushes more blood. My head swims with regrets.

I should have studied medical care.

I shouldn't have gotten involved with Ally.

I should have killed Marco the first time I saw him.

"Sir? Sir, the EMTs are coming," the officer says.

"Three dead bodies," one of the other officer calls out. "All murdered. Fucking horrific."

I hear the sound of another car pulling up. I close my eyes. "Just please find Marco Colosimo," I tell the female police officer. "He has Allison Harrington."

"Get out of the way," a rough voice demands.

Peter Harrington.

He grabs the front of my shirt and yanks me up. His eyes are bloodshot.

"What have you fucking done with my daughter?" he says, through bared teeth. "I don't give a fuck who's here; I will kill you if you don't tell me where she is."

"It's the Colosimos," I tell him. His fist comes out of nowhere, knocking me down to my knees. He's not as strong as Marco, but after all of the previous hits, the pain is the same.

The female officer tries to push Peter Harrington back, but he shrugs her off. I slowly get to my feet, my hands still locked behind my back.

"This is why I didn't want her near you. I knew this would happen. Tell me where she is or I swear to God—"

"Do you think I blew up my own house?" I snap back. "Do you think I beat myself up? Ask your officer. I was restrained. You think I'd kill three people in my own childhood home? This is the Colosimos. Marco Colosimo took her. They left about eight minutes ago. This is my fault, but I'm not the person who took her. We can't argue about this right now. I need to get to her."

"You're a lying sack of shit," Peter says. His eyes dart back and forth as he takes in what I said. "I just want my daughter back."

"Then let me go, so I can find her. You know who I am. You know I'll do what it takes to get her back, but I need to do it on my terms."

He stares at me. He's been my enemy for a long time, but in this moment, I know we're the same—two people who love Ally, who would do anything to save her life.

He turns to the female officer.

"Help the other men secure the scene inside," he says.

"Sir," she says, gazing between us. "Are you sure …"

"Do what I said," he snarls. She retreats into the house. He takes a key off his utility belt and indicates for me to turn around. He unlocks the cuffs, catching them before they fall to the floor.

Then he hands me another pair of keys. His car keys.

"You better kill Marco Colosimo," he says. "I'm betting my career on you getting my daughter back, so make it worth it."

I nod and start toward the car, only to be pulled up short by the chief's rough hand on my arm. "Wait," he growls, and yanks off his belt. Next thing I know, he's tying up my wound and issuing a gruff warning. "You can't leave that on long, or you'll lose the leg. But if I don't tie it off, you'll be dead before you drive a block. So you better break every speed limit to get to my daughter, Alekseiev."

Nodding again, I hobble to his car, lightheadedness starting to sink its claws in me in spite of the tourniquet.

---

105 on the speedometer, the police siren blaring, and passing dozens of cars. I should have found Marco or Ally by now. Marco owns a black BMW, but it's unlikely to be the vehicle he's driving. The only indication I have for where he's going is his comment about the Mexican cartel.

The Bratva doesn't fuck around with the Mexican cartel. They're careless, unnecessarily brutal, and they're involved in human trafficking. It's not a moral decision. We're just not stupid enough to get involved in a product that can testify against us.

However, my father had some deals with them back in the day, so I know they hide in the northern part of the city and there's only one direct route to it from here.

I pass two more cars as they pull over to let me by. No Marco. No Ally.

If he drove at the speed limit, he'd still be on this road. If he didn't, I'm going to have to improvise once I'm in the city.

A red sports car. No Marco. No Ally.

The pain is creeping back as my adrenaline is replaced with frustration. My leg, my ribs, my face—a stream of pain that flickers, twists, stabs, and pulsates.

White van. No Marco. No Ally.

Closer to the city, two cars pull out of the way, the siren on top of Peter Harrington's SUV acting like Moses' staff, parting the Red Sea.

As I'm preparing to pass them, the passenger door from the second car opens. A thin arm and dark hair whip out. Ally gets halfway out before her body is yanked back into the car.

The car speeds up again, ignoring the siren. I pass the other car. I watch the sedan, waiting to see if Ally can escape again. I stare at the passenger door. He must have restrained her somehow. She wouldn't give up the fight that easy.

I could ram into the car, but there's a decent chance it would kill Ally—even higher if she's not secured in her seat. But if I don't get the car to stop, he could kill her himself.

The sedan speeds up, hitting at least ninety. Marco is fleeing. He could have recognized me or he just knows he can't get pulled over by a policeman while he has Ally beside him.

I'm not going to lose him.

I'm not going to lose her.

I let the pain consume me for a split second before I stomp on the gas and jerk the wheel, switching lanes. The sedan tries to outspeed me, but I reach close enough to the driver's side that I can see Marco's hand on the steering wheel.

I yank the wheel to the right, slamming into his door. The sedan lifts off the road before crashing down on the roof and rolling off the road.

~

Shattered glass surrounds the overturned sedan. I run to the car, stopping on the passenger's side. Allison is hanging upside down, her seat belt on. Her eyes are wide, but she appears fine. My thoughts race to our baby, but I can't let the panic overwhelm me. That won't help them.

I grab her shoulders before unbuckling her seat belt, guiding her so she doesn't crash into the ceiling, then lifting her out and carrying her a few feet away from the totaled vehicle.

"Are you okay?" I ask, helping her to sit on the ground.

"Fine," she says, but she's cradling her arm. I run my hand over it. Blossoms of red are spreading near her elbow and wrist. Broken. She grabs me with her other hand. "You should be in a hospital. Call an ambulance."

"I don't have my phone," I say. I look down the road. No cars now.

A flicker of movement.

I spin around, my leg killing me.

Marco points his gun at me, blood trickling from the crown of his head. "Tell your whore to remove any of your weapons," he rasps.

"I don't have anything," I say. He shifts his body, aiming the gun at Ally. I slowly lift my shirt, showing there's nothing in my waistband. I lift my pants legs, pain burning up the sides of my body. "Nothing."

Ally steps in front of me. I try to push her out of the way, but she only steps closer to Marco.

"Please don't kill him, Marco," she begs. "I can get Lev sent to prison. He'll be more humiliated there than if he's dead. You know my father is the chief of police and I'm close to the district attorney. I'm getting an internship at the DA's office. Once I'm there, I can help you and your men get out of any legal trouble."

"Bitch, you think I trust you?" he sneers. "You've fucked me over every step of the way. Once you're in the hands of the cartel, it's your turn to get fucked over until you're dead."

Ally gets onto her knees. She crawls to him. I grind my teeth, my fist clenching together so tightly I expect my fingers to break. I'd kill him now, but the sudden movement might cause his trigger finger to move. She's alive right now. That's what matters.

"Please," she says, on her knees. "There's a part of you that knows this is wrong. I know it. What Lev did to your father is unforgivable, but you don't need to do the same thing. Don't let his actions affect yours. It's—"

"It's too late," Marco interjects, his gaze switching between her and me.

"I'll do anything you want," she says. "We could get married. I'll convince everyone that you saved me from Lev. I just don't want anyone else to die. I'll even let you sell me to the Mexican cartel. I'll be a willing participant. I'll be their best slave. I'll let them fuck me in every way possible and I'll act like I love it. I'll do anything if you—"

She jerks upward, grabbing Marco's arm that's holding his gun. His arm swings wildly, his other hand punching her head and neck. I dive toward the car wreck, grabbing a piece of twisted metal.

I see nothing except Ally, too close to the gun and Marco's fist, but I manage to grab his head, gripping his hair. I yank his head away from me. He struggles, the sound of gunshots ripping through the air.

Then I stab the piece of metal into his throat. It cuts into my hand, but I swing again and again, until I'm bleeding and he's bleeding.

Until there's no blood left in his body to escape.

Then I let him go. He crumples to the ground, pale and dead.

I grab Ally. "Are you okay?" I run my hand over her body, searching for gun wounds, but all I do is leave a trail of blood. Some of it mine, some of it not.

"He didn't hit me," she murmurs. As my hand ends on her one good wrist, I stumble. She grabs my elbow, helping to lower me to the ground. I see her face, a glowing light as everything around her turns blurry. "You're good, you're good. We just need to find a phone …"

I get back onto my feet, though everything feels illusory now.

"The car," I say. "Your father's car. Come on …"

I lead her back to the police car, my hand on her back and her hand on my arm. I open the driver's door.

Then I fall, the world slipping by me and Ally's anxious face bending closer before darkness takes over.

24

ALLISON

The baby is okay. In the space of an hour, I not only learn that there is, in fact, a baby for sure, but also that everything that happened tonight didn't hurt it. I want to weep with relief but can't. Lev is in surgery. He needs me to hold it together so I can be there for him when he wakes up.

The splint on my arm lies awkwardly on the waiting room chair's armrest. I watch Garner Hospital's staff move back and forth through large swinging doors. I try not to feel frustrated as they chat with each other, laughing and flirting. People are dying in this hospital and they're trying to get laid.

I move my splinted arm up, clasp my hands together, and close my eyes.

God, I'll give up my dreams of being a prosecutor if Lev survives. I'll do anything. Just don't let him die.

I open my eyes. Nothing feels different, just more desperate. If the Holy Spirit dropped by while I was praying, it didn't linger.

I stand up, walking down the hall to the vending machine. I don't have any money, but the multitude of choices seems like a decent distraction.

I have no idea what Lev's favorite food is. Somehow, it's never a discussion we touched on when we were quizzing each other.

"Ally!"

I turn. My father comes running to me. He hugs me, carefully avoiding my splintered arm.

"What are you doing here?" I ask.

"The officer who arrived at the scene called me," he says. "Are you okay?"

My mind flickers to Lev, still in surgery. "I'm fine."

He checks my splint and my face.

"You told the first responders … you said that Alekseiev was kidnapped by the Italian Mafia and that he saved your life," he says. "Is that true?"

His apprehension gets under my skin. I tap against the vending machine's glass, biting back all of the sarcastic answers I want to give.

"It's the truth," I say.

"Is it the full truth?"

He wants me to tell him about the Bratva. It means, at the very least, he suspects I know more than I let on I knew at the gala. And, if everything hadn't changed, I might have broken down and told him everything.

"It's the truth," I repeat. There's a flicker of disappointment across his face, but he hugs me again.

"I'll deal with everything," he says. "The media has already caught wind of what happened. One of the EMTs must have talked. I'll have to tell them what you said."

He hesitates, tucking a strand of my hair behind my ear. "Are you waiting for Alekseiev to get out of surgery?"

I nod.

"I'll stay with you."

I take a deep breath. "When you talk about Lev, can you refer to him as my fiancé?"

He looks down at his hand, which is holding mine. "If that's what you want, I'll do it."

"You need to know," I say. "He only stole your car to save me."

His forehead furrows. "Alekseiev didn't steal my car, darling. I gave it to him."

I replay the scenario that had been in my head. My father handing over his keys had never entered my imagination.

"Why would you give him your car?" I ask.

He shrugs. "He and I were both willing to do what it took to get you back safely. And, if we're being honest, Alekseiev was willing to do a lot more terrible things without thinking twice than me, so it only made sense to give him the keys. I never thought having a criminal working for me would be a blessing."

A man in blue scrubs walks up to me. "Miss Harrington? Mr. Alekseiev is out of surgery. It was touch- and-go for a while, but he made it through. It will take him some time to wake up from the sedatives, but considering what happened, we're willing to let you see him now."

"I'm going to go talk to the press," my father says. His hand rests on my shoulder and he kisses my forehead. "I'll make sure they know about you and your fiancé."

At Lev's hospital bed, I watch him. The bruises on his face and the tubes sweeping over his body don't make him appear any less strong and he still makes me feel like I've taken every amphetamine under the sun. Everything is different, but all those euphoric feelings have only amplified.

His hand twitches over his thigh. I lean forward, placing my hand over his and kissing his cheek. His other hand slides up into my hair, pulling me closer. I get into his hospital bed as he carefully shifts to make more space for me.

He kisses the side of my mouth, stroking the side of my face. His eyes stay closed.

"I want you to be the one to prosecute me," he says, his voice hoarse. "I'll tell the police that I'll only confess if that's the case. It will ensure that nobody connects the two of us in a way that will hurt your reputation and it will be a great start to your career."

"You're not going to be arrested," I tell him.

"It's fine, Ally. I deserve it for a thousand things I've done."

"That's not what I mean," I say. "I told first responders that you saved me from Marco. I told them everything that happened—I just didn't mention why he was coming after you. I made it sound like he only went after me because of my father. My dad knows all that, too. He's going to take care of it. And your plan is going to work because my father is going to refer to you as my fiancé. Nobody will question the story after that."

His eyes flicker open. The green of his eyes sends a shock of electricity under my skin.

"I can't risk your career and your father's career like that. You deserve—"

"I deserve every damn thing I want," I snap. "And I don't want you to go to prison."

"Ally ... you're confused. This whole thing was my fault. I deserve life in prison just for that. I'll plead guilty. I don't have a problem with that. If—"

"If you don't go along with my plan, I'll go to the media and tell them the whole truth," I say. "That includes the fact that I caused a man to die and collaborated with you to cover it up. And then I covered up your involvement in a certain criminal organization when I talked to my father and first responders."

He frowns at me but it slowly twists into a half smile. "You're learning fast."

"You taught me well. Never thought I'd use your blackmail against me to blackmail you, did you?"

"Can't say I did." He kisses me, his lips dry, but it still makes me want more. He pulls me closer to him, his fingertips finding a home on my hips. "If that's the path you want to go down, then I have to ask you something."

"Mmm?"

He takes my hand, one of the thinner tubes nearly getting caught on the side rail.

"I know our relationship didn't start in a good way," he says, his thumb rubbing the skin between my thumb and index finger. "I know I forced you to agree to marry me. That's off the table. It doesn't matter. But I want you to know that the moment you want to marry me—to really marry me—I'm ready. I'd drop everything to make you mine. I want everybody to know you're mine, not as a bargaining chip, but because I want to be able to point to you and proudly say that you're my wife. I want everyone to know that I love you and I'm committed to that for the rest of my life."

I lay my head on his arm, letting his words sink in. He caresses my hair as the sound of beeping and the bustle of the hospital surrounds us. Thoughts of the baby tumble through my mind but I don't tell him yet. He's dealt with enough shocks today.

Finally, I look up at him, tears of happiness in my eyes. "How about next month?"

EPILOGUE

LEV

A month later

When Ally walks down the aisle, it scares the shit out of me. I could spend a fortune on an army of bodyguards and jiujitsu training for Ally, I could have every preparation in place, and my enemies could still find a way to hurt her.

She is so beautiful, so intelligent, and so *good* that it's terrifying. Her dark hair is decorated with various small braids and beads, pulled into a bun. Her white dress is embellished with the same beads. The Tide & Shore Hotel's beach carries a strong breeze as she walks toward me, but it still feels like it's the undertow filling my lungs. It feels like an impossible task to keep her safe and the risk is impossibly high.

As she stops, turning to face in me in front of the pastor, the expression in her eyes is a riptide of love. My panic calms. All the pieces I'm juggling in my head—her protection, the Bratva, Mariya's Revenge, my physical rehabilitation—fall away and all that's left is this deep-seated need.

Ally makes faces at me as the pastor speaks about love and other promises. It reminds me that Ally is dedicating her love to me, in front of all of our closest friends and families. Out of everyone on earth, she's decided that I'm the person she wants to be united with. It's not something I deserve—she's not someone I deserve—but I'll take it because I'm a selfish asshole.

In the front row, I see Ally's parents and I know that, even though there's little love lost between us, we all love Ally and they're entrusting me to take care of her. That's a trust I will never break.

"Now, you've both written vows," the pastor says. "So, I'll let you take over. Lev?"

"I love you," I say bluntly to Ally. "I'll do everything within my power to protect you and take care of you. You're letting me into your life in a way that is more than I could ever ask for and you're trusting me to be a good husband, so that's what I'm going to be. I promise you that I'm going to be good to you for the rest of our lives."

She smiles at me, the faintest shine in her eyes.

"Allison?" the pastor prompts.

"I love you," she echoes. "Sometimes, I've had this fear that one day we'll drift apart—that we're swept away by infatuation or everything we've been through. I'm afraid to lose this intimacy that I've never had with anyone else because I can't imagine feeling it with anyone else and it's … it feels like part of me. It's the only time I feel complete. But when we're together, that fear is gone. And I know we might go through hard times, but I also know I want to spend the rest of my years with you. I want to struggle with you, to feel pain with you, to feel that intimacy with you, and I want to love you forever. It's all I want."

"Wonderful," the pastor says, clapping his hands together. "Lev, do you swear to love Allison, to cherish her, and to walk with her throughout her best and worst days? If so, say I do."

"I do," I say.

"Allison. Do you swear to love Lev, to cherish him, and to walk with him throughout his best and worst days? If so, say I do."

"I do," she says.

As the pastor talks about the wedding rings and how they're a sign of our love, Ilya steps up to give me Ally's ring while Julia steps up to give Ally mine.

When we exchange them, her hands are shaking. I grasp her fingers, squeezing them for a second before I let my arms drop and her hands clasp in front of her. They stop trembling.

The pastor claps his hands together again. "Beautiful. By the power vested in me by the city of New York, it is with great pleasure that I declare you husband and wife. You may kiss the bride."

We kiss. I scoop up my new wife and she wraps her arms around my neck. We kiss again, only letting the wind come between us.

∼

After everyone has fallen asleep and the exterior lights behind Tide & Shore have shut off, Ally and I run out onto the beach.

She unzips her wedding dress as she runs. All that remains after it falls is her underwear—white lace—as she bounds toward the beach. She glances behind her, giving me a shameless smile as she runs straight into the waves, barely letting them slow her down before she dives.

I shed my tie, my shirt, and my pants. I take a deep breath before running into the ocean with her.

Ally has swum out further, her dark hair nearly invisible in the water but her skin glowing like a reflection of the moon.

I swim out toward her, the water starting to feel warmer. She sinks down, so only her eyes are visible above the water. Bubbles form in front of her. Then she launches herself at me, grabbing my shoulders and wrapping her legs around my waist.

We kiss, the taste of salt on her lips. The wedding was intense and gratifying, but I'd rather be alone with Ally for a night than have a dozen weddings.

I am in love with this woman.

She dives under the water. She tugs on my boxer briefs until she gets them down to my knees. Treading water, I pull my knees up to get them off the rest of the way. Her head bobs back up to the surface, her dark hair slick as it clings to her shoulders. She tugs on my arm until it's straight in front of me. She slides her underwear onto my wrist before diving back underwater. I watch her swim back up, heading back toward the shore. I pursue her, deeply invested in whatever her intentions are.

When her feet hit the sand, I watch her ass bounce as she runs. She settles onto her dress, lying down on her back with her knees up.

I collide against her knees, but she quickly opens them, inviting me in. My hard cock rubs against her wetness. I'm drunk on everything —her beauty, her warmth, the night, the ocean, the thought of making love to her on her wedding dress on our wedding night.

"I have to tell you something," she says as my lips move down to her throat.

I stop, looking up at her. "Should I be worried?"

"I don't think so. I don't know," she says. "Lev, when I was in the hospital, the doctors confirmed something for me. I've been waiting to tell you ... I should've told you immediately that day, but you were so exhausted after surgery. And then you needed all your energy for rehab—"

I sit up. "Ally. Just tell me what's going on. Are you okay?"

"Yes, I'm sorry, yes," she says. "Lev ... we're pregnant."

The cold water shocked me less than this. Last month it was on my mind constantly, after she first told me she might be, but after everything that happened, it got buried.

But, goddamn, a child being brought into our lives, into the violent, chaotic, and unjust world—it hits me now that it's just another fear for me to carry around.

She touches my cheek, and when I look into her eyes, the fear fades.

I see how great she'll be as a mother, how she'll help me be a better father than my dad could ever be.

"Is that okay?" she asks. "And do you mind that I didn't tell you immediately?"

"It's great," I say. "And it's fine. I get it. We had a lot going on the last month. I was just thinking about how we're going to protect this child."

"We'll protect him or her," she says, "in the same way that we take care of each other."

I kiss the spot underneath her ear. "Absolutely."

Her thighs open wider. When I push into her, her tightness coaxes me in. It's exactly where I need to be.

Her back arches to meet me as I move in her. My hands cradle the back of her head. She makes small noises in the back of her throat, somewhere between crooning and moaning. Her hands slide over my ribs and up to my shoulder blades.

Gazing down at her, she's stunning. The white dress contrasts with her dark hair and the tiny muscle contractions on her face as I thrust into her makes me love her even more.

I kiss her lips, her throat, her clavicle. I thrust deep inside her as my tongue flicks over her nipple. As I blow against it, her body jolts.

I drive into her again, burying myself in her before I grind against her slowly. Her teeth sink into my shoulder, sending a spark of adrenaline through me. I grind faster against her. Her nails sink into my shoulder blades and her moans become longer and louder. I switch back to thrusting, catapulting into her. As she starts to move farther up the dress, I grab her hips, tugging her back toward me.

Her moans start to become higher pitched, her eyes squeeze shut, and her fingernails cut into my skin. Her body tenses underneath me, so I keep thrusting over her, feeling myself reaching the edge too.

When she comes, her pussy pulsates rapidly against my cock. The sensation and the pleasure on her face push me over the peak. The orgasm shatters everything in my head except the overwhelming ecstasy that carries me far longer than any orgasm ever has.

After several minutes pass, I gaze down at her, nearly gasping for breath. She looks up at me for a moment before her hand winds around my neck and pulls me closer to her. She kisses me, leaving her mark on my mouth.

I know that companies crash, empires burn, and that I will love her through all of it.

She is mine.

THE END

Thanks for reading! But don't stop now – there's more. Click the link below to receive the FREE extended epilogue to **UNPROTECTED WITH THE MOB BOSS**. You'll also get a free sneak preview of another bestselling mafia romance novel.

So what are you waiting for? Click below!

https://dl.bookfunnel.com/3jiy2dkqpj

SNEAK PREVIEW (BROKEN VOWS)

Keep reading for a sneak preview of BROKEN VOWS by Nicole Fox!

She's my fake wife, my property... and my last chance at redemption.

She's beautiful. An angel.

I'm dangerous. A killer.

She's my fake bride for a single reason – so I can crush her father's resistance.

But marrying Eve brings me far more than I bargained for.

She's fiery. Feisty. Won't take no for an answer.

She makes me believe that I might be worth redemption.

Until I discover a past she's been hiding from me.

One that threatens everything.

Now, I know that our wedding vows are not enough.

I need to make sure she's mine for good.

A baby in her belly is the only way to seal the deal.

In the end, the Bratva always gets what it wants.

~

Luka

Their fear tingles against my skin like a whisper. As my leather-soled shoes tap against the concrete floor, I can sense it in the way their eyes dart towards and away from me. In the way they scurry around the production floor like mice, meek and unseen in the shadows. I enjoy it.

Even before I rose through the ranks of my family, I could inspire fear. Being a large man made that simple. But now, with brawn and power behind me, people cower. These people—the employees at the soda factory—don't even know why they fear me. Other than me being the owner's son, they have no real reason to be afraid of me, and yet, like prey in the grasslands, they sense the lion is near. I observe each of them as I weave my way around conveyors filled with plastic bottles and aluminum cans, carbonated soda being pumped into them, filling the room with a syrupy sweet smell.

I recognize their faces, though not their names. The people upstairs don't concern me. Or, at least, they shouldn't. The soda factory is a cover for the real operation downstairs, which must be protected at all costs. It's why I'm here on a Friday evening sniffing around for rats. For anyone who looks unfamiliar or out of place.

The floor manager—a Hispanic woman with a severe braid running down her back—calls out orders to the employees on the floor below in both English and Spanish, directing attention where necessary. She doesn't look at me once.

Noise permeates the metal shell of the building. The whirr of conveyor belts and grinding of gears makes the concrete floors feel like they are vibrating from the sheer power of the sound waves. A lot of people find the sights and smells overwhelming, but I've never minded. You don't become a mob underboss by shrinking in the face of chaos.

A group of employees in blue polos gather around a conveyor belt, smoothing out some kink in the production line. They pull a few aluminum cans from the line and drop them in a recycling bin, jockeying the rest of the cans back into a smooth line. The larger of the three men—a bald man with a doughy face and no obvious chin—flips a red switch. An alarm sounds and the cans begin moving again. He gives the floor manager a thumbs up and then turns to me, his hand flattening into a small wave. I raise an eyebrow in response. His face reddens, and he turns back to his work.

I don't recognize him, but he can't be in law enforcement. Undercover cops are more fit than he could ever dream to be. Plus, he wouldn't have drawn attention to himself. Likely, he is just a new hire, unaware of my position in the company. I resolve to go over new hires with the site manager and find out the man's name.

When I make it to the back of the production floor, the lights are dimmed—the back half of the factory not being utilized overnight—and I fumble with my keys for a moment before finding the right one to unlock the basement door. The stairway down is dark, and as soon as the metal door slams shut behind me, I'm left in blackness, my other senses heightening. The sounds of the production floor are but a whisper behind me, but the most pressing difference is the smell. Rather than the syrupy sweetness of the factory, there is an ether, chemical-like smell that makes my nose itch.

"That you, Luka?" Simon Oakley, the main chemist, doesn't wait for me to answer. "I've got a line here for you. We've perfected the chemistry. Best coke you'll ever try."

I pull back a thick curtain at the base of the stairs and step into the bright white light of the real production floor. I blink as my eyes adjust, and see Simon alone at the first metal table, three other men working in the back of the room. Like the employees upstairs, they don't look up as I enter. Simon, however, smiles and points to the line.

"I don't need to try it," I say flatly. "I'll know whether it's good or not when I see how much our profits increase."

"Well," Simon balks. "It can take time for word to spread. We may not see a rise in income until—"

"I'm not here to chat." I walk around the end of the table and stand next to Simon. He is an entire head shorter than me, his skin pale from spending so much time in the basement. "There have been nasty rumors going around among my men."

His bushy brows furrow in concern. "Rumors about what? You know we basement dwellers are often the last to hear just about everything." He tries to chuckle, but it dies as soon as he sees that I'm not here to fuck around.

"Disloyalty." I purse my lips and run my tongue over my top teeth. "The rumbling is that someone has turned their back on the family."

Fear dilates his pupils, and his fingers drum against the metal tabletop. "See? That is what I'm saying. I haven't heard a single thing about any of that."

"You haven't?" I hum in thought, taking a step closer. I can tell Simon wants to back away, but he stays put. I commend him for his bravery even as I loath him for it. "That is interesting."

His Adam's apple bobs in his throat. "Why is that interesting?"

Before he can even finish the sentence, my hand is around his neck. I strike like a snake, squeezing his windpipe in my hand and walking him back towards the stone wall. I hear the men in the back of the room jump and murmur, but they make no move to help their boss. Because I outrank Simon by a mile.

"It's interesting, Simon, because I have reliable information that says you met with members of the Furino mafia." I slam his head against the wall once, twice. "Is it true?"

His face is turning red, eyeballs beginning to bulge out, and he claws at my hand for air. I don't give him any.

"Why would you go behind my back and meet with another family? Have I not welcomed you into our fold? Have I not made your life here comfortable?"

Simon's eyes are rolling back in his head, his fingers becoming limp noodles on my wrist, weak and ineffective. Just before his body can sag into unconsciousness, I release him. He drops to the floor, falling onto his hands and knees and gasping for air. I let him get two breaths before I kick him in the ribs.

"I didn't meet with them," he rasps. When he looks up at me, I can already see the beginnings of bruises wrapping around his neck.

I kick him again. The force knocks the air out of him, and he collapses on his face, forehead pressed to the cement floor.

"Okay," he says, voice muffled. "I talked with them. Once."

I pressed the sole of my shoe into his ribs, rolling him onto his back. "Speak up."

"I met with them once," he admits, tears streaming down his face from the pain. "They reached out to me."

"Yet you did not tell me?"

"I didn't know what they wanted," he says, sitting up and leaning against the wall.

"All the more reason you should have told me." I reach down and grab his shirt, hauling him to his feet and pinning him against the wall. "Men who are loyal to me do not meet with my enemies."

"They offered me money," he says, wincing in preparation for the next blow. "They offered me a larger cut of the profits. I shouldn't have gone, but I have a family, and—"

I was raised to be an observer of people. To spot their weaknesses and know when I am being deceived. So, I know immediately Simon is not telling me the entire story. The Furinos would not reach out to our chemist and offer him more money unless there had been communication between them prior, unless they had some connection Simon is not telling me about. He thinks I am a fool. He thinks I will forgive him because of his wife and child, but he does not know the depths of my apathy. Simon thinks he can appeal to my humanity, but he does not realize I do not have any.

I press my hand into the bruises around his neck. Simon grabs my wrist, trying to pull me away, but I squeeze again, enjoying the feeling of his life in my hands. I like knowing that with one blow to the neck, I could break his trachea and watch him suffocate on the floor. I am in complete control.

"And your family will be dead before dawn unless you tell me why you met with the Furinos," I spit. I want nothing more than to kill Simon for being disloyal. I can figure out the truth without him. But it is not why I was sent here. Killing indiscriminately does not create the kind of controlled fear we need to keep our family standing. It only creates anarchy. So, reluctantly, I let Simon go. Once again, he falls to the floor, gasping, and I step away so I won't be tempted to beat him.

"I'll tell you," he says, his voice high-pitched, like the words are being released slowly from a balloon. "I'll tell you anything, just don't hurt my family."

I nod for him to continue. This is his only chance to come clean. If he lies to me again, I'll kill him.

Simon opens his mouth, but before he can say anything, I hear a loud bang upstairs and a scream. Just as I turn around, the door at the top of the stairs opens, and I know immediately something is wrong. Forgetting all about Simon, I grab the nearest table and tip it over, not worrying about the potential lost profits. Footsteps pound down the stairs and no sooner have I crouched down, the room erupts in bullets.

I see one of the men in the back of the room drop, clutching his stomach. The other two follow my lead and dive behind tables. Simon crawls over to lay on the floor next to me, his lips purple.

The room is filled with the pounding of footsteps, the ring of bullets, and the moans of the fallen man. It is chaos, but I am steady. My heart rate is even as I grab my phone, turn on the front facing camera, and lift it over the table. There are eight shoulders spread out around the room, guns at the ready. Two of them are at the base of the stairs, the other six are spread out in three-foot increments, forming a barrier in front of the stairs. No one here is supposed to get out alive.

But they do not know who is hiding behind the table. If they did, they'd be running.

I look over at one of the chemists. They are not our family's soldiers, but they are trained like anyone else. He has his gun at the ready, waiting for my order. I nod my head once, twice, and on three, we both turn and fire.

One man falls immediately, my bullet striking him in the neck, blood spraying against the wall like splattered paint. It is a kind of artwork, shooting a man. Years of training, placing the bullet just so. Art is meant to incite a reaction and a bullet certainly does that. The man drops his weapon, his hand flying to his neck. Before he can experience too much pain, I place another bullet in his forehead. He drops to his knees, but before he falls flat on his face, I shoot his friend.

The men expected this ambush to be simple, so they are still in shock, still scrambling to collect themselves. It makes it easy for my men to knock them off. Another two men drop as I chase my second target around the room, firing shot after shot at him. He ducks behind a table, and I wait, gun aimed. It is a deadly game of Whack-a-mole, and it requires patience. His gun pops up first, followed shortly by his head, which I blow off with one shot. His scream dies on his lips as he bleeds out, red seeping out from under the table and spreading across the floor.

There are three men left, and I'm out of bullets. I stash my gun in my pocket and pull out my KA-BAR knife. The blade feels like an old friend in my hand. I crawl past a shivering Simon, wishing I'd killed him just so I wouldn't have to see him looking so pathetic, and out from behind the table. I slide my feet under me, moving into a crouch. The remaining men are wounded, and they are focused on the back corner where shots are still coming from my men. They do not see me approaching from the side.

I lunge at the first man—a young kid with golden brown hair and a tattoo on his neck. It is half-hidden under the collar of his shirt, so I cannot make it out. When my knife cuts into his side, he spins to fight me off, but I knock his gun from his hand with my left arm and then drive the knife in under his ribs and upward. He freezes for a moment before blood leaks from his mouth.

The man next to him falls from multiple bullets in the chest and stomach. I kick his gun away from him as he falls to the floor, and advance on the last attacker. He is hiding behind a metal table, palm pressing into a wound on his shoulder. He scrambles to lift his gun as I approach, but I drop to my knees and slide next to him, knife pressed to his neck. His eyes go wide, and then they squeeze shut as he drops his weapon.

The blade of my knife is biting into his skin, and I see the same tattoo creeping up from beneath his collar. I slide the blade down, pushing his shirt aside, and I recognize it at once.

"You are with the Furinos?" I ask.

The man answers by squeezing his eyes shut even tighter.

"You should know who is in a room before you attack," I hiss. "I am Luka Volkov, and I could slit your throat right now."

His entire body is trembling, blood from his shoulder wound leaking through his clothes and onto the floor. Every ounce of me wants this kill. I feel like a dog who has not been fed, desperate for a hunk of flesh, but warfare is not endless bloodshed. It is tactical.

"But I will not," I say, pulling the blade back. The man blinks, unbelieving. "Get out of here and tell your boss what happened. Tell him this attack is a declaration of war, and the Volkov family will live up to our merciless reputation."

He hesitates, and I slash the blade across his cheek, drawing a thin line of blood from the corner of his mouth to his ear. "Go!" I roar.

The man scrambles to his feet and towards the stairs, blood dripping in his wake. As soon as he is gone, I clean my knife with the hem of my shirt and slide it back into place on my hip.

This will not end well.

Eve

I hold up a bag of raisins and a bag of prunes a few inches from the cook's face.

"Do you see the difference?" I ask. The question is rhetorical. Anyone with eyes could see the difference. And a cook—a properly trained cook—should be able to smell, feel, and sense the difference, as well.

Still, Felix wrinkles his forehead and studies the bags like it is a pop quiz.

"Raisins are small, Felix!" My shouting makes him jump, but I'm far too stressed out to care. "Prunes are huge. As big as a baby's fist. Raisins are tiny. They taste very different because they start out as different fruits. Do you see the problem?"

He stares at me blankly, and I wonder if being sous chef gives me the authority to fire someone. Because this man has got to go.

"You've ruined an entire roast duck, Felix." I drop the bags on the counter and run a hand down my sweaty face. I grab the towel from my back pocket and towel off. "Throw it out and start again, but use *prunes* this time."

He smiles and nods, and I wonder how many times he must have hit his head to be so slow. I motion for another cook to come talk to me. He moves quickly, hands folded behind his back, waiting for my order.

"Chop up the duck and make a confit salad. We can toss it with more raisins, fennel—that kind of thing—and make it work."

He nods and shuffles away, and I mop my forehead again.

At the start of my shift, I strode into the kitchen like I owned the place. I was finally sous chef to Cal Higgs, genius chef in charge at The Floating Crown. After graduating culinary school, I didn't know where I'd get a job or where I'd be on the totem pole, and I certainly never imagined I'd be a sous chef so soon, but here I am. And now that I'm here, I can't help but wonder if it wasn't some sort of trick. Did Cal give into my father's wishes easily and give me this job because he needed a break from the insanity?

I've been assured by several members of staff that the dishwasher, whose name I can't remember, has been working at the kitchen for over a year, but he seems to be stuck on slow motion tonight. He is washing and drying plates seconds before the cooks are plating them up and sending them back out to the dining room. And two of the cooks, who were apparently dating, decided that the middle of dinner rush would be the perfect time to discuss their relationship, and they broke up. Dylan stormed out without a word, and Sarah, who should be okay since she was the dumper, not the dumpee, is hiding in the bathroom bawling her eyes out. I've knocked on the door once every ten minutes for an hour, but she refuses to let me in. Cal has a key, but he has been shut away in his office all night, and I don't want to go explain what a shitshow the kitchen is, so we are making do. Barely.

"Sarah?" I knock on the door. "If you don't come out in five minutes, you're fired."

For the first time, there is a break in the crying. "You can't do that."

"Yes, I can," I lie. "You'll leave here tonight without your apron. Single and jobless. Just imagine that shame."

I feel bad rubbing salt in her wound, threatening her, but I'm out of options. I tried comforting her and offering her some of the dark chocolate from the dessert pantry, but she refused to budge. Threats are my last recourse.

There is a long pause, and I wonder if I'm going to have to admit that I actually can't fire her—I don't think—and tell the staff to start using the bathrooms on the customer side, when finally, Sarah emerges. Mascara is smeared down her cheeks, and her eyes are red and puffy from crying, but she is out of the bathroom. As soon as she steps through the doorway, one of the waitresses darts in after her and slams the door shut.

"I'm sorry, Eve," she blubbers, covering her face with her hands.

I grab her wrists and pry her palms from her eyes. When she looks up, her eyes are still closed, tears leaking from the corners.

"Go to the sinks and help with the dishes," I say firmly. "You're in no state to cook right now. Just focus on cleaning plates, okay?"

Sarah nods, her lower lip wobbling.

"Everything is fine," I say, speaking to her like she is a wild animal who might attack. "You won't lose your job. Cal never needs to know, okay? Just go wash dishes. Now."

She turns away from me in a daze and heads back to help the dishwasher whose name I can't for the life of me remember, and I take a deep breath. I've finally put out all the fires, and I lean against the counter and watch the kitchen move around me. It is like a living, breathing machine. Each person has to play their part or everything falls apart. And tonight, I'm barely holding them together.

When the kitchen door swings open, I hope it is Makayla. She has been a waitress at The Floating Crown for five years, and while she has no formal culinary training, she knows this kitchen better than anyone. I've asked her for help tonight more times than I'm comfortable with, but at this point, just seeing one, capable, smiling face would be enough to keep me from crying. But when I turn and instead see a man in a suit, the tie loose and askew around his neck, and his eyes glassy, I almost sag to the floor.

"You can't be back here, sir," I say, moving forward to block his access to the rest of the kitchen. "We have hot stoves and fire and sharp knives, and you are already unstable on your feet."

Makayla told me a businessman at the bar had been demanding macaroni and cheese all night between shots. Apparently, he would not take 'no' for an answer.

"Macaroni and cheese," he mutters, falling against my palms, his feet sliding out from underneath him. "I need macaroni and cheese to soak up the alcohol."

I turn to the nearest person for help, but Felix is still looking at the bags of raisins and prunes like he might seriously still be confused which is which, and I don't want to distract him lest he ruin another duck. I could call out for help from someone else or call the police, but I don't want to cause a scene. Cal is just in the next room. He may have hired me because my father is Don of the Furino family, but even my father can't be angry if Cal fires me for sheer incompetence. I have to prove that I'm capable.

"Sir, we don't have macaroni and cheese, but may I recommend our scoglio?"

"What is that?" he asks, top lip curled back.

"A delicious seafood pasta. Mussels, clams, shrimp, and scallops in a tomato sauce with herbs and spices. Truly delicious. One of my favorite meals on the menu."

"No cheese?"

I sigh. "No. No cheese."

He shakes his head and pushes past me, running his hands along the counters like he might stumble upon a prepared bowl of cheesy pasta.

"Sir, you can't be back here."

"I can be wherever I like," he shouts. "This is America, isn't it?"

"It is, but this is a private restaurant and our insurance does not cover diners being back in the kitchen, so I have to ask you—"

"Oh, say can you see by the dawn's early light!"

"Is that 'The Star-Spangled Banner'?" I ask, looking around to see whether anyone else can see this man or whether I'm having some sort of exhausted fever dream.

"What so proudly we hailed at the twilight's last gleaming?"

This is absurd. Truly absurd. Beyond calling the police, the easiest thing to do seems to be to give in to his demands, so I lay a hand on his shoulder and lead him to the corner of the kitchen. I pat the counter, and he jumps up like he is a child.

I listen to the National Anthem six times before I hand the man a bowl of whole grain linguini with a sharp cheddar cheese sauce on top. "Can you please take this back to the bar and leave me alone?"

He grabs the bowl from my hands, takes a bite, and then breaks into yet another rousing rendition of "The Star-Spangled Banner." This time in falsetto with accompanying dance moves.

I sigh and push him towards the door. "Come on, man."

The dining room is loud enough that no one pays the man too much attention. Plus, he has been drunk out here for an hour before ambushing the kitchen. A few guests shake their heads at the man and then smile at me, giving me the understanding and recognition I sought from the kitchen staff. I lead the man back to the bar, tell the bartender to get rid of him as soon as the pasta is gone, and then make my way back through the dining room.

"She isn't the chef," says a deep voice at normal volume. "Chefs don't look like *that*."

I don't turn towards the table because I don't want to give them the satisfaction of knowing I heard them, of knowing they had any kind of power over me.

"Whatever she makes, it can't taste half as good as her muffin," another man says to raucous laughter.

I roll my eyes and speed up. I'm used to the comments and the cat calls. I've been dealing with it since I sprouted boobs. Even my father's men would whisper things about me. It is part of the reason I chose a path outside the scope of the family business. I couldn't imagine working with the kind of men my father employed. They were crass and mean and treated women like possessions. Unfortunately, the more I learn of the world beyond the Bratva, the more I realize men everywhere are like that. It is the reason I'll never get married. I won't belong to anyone.

I hear the men's deep voices as I walk back towards the kitchen, but I don't listen. I let the words roll off of me like water on a windowpane and step back into the safe chaos of the kitchen.

The kitchen seems to calm down as dinner service goes on, and I'm able to take a step back from micro-managing everything to work on an order of chicken tikka masala. While letting the tomato puree and spices simmer, I realize my stomach is growling. I was too nervous before shift to eat anything, and now that things have finally settled into an easy rhythm, my body is about to absorb itself. So, I casually walk over to where two giant stock pots are simmering with the starter soups for the day and scoop myself out a hearty ladle of lobster and bacon soup. Cal doesn't like for anyone to eat while on service, but he has been in his office all evening, and based on the smell slipping out from under his door, he will be far too stoned to notice or care.

The soup is warm and filling, and I close my eyes as I eat, enjoying the blissful moment of peace before more chaos ensues.

The kitchen door opens, and this time it really is Makayla. I wave her over, eager to see how everyone is enjoying the food and whether the drunk patriot finally left the restaurant, but she doesn't see me and walks with purpose through the kitchen and straight to Cal's office door. She opens it and steps inside, and I wonder what she needed Cal for and why she couldn't come to me. Lord knows I've handled every other situation that arose all night.

I'm just finished the last bite of my soup when Cal's office door slams open, bouncing off the wall, and he stomps his way across the kitchen.

"Eve!"

I shove the bowl to the back of the counter, throwing a dish towel over top to hide the evidence, and then wipe my mouth quickly.

"Yes, chef?"

"Front and center," he barks like we are in the military rather than a kitchen.

Despite the offense I take with his tone—especially after everything I've done to keep the place running all night—I move quickly to follow his order. Because that is what a good sous chef does. I follow the chef's orders, no matter how demeaning.

Cal Higgs is a large man in every sense of the word. He is tall, round, and thick. His head sits on top of his shoulders with no neck in sight, and just walking across the room looks like a chore. I imagine being in his body would be like wearing a winter coat and scarf all the time.

"What is the problem, Chef?"

He hitches a thumb over his shoulder, and Makayla gives me an apologetic wince. "Someone complained about the food, and they want to see the chef."

I wrinkled my forehead. I'd personally tasted every dish that went out. Unless Felix managed to slide another dish past me with raisins in it instead of prunes, I'm not sure what the complaint could be.

"Was there something wrong with the dish or did they simply not like it?"

"Does it matter?" he snaps. His eyes are bloodshot and glassy, yet his temper is as sharp as ever. "I don't like unhappy customers, and you need to fix it."

"But you're the chef," I say, realizing too late I should have stayed quiet.

Cal steps forward, and I swear I can feel the floor quake under his weight. "But you made the food. Should I go out there and apologize on your behalf? No, this is your mess, and you will take care of it."

"Of course," I say, looking down at the ground. "You're right. I'll go out there and make this right."

Before Cal can find another reason to yell at me, I retie my apron around my waist, straighten my white jacket, and march through the swinging kitchen doors.

The dining room is quieter than before. The drunk man is no longer singing the National Anthem at the bar and several of the tables are empty, the bussers clearing away empty plates. Happy plates, I might add. Clearly, they didn't have an issue with the food.

I didn't ask Makayla who complained about the food, but as soon as I walk into the main dining area, it is obvious. There is a small gathering at the corner booth, and a salt and pepper-haired man in his late fifties or early sixties raising a hand in the air and waves me over without looking directly at me. I haven't even spoken to the man yet, and I already hate him.

I'm standing at their table, staring at the man, but he doesn't speak to me until I announce my presence.

"I heard someone wanted to speak with the chef," I say.

He turns to me, one eyebrow raised. "You are the chef?"

I recognize a Russian accent when I hear one, and this man is Russian without a doubt. I wonder if I know him. Or if my father does. Would he be complaining to me if he knew my father was head of the Furino family? I would never throw my family name around in order to scare people, but for just a second, I have the inclination.

"Sous chef," I say with as much confidence as I can muster. "I ran the kitchen tonight, so I'll be hearing the complaints."

His eyes move down my body slowly like he is inspecting a cut of meat in a butcher shop. I cross my arms over my chest and spread my feet hip-width apart. "So, was there an issue with the food? I'd love to correct any problems."

"Soup was cold." He nudges his empty bowl to the center of the table with three fingers. "The portions were too small, and I ordered my steak medium-rare, not raw."

Every plate on the table is empty. Not a single crumb in sight. Apparently, the issues were not bad enough he couldn't finish his meal.

"Do you have any of the steak left?" I ask, making a show of looking around the table. "If one of my cooks undercooked the meat, I'd like to be able to inform them."

"If? I just told you the meet was undercooked. Are you doubting me?"

"Of course not," I say. *Yes, absolutely I am.* "It is just that if the meat was undercooked, I do not understand why you waited until you'd eaten everything to inform me of the problem?"

The man looks around the table at his companions. They are all smiling, and I can practically see them sharpening their teeth, preparing to rip me to shreds. When he turns back to me, his smile is acidic, deadly. "How did you get this position—sous chef? Surely not by skill. You are pretty, which I'm sure did you a favor. Did you sleep with the chef? Maybe—" he moves his hand in an obscene gesture—"'service' the boss to earn your place in the kitchen?

Surely your 'talent' didn't get you the job, seeing as how you have none."

I physically bite my tongue and then take a deep breath. "If you'd like me to remake anything for you or bring out a complimentary dessert, I'm happy to do that. If not, I apologize for the issues and hope you will not hold it against us. We'd love to have you again."

Lies. Lies. Lies. I'm smiling and being friendly the way I was taught in culinary school. I actually took a class on dealing with customers, and this man is being even more outrageous than the overexaggerated angry customer played by my professor.

"Why would I want more food from you if the things you already sent out were terrible?" He snorts and shakes his head. "I see you do not have a ring on. That is no surprise. Men like a woman who can cook. Men don't care if you know your way around a professional kitchen if you don't know your way around a dinner plate."

The older gentleman is speaking, but I hear my father's words in my head. *You do not need to go to culinary school to find a husband, Eve. Your aunties can teach you to cook good food for your man.*

My entire life has been preparation for finding a husband. The validity of every hobby is judged by whether it will fetch me a suitor or not. My father wants me to be happy, but he mostly wants me to be married. Single, I'm a disappointment. Married, I'm a vessel for future Furino mafia members.

Years of anger and resentment begin to bubble and hiss inside of me until I'm boiling. My hands are shaking, and I can feel adrenaline pulsing through me, lighting every inch of me on fire. This time, I don't bite my tongue.

"I'd rather die alone than spent another minute near a man like you," I spit, stepping forward and laying my palms flat on the table. "The fact that you ate all of the food you apparently hated shows you are a pig in more ways than one."

In the back of my mind, I recognize that my voice is echoing around the restaurant and the chatter in the rest of the room has gone quiet, but blood is whirring in my ears, and I can't stop. I've stayed quiet and docile for too long. Now, it is my turn to speak my mind.

"You and your friends may be wealthy and respected, but I see you for what you are—spineless, cowardly assholes who are so insecure they have to take their rage out on everybody else."

I want to spin on my heel and storm away, making a grand exit, but in classic Eve fashion, my heel catches on the tablecloth, and I nearly trip. I fall sideways and throw an arm out to catch myself, knocking a nearly full bottle of wine on the table over. The glass shatters and red wine splashes across the tablecloth and onto the guests in the booth like a river of blood.

I pause long enough to note the old Russian man's shirt is splattered like he has been shot before I continue my exit and head straight for the doors.

I suck in the night air. The evening is warm and humid, summer strangling the city in its hold, and I want to rip off my clothes for some relief. I feel like I'm being strangled. Like there is a hand around my neck, squeezing the life out of me.

Breathing in and out slowly helps, but as the physical panic begins to ebb away, emotional panic flows in.

What have I done? Cal Higgs is going to find out about the altercation any minute, and then what? Will he fire me? And if he does, will I ever be able to get another chef position? I was only offered this position because of my father, and I doubt he will help me earn another kitchen position, especially since I'm no closer to finding a boyfriend (or husband) since I left for culinary school.

Despite it all, I want to call my dad. He has always made it clear he will move heaven and earth to take care of me, to make sure no one is mean to me, and I want his support right now. But the support he offered me when a girl tripped me during soccer practice and made me miss the net won't apply here. He will tell me to come home. To put down my apron and knife and focus on more meaningful pursuits. And that is the last thing I want to hear right now.

I pull out my phone and scroll through my contacts list, hoping to see a spark of hope amidst the names, but there is nothing. I've lost touch with everyone since I started culinary school. There hasn't been time for friends.

This is probably the kind of situation where most girls would turn to their moms, but she hasn't been in the picture since I was six years old. Even if I had her number, I wouldn't call her. Dad hasn't always been perfect, but at least he was there. At least he cared enough to stay.

I untie my apron and pull it over my head, leaning back against the brick side of the restaurant.

"Take it off, baby!"

I look up and see a man on a motorcycle with his hair in a bun parked along the curb. He is waggling his eyebrows at me like I'm supposed to fall in love with him for harassing me on the street, and the fire that filled my veins inside hasn't died out yet. The embers are still there, burning under the skin, and I step towards him, lips pulled back in a smile.

He looks surprised, and I'm sure he is. That move has probably never worked for him before. He smiles back at me, his tongue darting out to lick his lower lip.

"Is that your bike?" I purr.

He nods. "Want a ride?"

My voice is still sticky sweet as I respond, "So sweet of you to offer. I'd rather choke and die on that grease ball you call a man bun, but thanks anyway, hon."

It takes him a second to realize my words don't match the tone. When it hits him, he snarls, "Bitch."

"Asshole." I flip him the bird over my shoulder and start the long walk home.

∽

Click here to keep reading BROKEN VOWS.

MAILING LIST

Sign up to my mailing list!
New subscribers receive a FREE steamy bad boy romance novel.

Click the link below to join.
https://readerlinks.com/l/1057996

ALSO BY NICOLE FOX

Kornilov Bratva Duet

Married to the Don

Til Death Do Us Part

Heirs to the Bratva Empire

*Can be read in any order

Kostya

Maksim

Andrei

Tsezar Bratva

Nightfall (Book 1)

Daybreak (Book 2)

Russian Crime Brotherhood

*Can be read in any order

Owned by the Mob Boss

Unprotected with the Mob Boss

Knocked Up by the Mob Boss

Sold to the Mob Boss

Stolen by the Mob Boss

Trapped with the Mob Boss

Volkov Bratva

Broken Vows (Book 1)

Broken Hope (Book 2)

Other Standalones

Vin: A Mafia Romance

Printed in Great Britain
by Amazon